Before her death in July 1997, beloved lesbian-feminist author Chris Anne Wolfe published two Amazon adventure novels – *Shadows of Aggar* and *Fires of Aggar*. But these two volumes are only the first half of the four-part Aggar cycle. Chris Anne also published two stand-alone novels – a time-bending romance, *Annabel and I*, and a retelling of Beauty and the Beast, *Roses and Thorns*.

As her publisher and friend, I was honored to inherit the manuscripts of Chris Anne's remaining novels, short stories, poetry and songs. These hand-written volumes include both remaining Aggar books – *Sands of Aggar* and *Oceans of Aggar* – and more than a dozen retold fairy tales, and original fantasy and contemporary novels. Only Blue Forge Press has the right to publish Chris Anne's work and we take great pride in that mission.

Jennifer DiMarco
Publisher
Blue Forge Press

More by Chris Anne Wolfe

Amazons of Aggar

Book 1: Shadows of Aggar
Book 2: Fires of Aggar
Book 3: Sands of Aggar
Book 4: Oceans of Aggar
Book 5: Bonds of Aggar
Book 6: Wilds of Aggar

Annabel and I

Roses and Thorns

Talismans & Temptations

www.BlueForgePress.com

SANDS OF AGGAR

Chris Anne Wolfe

BLUE FORGE PRESS
Port Orchard * Washington

Blue Forge Press is the print division of the volunteer-run, federal 501(c)3 nonprofit company, Blue Forge Group, founded in 1989 and dedicated to bringing light to the shadows and voice to the silence. We strive to empower storytellers across all walks of life with our four divisions: Blue Forge Press, Blue Forge Films, Blue Forge Gaming, and Blue Forge Records. Find out more at www.BlueForgeGroup.org

Blue Forge Press
7419 Ebbert Drive Southeast
Port Orchard, Washington 98367
blueforgepress@gmail.com
360-550-2071 ph.txt

SANDS OF AGGAR

Chris Anne Wolfe

Prologue

Excerpt from Audio Logs
Artemisia n'Minona
Valley Bay
Sixth Tenmoon A.C.

As a storyteller of Valley Bay, I've tried to keep my skills of weaving words alive. It's difficult at times to find the light... the energy... to do this weaving but I know the words keep me alive. History... our herstory... must be preserved. For Valley Bay is no more and the wind howling through forests and ruins still burns my eyes with ash. I know it isn't real but that doesn't stop the tears.

"I've been hiding in the ruins of the Council's Keep for fourteen days, but I'll be leaving at dawn. It's too dangerous to stay. New hunters come every day, searching for survivors. They'll kill me if they find me.

"I don't know how many of our records will survive the purging. I hope someday someone hears my story and remembers once there were Amazons on Aggar. Once we stood with Blue Sights and seers to defend against the Terran invasion and we were rewarded with death and disease.

"It's been three years now since the Terrans attacked. We thought we'd seen the last of them hundreds of years ago, but it was only a stalemate.

"One hundred fifty years ago, the rulers of the Ramains moved the marauding Clan, survivors of the first Terran occupation, into the north. They didn't consider the Changelings who already lived there. The Clan and Changelings destroyed each other and the Changelings were all but eradicated. What was left of the Clan hid for generations, developing technologies and sending wayward messages to Terran homeworlds. When they were finally heard by their brethren, they threw us away as we had thrown them away. They helped the Terrans circumvent the forces and defenses of Aggar. They helped them invade.

"The invaders targeted the Blue Sights first. A shower of biochemical warfare, nanobots unleashed into the atmosphere programmed to assassinate anyone with the Sight or carrying the gene. We weren't able to counter it. It was a massacre. Our sisters and friends dropped dead by the hundreds. Almost all the gifted perished.

"And then the ships descended, as if falling from the sky. I was there when Valley Bay burned. My *soroi...* she died when the Council Keep fell. All that's left of the ancient stronghold is dust and debris, broken rooms and hidden spaces filled with shadows.

"In the end, we were victorious. I suppose. Though it hardly felt that way. Through magic and military tactics we fought back, forcing the Terrans off Aggar but the cost was great. Perhaps too great.

"Our seers are dead now. I fear the Blue Sights are lost forever. Valley Bay is ash and my sisters are scattered. The residents of Aggar have blamed the invasion on the Amazons and hunt us down, trying to remove all non-natives from their brutalized land.

"I hear rumors on the wind. There are sympathetic tribes in the deserts willing to hide the sisters of *Dey Sorormin*. I intend to find them if I can survive the journey. Perhaps some of my sisters have found safe harbor there as well.

"We have been on Aggar now for centuries. My ancestors were born and raised here. I thought we were one people. That we were one with this world. But angry eyes, eyes still mourning, see us no differently than the Terrans that wanted to pillage Aggar for her resources.

"I pray to the Goddesses that this record is found in a more peaceful time. That sisters who come after me will discover these words and be amazed that Aggar – our Aggar – was once so hostile to our kind."

PART ONE

RISE FROM THE DEAD

Chapter One

The music was frenzied with the tin rhythms of shaker bells and tambourines. The pipes, then the fiddles, were lost in a quickening, dizzying, rushing beat that drove the dancer faster and faster. Jacquin's hair swirled in long ebony tangles, the muscles in her calves and thighs taut as she sprang, her back arched almost impossibly, weaving her body into a living tapestry, tangled and spinning across the desert square. Crimson silks slid across dark, oiled skin, tanned by the sun in a way that betrayed her Amazon heritage, and skimmed across tight muscles and pointed toes as she moved.

Fire dancers, members of her Tribe clothed in hand-spun silks and crafted leathers, moved in time with her, creating a solid ring of light, the flames licking the air, warming Jacquin's skin, infusing the evening with the scent of ash and sweat. Jacquin lost herself in movement, the world fading until it was nothing but flame and rhythm, the sand coarse and light beneath her bare feet, and the tension in her body.

She didn't notice as the crowd gathered or faded, the audience a blur of merchants' colors and clapping hands, smiles and eyes wide with awe. She didn't hear their cheers. She simply closed her eyes and spun, her arms stretched high over her head, reaching out to the sky, gold and orange like cactus blossoms as dusk fell. Her heart pounded behind her ears, leaping in time with her feet, beating a steady rhythm against her ribs, pulling the beat of the drum circle deep beneath her bones. She was one with the music, one with the night. Dancer. Amazon. Tribe.

In an instant, the light of day faded to darkness, eclipsed by an oncoming vision. A deep chill settled into her skin, the scent of dust and musk – of constant travel – flooded her nose and mouth. A warrior woman, tall and silent... a silver glow from the brim of her hood to her booted toe. A sword shimmered in her hand as she swung, the blade slicing through the air as Jacquin recoiled in fear.

Jacquin's chestnut eyes blinked – startled. The present returned. She was still, resting on her knees, her back arched so far her hair was a rippling pool on the desert floor. The crowd was applauding, laughter tinged with amazement. A few coins thudded across the ground like shattering starlight.

So – she had completed the dance.

Jacquin fixed a sparkling smile to her face, masking the disoriented feeling that always followed a vision, and rose with a spin, like a flame bursting to life. The acrobats and sword dancers were moving into the circle, their bodies lithe and agile like serpents. Her sisters were collecting her coin. Her part for the evening was done.

Khalisa greeted her with a thick blanket and pulled her further from the performers toward the rows of wagons where the Tribe lived. The temperature was dropping rapidly as night spread across the small desert town of Oasis and the beads of Jacquin's sweat were turning cold; the scraps of ribbon and string that covered her breasts and hips were not worn for warmth.

"You danced a vision again, didn't you?" Khalisa pressed, rubbing her sister's arms through the blanket. Another of their Tribe hurried past, a lithe youth with deep amber hair, handing a mug of brewed tea to Jacquin with a quick grin.

Khalisa slanted a look at her sister; it was half teasing, half serious. Sometimes Jacquin did not leave her visions behind when she left the dancing.

"I'm fine." Jacquin's elven-slim brows lifted with sudden mischief. "Since when do you have such an interest in another's visions? Or did my feet lose time while my mind wandered?"

Khalisa laughed and spun her sister to face the crowd. "Since I'm wondering if that one there has taken your fancy? You seemed to be using him for your focal point."

Jacquin pulled the blanket tighter around her shoulders, her lip curled in a subtle sneer as she looked him over. Fine jerkin and breeches. A solid ruby ring on his finger. "Only his coinpurse."

Khalisa chuckled, low and husky. "I had my attention on other charms."

"You're too brazen with men, sister. You're a descendant of *Dey Sorormin!*"

Khalisa laughed, her fingers squeezing her sister's shoulders through the blanket, the tension in her hands betraying her excitement. "Your fascination with the Amazons is making you dull. Do you think he'd share my bed tonight?"

"Of course. He came here looking for *sha'mala.*"

"Jacquin!" Khalisa blushed at the slang term used to objectify the women of the desert tribes. "Why would you say that?"

"It's how he sees us."

"Don't be a hypocrite. You've shared a bed with more than a few merchants' daughters. Do you think it's only men who come here to be seduced?"

The sandy-haired merchant moved aside. His grin took on a knowing, good-natured quirk, and he nodded to direct his companion's attention toward the sisters.

"Maybe your bitterness will fade when you see his companion," Khalisa murmured impishly. "She more your type?"

Jacquin turned her attention and a wicked grin tugged at the corners of her scowl, smoothing it into something almost feral.

The woman was lanky with a short cap of honey-blond hair. She met Jacquin's bold stare and then blushed brightly, backing a step away and out of sight.

"She looks awfully young–" Khalisa mused warily. Her eyes, however, were still plainly glued to the man. "Sibs do you think? Or are we about to walk into something unpleasant?"

"She's not young," Jacquin corrected absently. A very small, very pleased – slightly wicked, smile grew on her narrow-chinned face.

Something in her sib's voice caught Khalisa's attention. She peered over Jacquin's shoulder, looking more closely as the woman ventured back into view. This time the woman managed to withstand the sisters' scrutiny, but there was something about her blush, her shy eyes, her lack of bravado that captured Jacquin's interest.

"You're right," Khalisa conceded slowly. "Not young at all. Merely that 'always do right and be a good little merchant' sort of girl."

"And they are sibs. Look at the set of those eyes – those straight noses." Jacquin turned, sliding the blanket from her shoulders and dumping it back into Khalisa's hand. From Khalisa's own belt, she untied a flat, folded pouch of aromatic soaps and herbs Khalisa sold in the Oasis market. "And I'll bet the whole family is the very 'good little merchant' type."

"I can't tell if you plan to bed her or steal her money."

Jacquin rumbled a deep throated purr, her gaze seeking the woman in question. Her fingers fastened the small pouch to her hip by a slender thread of silk. "I would never steal from her. But her brother..."

"Jacquin! You wouldn't! I told you I fancy him!"

"I'll read for him. Or trade with him. Then he's yours."

"And the sister?"

"The sister...," Khalisa drawled slow, smiling yet slower, "Well, that's up to her, yes?"

Their laughter rang low, their brown eyes sparkling with mischief.

The music played. The drums had been left dormant, exchanged for softer pipes and strings as night settled over Oasis. Jacquin felt her pulse match the tempo again. Her feet, delicate yet strong instinctively stepped into rhythm even as she walked. The air was crisp, the scents of sand and wind mingling with the darkly sweet spices from the soap at her waist. The audience was happy, their joy and wonder about to turn to reckless abandon.

Jacquin smiled at each visitor as she passed through the crowd, beaming at the children cheering as they held hands and spun across the desert floor, sending waves of sand into the air like a dust devil fighting for life. She glanced longingly at the lovers, holding each other close, her crimson velvet gown pressing tight against his gold-embroidered tunic, seeking the lines of each other's bodies through the cloth. She nodded a warm welcome to the old man, bent with age, his arms and legs covered by thick sable robes to keep out the oncoming cold, his dark eyes kind and deep. He lived in the town proper, but he came to watch her dance every night. He had never told her his name.

Jacquin's smile curled into a delicious invitation as she approached the young woman she'd spied before. The woman – undoubtedly the daughter of a traveling merchant – turned to spy Jacquin's approach and in that instant everyone else – the audience, the woman's leering brother – seemed to disappear.

Jacquin felt the breath catch in the younger woman's throat as if it was her own, could see the emotions tangle like the woman's wind-tossed hair in the stranger's green eyes – fear, lust, wonder. But the music captured her in its rhythm – held her bound still in Jacquin's unspoken vow... in the magic of the enchantress.

Jacquin smiled, the corners full mouth pursed and her eyes beckoning, extending a slim-fingered hand. "Tell me, child, have you ever had your fate read in the cards?"

Jacquin ran her hands over the tattered, worn, cards. She knew every line, every crease, their scent as deep and musty as ancient books, and with just as much history. The designs and symbols had been faded even when they'd been passed to her; the images were drawn from the records of the Amazons, held and cherished by the Tribe.

She turned one card with a graceful twirl of her wrist, the click of the cards echoed through the large, round wooden wagon built from silverpine trees in the far north. The light from a half dozen lanterns, the panels made of glass stained burnt orange and scarlet, bathed the carvings of eitteh, sandwolves, mountains and sunlight etched into the ceiling and walls by Jacquin and Khalisa as children, proof the wagon had been a family home before Jacquin had started using it to swindle ignorant strangers. "The sandwolves. A profitable business venture awaits."

"We're meeting with a patron in less than a fortnight. Do you see it going well?" The young tradesman, who had introduced himself as Tristan, leaned over the cards, searching Jacquin's face for answers, his eyes wide with belief and naiveté. His sister, Dani, stood on his left, Khalisa on his right, her arm draped over his shoulders.

Jacquin ran the remaining stack of cards between her fingers, tapping the edges absent-mindedly with short, filed nails. "The hour is late, my young friend, and your session has ended. Perhaps you should be getting to bed?" Jacquin lifted a single, slender eyebrow, her gaze fixed on Tristan's coinpurse, now less than half the weight it was when he'd entered.

"Of course he wants to hear more," Khalisa insisted, sliding another coin across Jacquin's table, where Jacquin palmed it and added it to the growing pouch at her waist, the money kept out of sight so as not to alert her customers to how much they'd spent.

Even when she fancied Jacquin's mark, Khalisa prioritized her dedication to her sister over a tryst. She dispensed the merchant's money amid a tangle of kisses, whispers, and praise so genuine Tristan never realized what was lost. Of course, Jacquin was an expert at baiting, speaking vaguely enough to make every promise relatable, hooking her prey just as time was running out, urging more questions and more gold with each tale.

She grinned gently at her sister. Who said they were stealing? They worked hard for their pay. Perhaps it was time to give her sister what she wanted.

"Indeed. Your efforts have not been lost on your future patron. You will soon see the fruit of your labors." Jacquin expertly palmed the deck, finding the thin card with the corner worn into a smooth curve the same shape as her thumbnail. She pulled it from the deck with some light slight-of-hand, revealing an image of two women embracing, one with hair like a thick, ebony cloak, the other an Amazon with close-cropped golden hair. "The lovers. You are marked for passion tonight."

Khalisa moved closer with each word, laying a gentle kiss across Tristan's cheek, her bare skin brushing his arm, the smell of her perfume, like desert flowers and rich spices, and silken hair encircling him. He was already won over. He was barely listening to Jacquin anymore.

As Jacquin watched her sister exit the wagon with her new lover, Dani sat across from her. Her wide eyes were unsure, her thin lips pursed with an unspoken question. "Will you read my fate next?"

Jacquin turned slowly to the young woman, meeting her attempt at boldness with a slow smile. "The cards aren't for you, *Min* Dani. Have you ever had your palm read?"

Dani blushed lightly as she slid her arm across Jacquin's table, slowly uncurling her long fingers to reveal her palm. Even without touching it Jacquin knew her skin was smooth, unused to hard labor. Jacquin had never trusted a woman with smooth hands. But it wasn't trust she was after tonight.

"Are you really an Amazon?"

Jacquin smirked at the abrupt question, Dani's face an open book.

"What have you heard about Amazons, Dani?" Jacquin traced her fingers over the lines of Dani's palm and fingers, lingering over sensitive places with the lightest touch. Dani's blush deepened, her skin darkening to a deep cinnamon with desire, but she didn't attempt to remove her hand.

Jacquin cautiously lifted Dani's hand to her mouth, running lips and teeth gently over the lines of her fingers, her eyes never leaving Dani's face.

"I just... I didn't know Amazons were dancers, too. The stories... they're all warriors." Dani's voice was soft and breathless.

Jacquin grinned against Dani's skin. "There are all kinds of Amazons. Warriors. Explorers. Healers. Diplomats. And yes, dancers."

"You're a beautiful dancer."

"You're a beautiful woman."

Dani's skin was as dark as Jacquin's, her heart pounding in her wrist beneath Jacquin's lips. Her skin was warm and familiar with the scents of spice and warm tea. It was a blend Khalisa used in her soaps. Still, hiding just beneath the scents of Jacquin's home was a scent that refused to be overpowered, one of forest, of cold and pine and damp earth. The smoothness of her palms, the old calluses on the tips of her fingers that only belonged to a well-trained player of a string instrument, the clean taste of her, even after a night in the desert all wove the story of Dani's life beneath Jacquin's tongue and hands. Dani's skin was far more intoxicating than her delicate face and wide eyes.

As Jacquin's lips nipped toward Dani's wrist, her senses were suddenly assaulted by a vision. The wagon disappeared, replaced by a dark void, thick and endless as no night, no cave, could ever be.

Dani stared up at her in shock and terror, a glass arrow protruding from her chest, blood seeping through her fine, white linen nightshirt. The earthy scent of her skin had soured, replaced with the smell of fear. Of death. *Soon.*

"Jacquin?" Jacquin blinked at the sound of her name, the vision gone. Dani looked up at her in concern. The lust had disappeared from Jacquin's eyes, her hand gone slack. She felt tears roll down her cheeks. "What's wrong?"

Jacquin curled Dani's hand between both of her own, trying not to notice the small scar on the back of her right hand, the slight bend in her small finger that spoke of an active, daring youth. She didn't want to know more of this woman's story. The more she explored her, the more she delved into the story of her life written across her body, the more she'd mourn her. Dani had shared nothing with Jacquin but her name, and already Jacquin's heart was breaking for her. "I'm so sorry."

Dani's eyes clouded with confusion, her slender neck arching back in surprise. "What?"

Jacquin couldn't look at her without seeing her die, couldn't breathe her scent without it souring to the smell of blood. What was seen could not be unseen. Dani was a walking corpse. Jacquin's head swam, her stomach turned. "Excuse me. I have to go." Jacquin rushed out of her wagon and into the night, her bare feet landing heavily on the well-packed sand of the Tribe's market, leaving her confused would-be lover behind.

"Jacquin?" Dani climbed out of Jacquin's wagon awkwardly, unused to the steep stairs and rounded door, but the dancer was already gone, weaving between the tight rows of wagons and stalls with ease. She'd grown up here, on the dusty outskirts of Oasis. The Sorormin Tribe's settlement was dense, almost as big as the permanent market in town and twice as crowded after dark. Jacquin wouldn't be found unless she wanted to be.

She jogged to the edge of Oasis, skirting along the market where she could pass unnoticed while still drawing on the heat of the torches, the rippling sound of silks swaying in the night breeze, the scents of fresh meat and spices that would calm her soul, take the edge off the lingering pain of her vision.

She'd barely made it out of the market before her stomach rolled again and she fell to the ground and vomited into the sand, the acid from an empty stomach, never sated after her dance, burning her throat. She could still feel the vision's claws in her muscles and bones, replaying in her mind. She felt out of her skin, dizzy with heat, hunger and exhaustion.

She stumbled to the far edge of Oasis, past the market and Tribal homes, to where the tall, stone wall of the city proper rose like a fortress, guarding the town from the desert's predators. Jacquin didn't feel the cold any more. She could barely feel her own body over the noise in her mind.

She followed the wall, leaning against it for support until she reached a mass of broken wagons, wheels and axels, stacked in a mountainous pile, many too dilapidated to be used again. It was a scrap yard. A graveyard of memories and traditions wearing down in the desert sun.

The moon flooded blue light over each spoke, casting deep shadows in every chip and crack, turning hand-carved designs and family symbols into something much darker, like ancient curses scrawled in a necromancer's book. Most of the Tribe refused to come here after dark. The children whispered it was haunted. But it was the only place Jacquin could find peace.

Jacquin climbed deep into the pile, burying herself in looming stacks of wood and steel, thankful to be barely clothed as she wove and danced deep into the twisting heap. Soon the moon was hidden from view, its light slipping between cracks and wheel spokes until Jacquin's skin was a puzzle of moonlight and shadow.

There, in the corner where the north and east wall of Oasis met, was a small wagon wedged in the sand. The wheels had been removed, the windows boarded long before being cast into the pile. A single lantern post above the door hung lopsided, clinging to the wood by a single nail. The other pieces and taller wagons loomed overhead; no one passing would see the broken sanctuary. It had been here since Jacquin was a child, too dilapidated and broken to be a priority for repairs.

Jacquin stepped through the door, her feet sliding over the soft carpet she'd laid years ago to cover the base of the wagon, now worn away, consumed by the desert. She lit a glass lantern, casting the room, the worn pillows and soft blankets, in flickering shadows. She collapsed on the pillows, ignoring the grit of sand that shifted and scattered across the carpet from the abrupt movement. The dusty smell, the ghosts of her tears, her screams and finally the shattered tension of letting go, the private aftermath of her most deadly and heartbreaking visions, started to ease deep into her heart, seeking to soothe Dani's death into the back of her mind, to heal Jacquin's soul like cauterizing fire.

She closed her eyes and breathed deep into her stomach, trying to smell more than Dani's lifeblood oozing from her heart, feel more than the phantom pain of an arrow piercing her chest. Even in the vision Dani's eyes had been so young, if not in years then in experience. Her death was a waste.

Jacquin pressed her face against a soft down pillow embroidered in gold until she stopped trembling. Her visions were becoming increasingly more violent. At least once a day for the last monarc she'd touched someone to watch them die by sword or arrow. She had never seen when or how beyond the direct assault. She assumed they were going to be waylaid by bandits after leaving Oasis, but the visions had become so common she feared the threat would target Oasis itself. Her home.

She closed her eyes, dreading once again the day she'd touch her sister and watch her die.

She opened her eyes and focused on the flame of her lantern. She wondered if the Amazons had prayed. Jacquin had never been religious, but as the vision continued to cling to her, she wished for divine direction.

Her face twisted in frustration at herself for becoming so broken over the vision, for the influence her magic had over her body and mind. "*Z'ki Sak, Diana!*" she sighed in exasperation, recalling a phrase from the books of Valley Bay. "What can I do?"

Her mind drifted toward her vision during her dance. The silver warrior, hooded and hidden in shadow. It wasn't the first time she'd danced a vision of the same figure, so strong and mysterious. She'd assumed the warrior to be a protector, a spirit guide, a touchstone that kept her sane. It had never moved until tonight.

"Help me," she whispered to the air, the memory of her warrior firm in her mind, pleading with the only deity she respected: her personal, supernatural protector in silver.

Chapter Two

It was miserably wet. Thunderstorms rumbled in the east, promising to turn the chilly spring drizzle into a torrential downpour before twilight completely faded. The cobbles were slick, and the steel shod hooves of the war mare chipped the stones with each heavy clop. But there was barely anyone to notice. The small town was shut tight against the rain. Timbers and gutters dripping, mortar sheeting wet, and mud running thick all made a slick and gravel sludge of swirling brown water that cautioned any traveler. Smoke was thicker, curling grey-blue as it was drafted down from chimney spouts to make a damp fog in alleys and dead air spaces. The place smelled of wood burning and sewage, but the rankness was muted by the wet cold; it would grow worse later beneath summer suns.

The blacksmith's doors were slanted open, the orange blazes dancing deep in the shadows. The ping-ping of the anvil's hammer echoed a strange sort of welcoming.

It was one Adrian accepted. She ducked low and rode Dread straight through the smithy's door. The rain tarp cowled both her and the gear across Dread's flanks. For a moment, the hammer's song stilled. Adrian slid out from beneath the oiled skin she wore as a cloak, stepping down from the saddle with a very mortal creak to the leather seat.

The hammer thunked against the stout floorboards, and the burly male picked up a towel to wipe the sweat from his hands. He passed the rag through the matted hair of his chest in an absent gesture, through damp fur that rivaled the growth on his face, then tossed it aside as Adrian took a stance across the anvil from him. She was nearly as hidden as she had been beneath the tarp. The heavy silverish-grey of her cloak covered her from calf to head. The hood was pulled forward and low, creating a dense shadow where her eyes should have been, and only the smoothness of her pale chin hinted at her sex.

"Cold day," the smithy noted. His hands curled into hammer-like fists on his hips.

"Cold enough," she returned levelly. Fingers gloved in grey, stitched leather underlined her resources as a gold bar the size of a thumb was extended to him. "She needs shoes, the padded sort to dull travel shock, but with sharp honed edges to the fore pair."

"Aye," he nodded and took the gold piece. "I've done the like for merchant guards and passing kings' men."

"And her tack needs a slow drying, not too near the fire. Then a good cleaning and oiling."

"Have a girl apprenticed to me, she'll do it right. If you like, I've stalls for boarding, too. Better'n the Red Griffin next door, although theirs aren't bad. Both are broad, fine boxes. But I've got a tack shelf and saddle bar in each, for your animal to guard your pieces."

It went without saying that Dread was the sort of steed to have that training.

"An' the side door's always open. You can leave at your own pleasure, waken me or not."

"Fair enough."

He picked up an iron length, clanging the triangle hanging from the ceiling as Adrian retrieved a smaller bag from beneath Dread's tarp. A squarely-built youngster of fourteen appeared as a door whacked shut in the back. Adrian noted the attentive glint in those hazel eyes and approved.

"You listen to these two," she murmured to Dread and her mare gave a snort, nodding consent. She turned to the smithy again. "Keep your movements slow. If she gets nervous, step back and keep your hands where she can see them. She'll calm by herself, if she's satisfied."

"An' if she isn't, you're not goin' need worry 'bout it anymore," the man warned his apprentice. The girl nodded but didn't flinch.

Adrian paused, watching as the apprentice came forward and led Dread away. The mare flicked her tail and tossed a chiding look back at Adrian, as if to remind her rider that she too was capable of distinguishing between children and dubious spies. It made Adrian smile. The youngster moved out of ear range, and Adrian amended, "There is another thing."

The smithy paused, his hot bladed knife angled above the gold bar ready to cut her change.

"A less tangible need."

He laid the blade aside and weighed the money in his hand. His sharp eyes darted back toward the stable hall to be sure his girl wasn't near enough to hear something that might get her hurt later. He grunted, hefting the gold piece again. He tossed it into the leather bucket with others and nodded for her to continue.

"Who has passed through and what routes out did they take?"

"How far back?"

There was a measuring silence, until finally, "You tell me."

He gave a short sigh, then another nod. "War party, fresh looting."

"That's the one."

"They split by two roads. East and Southeast. Most of 'em went east, but the dangerous ones maybe went separate."

"How so?"

"They were ridin' the faster horses. Every one of 'em carried barbed spears 'long with side sabers. No archers that I could see. They were meanin' business. Took food an' the saddle packs they could carry, but they left the pack animals an' the finery with the others. Looked like scouts, the lot of 'em... Travelin' so light."

Or a skirmish attack honed in on a target, Adrian corrected.

"Another thing. One circled back in from the East Road group. He came with a merchant's band, a big one from the Nor'west Way. He's dressed fancier. Last time he kept his cloak on and his face mostly covered, but we recognized 'im. The tender of Red Griffin as well as myself. A big fella with black beard goin' grey in streaks. He's got a good smile to 'im, but it's the kind that don't reach his eyes. An' he don't look at you much when he's talkin'. Instead, he's busy watchin' the doors an' roads beyond the windows."

Adrian recognized the description. Gryert. A battle-weaned sergeant grown into a general's strategist who'd worked for the Twins. He was circling around to ensure the battle party wasn't being followed before rejoining the marauders later. He was a mercenaries' delight; she was about to become his nightmare.

The smithy watched as she mutely picked up her bag and gave him a brief nod of thanks before stepping out into the rain. His eyes narrowed speculatively. He'd do best to keep the apprentice upstairs with his missus tonight. He'd take his hammer up as well. He never much liked looters, that more than the money had been his reason for talking to the stranger. But he wasn't a stupid man either, and he had to respect anyone wearing a sword the way that fellow in Red Griffin did. He hoped the woman knew what she was doing — for all their sakes.

Adrian entered from the side, near hidden in the smoke and shadows of the long bar's end. It was a common enough place to come from, since it was the door nearest the smithy's front and in such weather any traveler needing their horse re-shod would have chosen the same. But instead of joining the warmth and hustle of the center room, Adrian slipped further back into the corner to watch. She'd pushed her hood back some, enough to let the lack of whiskers and the angular cast of her features become clear, yet not enough to bring her whole face into view. Her angular, silver mane of hair was still covered.

She knew Gryert might not recognize her face – she had been a child when they'd last spoken – and she took magical precautions to hide her more distinguishing features. He'd recognize her silver hair, however, and he was no doubt charmed to see through all but the most complex of illusions. She didn't want to be recognized. She held no fantasies about toying with him or learning anything of value from him. He was here for the sole purpose of identifying the bandits sent from the Core.

Yellow light streamed in through the thick tobacco haze, bringing smells of greasy fats roasting and caramel sweets browning. Behind the bar, the kitchen opened in a yawning wide gape above the ale kegs, and food passed out as dirty trays slid in. The clanging of metal pots and cooks' curses mingled with the ruckus of the tavern customers. Lively betting on some card game vied with another table's rowdy celebration of a young soldier's merits. Ermine-cuffed jackets and stained sheepskin vests rubbed shoulders here. It was a merchant traveler's lodge where the better swords and the traders' offspring drank together even as they did on the journey roads, because the first were well paid and the second still too young to hate them for it.

Adrian noted the variety in meats served as she exchanged coin for ale. Their selection was impressive for so small a town, so far from the rest of humanity. It was also probably the only inn around with private rooms. The liveries she had passed on the outskirts had been lined with barracks above to allow goods, stock and guards to stay near enough to one another, and they were more than likely the caravans' first choice for crew lodgings. That explained why Gryert was here. He would want his privacy to discourage the locals' questions and yet need the access to the travelers' news.

She knew then, he would certainly be here... somewhere.

Across the room she finally saw him. A sable-clad man of older years who leaned to the side of his chair, a leg extended parallel to his table and his shoulder comfortably pressed against the stone wall. His back was mostly guarded by that wall. His fingers played with the jeweled hilt of the short sword at his hip. Above him, the upper stairs glowed brightly from lanterns in the stairwell, and the creak of the wood boards would have announced any's descent.

Before him, laughing and filling their short cups with spirits, a pair of merchant sons reveled in some story he was encouraging from them. His grin showed white teeth through his smooth, thick beard as he chewed on a mint taper. He nodded at something the two said, eyes rounding through the crowd haphazardly.

He was becoming lax in his assumptions, Adrian noted. The rains had begun to pour and the thunders lashed with lightnings outside. The weather was altogether too nasty for anybody of sense to be traveling in, and he was beginning to think he would be safely unhindered for at least another night.

She ordered a bowl of mushroom barley for dinner. She could afford to wait and let him grow assured.

He looked straight at her. But her face was not particularly hidden and her manner drew no attention. The bar was crowded with quieter locals towards her end, and her greyish cloak faded in with their drab browns and greens. She mimed the hunch of those about her well, their hoods bared just enough to invite a friend's conversation and hide enough to discourage a stranger's frivolity. Again his gaze swept past her.

Gryert had indeed become careless since the years she had known him. But then the Twins' magics had undoubtedly given him less need for caution.

Or perhaps, she was under-rating how her own skills had grown.

She watched, and as the night drew on his back inched further and further away from the wall. She ordered another ale and asked about rooms.

"Plenty, if you're willing to share?" the bar's tender prodded agreeably.

"The room yes, the bed no."

"Still got a few to choose from."

"Something with less noise would be best."

The jovial grin took on a somewhat more ironic twist. "You've got a choice 'tween kitchen clatter an' customer chatter."

A slow smile answered him, although he couldn't have said if it was good-natured or sarcastic. "The kitchen's will do fine."

"Good enough then." He fished a great ring of keys out from beneath his apron and extracted a wooden one from the set. He held it out of her reach. "Money up front."

She slid a pair of small, but flawed jewels across the bar to him. "Instead of coin stick?"

"Acceptable." On a merchant's route, it wasn't such an unusual thing. He pointed at the stairs behind Gryert. "Top floor, back hall not front. You'll find space in the double, third room on the left. Fire's not lit, but your wood's included. So's breakfast porridge an' breads."

She nodded and stood, pausing for a last pull on the weak ale as she saw Gryert rearranging his chair. She put her stein down as he faced himself towards his table, drinking a parting toast with his companions. She moved along the bar, slipping between elbows and shoulders unnoticed. The merchant boys left to join the dicing games, and Gryert reached across the table to grab a half-emptied glass and drain it. The motion freed his sword's pommel knob, an octagonal gem bright in its bloody redness, and she recognized the talisman from the Twins.

He stretched again to retrieve the bottle. This time she closed in, the slender length of her short sword skritching as it left its sheath. He rounded at the sound, hearing it even in the tavern's noise. His hand went down, but too slow, and the scabbard belt sliced, his sword falling. She grabbed for his hair as he shoved the chair back hard into her belly. She missed and the table went over in his scramble.

They faced each other then, across the width of the suddenly silent room. His long knife was drawn. His dark eyes squinted, his confusion apparent as he tried to fathom why a lone swordarm would be attacking him; he'd anticipated a mercenary crew. She unfastened her cloak and let it fall aside, covering the red gem of the weapon at her feet. Her baggage dropped with it.

With a silent command, she allowed the most intricate of her spells disguising the more recognizable features of her face to flicker, long enough that only he would see.

His stance widened as did his eyes, disbelief and fear mixing as he rasped, "But you're dead?!"

A knife flew from her hand, his blade angled up to deflect it. The second he never saw coming, and it pinioned his arm into the wood beam above him as the knife fell from his fist. She slammed his freed hand against the wall as the point of her blade jabbed beneath his sternum, barely stayed by the chain mail beneath his sable vest.

"Kin blood!"

"They said you were dead!"

"Not quite."

Intense, furious eyes stared into his fear, steady and unflinching. She could read his thoughts, images of the Twins dancing through his mind. All their plans, all their ambitions...

"Tell me who rides east and who southeast?"

He swallowed thickly, knowing what would come. In a

whisper he said, "No."

"*Aravin sith vin....*" The slender steel of her blade slid through the chain mail, her magic turning it to less than butter.

The room's silence was deafening save for that last gurgle of breath, and then his head rolled to the side. Only then did Adrian step back, letting his carcass fold down into a heap. She wiped the slender length of her sword clean on the silk of his blouse sleeve. Her blade returned to its sheath upon her right hip. Then she stood, shrugging as she did to resettle the heavier weight of the larger weapon strapped to her back. Most in the tavern had not even noticed she carried another sword before now; they'd all been too intent on the conflict itself. Adrian bent once more, snatching a leather tag from Gryert's neck and snapping its thong with a deft twist.

She looked around the hushed crowd slowly. "Who travels west?"

An uncomfortable murmur ran through her audience, but quiet fell again as a dwarf stood and stepped away from his table. Another of his kind followed, placing himself at his friend's elbow. Their unruly long beards were tucked into wide belts, and both were armed with short, fat knives and heavy, two-bladed axes.

"We do, Warmage," the first one rumbled, thumbs tucking into his belt as his chin thrust forward. "We go all the way to your capital city."

He surprised her. This far from her country's borders, Adrian had not expected to find any that knew of the Grey Exiles from the Core. She lifted the leather bit. "Will you take this with a message to the Tribunal?"

Her gentle tone was utterly surprising to the folks; she spoke clearly with question and gave no hint of command. The dwarf stalked forward, halting a pace from her outstretched hand to eye the tag cautiously. There was nothing more than the family seal embossed on it. He grunted and nodded. It made sense; she had cried for kin blood.

Adrian gave it to him and gestured at Gryert's body. "He'll carry gold stick in his purse. Whatever he has, it's payment for the favor."

A rumble assent of sorts accepted her terms. Then he faced her more squarely and prompted, "You said a message too."

"Tell them, it has begun." Their gazes met, and the dwarf understood. It would be the last thing her people ever heard from her; but it was a testimony more than a message. It meant at least some price had been extracted for the crimes, and her folk would not be forced to hire mercenaries to pursue the matter more.

He honored her with a waist deep bow, a thing almost unheard of with a dwarf's pride. She returned it in full.

He went to retrieve Gryert's purse as she rounded towards the bar and the tavern's tender. She flipped a gold stick through the air before he could protest the dueling. He sized it in his palm, then her in her grey leathers. His fist closed about the money, and he turned towards the patrons.

"House pays for the ale! Set yourselves down'n we'll bring it right to you!"

The tender sent a pair to clear away the body, and Adrian retrieved her things near the stairs. She took Gryert's sword, too, careful to keep her cloak draped about it. But she wasn't concerned that someone might accuse her of theft. She was wary of the talisman gem. It was still a thing to be dealt with.

In the dim passage above she found her room quickly. It wasn't surprising that it was empty; the hour was still early. Although, given her display downstairs, the one who'd paid for the bed next to hers might think twice about claiming it. That, and it wasn't the sort of room that one would generally spend a lot of time in. The place was clean, but stark. A pair of cots with worn but thick woven blankets and a small table with a single chair were its complete furnishings. There was also cut wood in a heavy ceramic pot next to the fireplace and a matching set of oil lamps suspended in sconces above the mantel. It was not a particularly comfortable place for entertaining. But it would serve Adrian's needs.

She dumped her gear on the bed, carefully laying the cloaked sword beside it and lit one of the wall lamps. Turning to the plank table next, she shoved its shorter end up against the wall. She took a step back, decided there was too much light and dimmed the wick some. There was no reason to tell the Twins where she was, if they should notice her use of their talisman. She wasn't certain they'd ward it against a stranger's use; she suspected arrogance might have made them too sure of Gryert's skills to bother with such charms.

From her rolled pack, she extracted a bundle of thin but sturdy hide tubes and chose one. The parchment map shook out and spread easily; she kept them well oiled so they'd be malleable and fairly waterproof. She hung the sheet over the table, tacking it into the wall with two small knives that had made a false buckle on her back sword's harness. Then she retrieved Gryert's weapon from the bed and beneath the cloak, unsheathed the blade. She drove the end into the table top with a thud and then cautiously moved away, holding her cloak up like a curtain behind the bespelled thing.

The red gem glittered atop the sword's hilt, bound by a little wire cage. With an unnatural splay of sparks, it spat and hissed for a moment. She waited patiently for it to settle into a steady, pink glow and then drew nearer again, still keeping the grey cloth high. A beacon-like stream of ruby-blood light began sweeping — rotating — in a full circle. Adrian watched from over the edge of her cloak with a growing satisfaction; there had been no warding.

"Questions for thee," she rasped in a low, low voice that mimicked an elderly sage or a hoarse demon tone. The jewel responded, drawing its auras back into its center in readiness. "Two masters thou have, aside from the fool bearer. Fashioned were thee as the eye for the Twins. Now comes the time, these Two must thee find. The First is Eldest, Laik by name..."

The red light flashed out, singeing a brown smote on the map's line of the East Trader's route.

"... and the Second, the younger. Foxsen by name."

Again the light burned the map. This time it lit a fainter mark on the Southeast Road. Adrian smiled grimly. "Now Fire Eye, another query of thee. Show the place they will meet, to join again as Two."

Beyond the denser forests, the red glow shadowed a village-small town labeled Cont. It was less than she had hoped, the light left no singed flecking; their plans were tentative, at best. She tried a last question, knowing those distant masters were probably already sensing something wrong.

"There are targets to be struck, precious goods to reap — all will come before the Two meet. Point to these places thy masters ride for, point to the rape and the war."

Lightening struck out in scarlet bolts and left smoke curling about a ragged, charred hole. It pointed deep into the deserts of the southern continents, a place unmarked on her maps. There wasn't even a nearby road's turn or a caravan's trail indicated in that sandy landscape. But there was something on that Southeastern route... something so vitally important to the Twins that their ambitions were completely united for it.

"Sleep now, thy rest is earned." Adrian was almost haphazard in remembering to cover the talisman again.

It was a puzzle that remained, even as she bound the gemmed hilt with shredded blanket cloth and laid it in the hearth. With her uttered spell, fires engulfed both sword and talisman in cold, white flames of magic. She stood, watching that steel and ruby weapon evaporate into harmless nothingness, and then when it was gone, she struck a match to the other candle sconce, carefully packed the map away, and drew a small bowl from her things. She settled on the hard wood floor, ignoring the cold drafts and emptied a bit of powdered incense into the blue-black swirls of the ceramic piece; the center depths looked like the starry sky on a clear night. She sat herself down solemnly, feet flat against the floor on either side of the bowl and elbows on knees. She drew a breath and clasped her hands, head bowing, and a tiny blue-white flame leapt into life in the shrine bowl.

And she prayed, for the soul of the boy Gryert had once been, for the waste of the man that had turned from gentler ways... for the potential of the life she had taken. Silent tears fell to sputter the flame, but it did not go out. She sent what she could of his soul to the Star Strider, what little good was left in the depths of his blackened heart, but she did it without reservations and the faint essence of what could-have-been crossed back into Her mercy at the plea.

Then the flame finally died. Adrian blinked the scorched, salty tears from her vision and steadied her breathing. She rose to find her bed.

She never thought to pray for herself. She had been through Hellthorns and returned whole; the Star Strider must have seen some use in unsheathing Her Weapon. Adrian had accepted the role without question, trusting that Her Need was great enough... even knowing that this was only the beginning and that she might very well lose her way — and her soul – before the end.

Chapter Three

Rox crept through the underbrush, her steps as silent as owl's wings. She scanned the trees as she moved, looking for the tell-tale footprints or crushed brush that would indicate the presence of other humans – anyone who might be tracking her party. A scuffle nearby caught her attention and she spotted the fluffy tail of a tree rodent leaping up a willowy sapling. The forests had been growing thinner the further she and the Circle traveled south, the massive silverpines of the north dwindling to the spindly trees she wove through now. If they traveled further south the land would open up into dense, hilly brushlands and then to the deserts that consumed most of the southern continent.

Rox's leather cloak was heavy and wet, the rainwater still clinging to the trees from the storms earlier in the day soaking her to the skin. Her rough, wool clothing rubbed uncomfortably against her skin, the scratchy fabric pressed tight against her by the heavy cloak. Her cropped, damp dark golden curls clung to her nape and forehead, sending tiny rivulets trickling down her narrow cheeks and chin. Still, she would rather be wet cold here in the forest than back with the Circle. There were worse things than skin burns from cheap clothing.

She paused in a small clearing of particularly tall trees and glanced up through the branches. Raccoons and other tree rodents slept in the branches, birds dozing in their nests. No sign of anything out of the ordinary. No bowmen. No warriors. Rox had always been able to see in the dark. Her green eyes glinted like a wolf's as she moved expertly through the night. If it was a form of magic, it was the only one she had. Still, she thanked the Mother for it as she easily scouted a perimeter around the Circle's camp. If there was anyone hiding in the forest, she'd find them. More than one assailant had been caught by assuming she couldn't see them and becoming careless.

She made her way back to camp, shrugging her bow off her shoulders to relieve some of the weight off her back. She traveled almost five hundred paces when the forest split open into a large clearing. The contrast between the forest and the camp was jarring, like stepping off the edge of the world.

The Circle's camp was sparse: a couple dozen bed mats laid

under waxed canvas tarps to ward off the storms. She stepped around the massive marauders, sleeping with their swords and daggers in their arms. A few held treasure they didn't trust a courier to take home, gold and jewels they'd gained through murder and destruction. Trinkets and tokens of their depravity. Their snores and muttered curses as they dreamed of raids and murder cast a heavy fog around the clearing that made it hard to breathe. Still, it would soon be worse: another dozen members would be arriving before dawn with messages from the Twins on where to reposition. Until then, they waited, and Rox ensured their safety.

She felt a tremble and silken sweep across the back of her neck as Fisk woke. He crept out of his safe haven between her nape and the folds of her hood to rest on her shoulder, his long, pointed nose sniffing at the air, his tiny claws digging into her sleeve for balance. As a waterferret, Fisk's sleek fur repelled the rain but he still hid in her cloak and jackets to avoid the storms.

Rox grinned wryly, the expression crooked, good-natured and rarely seen. "It stopped raining."

Fisk grunted deep in his chest and skittered down Rox's arm, dropping into the deep pocket at her hip with practiced ease. Rox patted her dear friend through her pocket and he emitted a rumbling sound not unlike an eitteh's purr. "You're lucky you found me. You never would have survived as a fishing ferret." Fisk nipped at her finger through the cloth of her pocket in response.

Rox laid out her thin, woven bedmat along the edge of camp, where she could see every member of her traveling party. Her scouting hadn't turned up any threats, but she was still cautious. She would have to keep consistent watch over the camp as new segments of their party rejoined the camp and do another perimeter sweep before dawn. There was always a chance an angry villager or assassin bent on vengeance would try tailing the raiding parties back to camp. Rox didn't blame them. She'd hunt them down, too if she'd lived in one of the villages the Circle targeted. Part of her wished she could let a few angry villagers pass, give them a chance at vengeance, but if even one member of the Circle died due to her negligence, she wouldn't get paid. And at the end of the day, that's all that mattered.

She scowled, the expression etched so deeply in her face the lines were becoming permanent. The scent of the camp was overwhelming: The odor of dozens of long-term travelers would be bad enough, but there was such a universal rejection of all forms of hygiene among the Circle's men that the smell made Rox's head spin. Rox thanked the Mother once more for her decision to spend some of her last coin on a charm that warded against lice and other parasites.

She could see the tiny bugs in the moonlight, leaping into the air off the men's hair and beards. She shuddered and turned away.

Rox turned and started tying down her canvas rain-guard. As she reached the last knot, she was shoved from behind. Rox fell with a hard crash, slamming into the ground with a grunt. Pine needles and gravel dug into her arms and scattered beneath her, clacking against nearby trees and bed mats. Fisk raced out of her pocket and into the bushes, confused by the fall and wary of an oncoming fight. She instantly leapt back to her feet, charging forward to meet the marauder who'd shoved her. Her small, lithe frame barely reached the man's shoulder, but the ferocity in Rox's sage green eyes made any difference in their size negligible.

In an instant, every member of the Circle was awake and on their feet, knives and swords at the ready, searching the darkness for the source of the crash.

Rox glared up at the man above her, his sharp, square jaw clenched in rage, his long, mud-brown hair streaked with grey tied at his nape. He wasn't much older than Rox, maybe 80 tenmoons, but he hadn't aged well. Rox's lips pulled back from her teeth in a feral growl. When had he gotten back? "Push me again, Calder."

"Gryert's dead. I found his body dumped outside Pinewood. Stripped of everything. Even his charms."

A tense silence fell over the clearing, every eye on Rox.

Rox's voice was cold and even. "Gryert left the party."

"You were hired to keep us safe."

Rox hissed between her teeth, the heat of rage and determination resting just under her skin, waiting to be unleashed at the slightest slip of control. "Only on the road. What you do at rest stops is your issue."

"It's your issue if we're being followed."

"We're not being followed. It was probably highwaymen." Rox snorted at the irony.

One of the younger marauders, Tyrius, shifted uncomfortably, making his blonde beard sway in time with his anxieties. He clenched his sword with a white-knuckled hand. "No highwayman could kill Gryert. He was a mage."

Calder glared down at Rox, his grey eyes slits of anger. "His sword was taken."

"Then the Twins will find whoever robbed him."

Tyrius fidgeted, his eyes growing wider as he muttered to a nearby companion. "Or he called up something. Something magical from his sword. A demon from the Fates' Cellar."

"The sword was a way to spy on us, not cast spells," Rox

groused, trying to stop Tyrius' line of thought before it spread through the party. Gryert had been using small tricks and flashy spells since they'd left the Core to keep the Circle nervous of his abilities. Rox had never taken him seriously. A good magician didn't need to show off. Still, the Circle was comprised of bullies and raiders; vicious fighters but often lacking in common sense. She could defend the party from physical attackers, but she was powerless against fears of the supernatural.

Calder wasn't as easily swayed as his companions. He wasn't a member of the Circle because he was a brute with no other path in life. He was a genuine psychopath. Rox had heard once he had been picked up by the Twins before he was to be executed for torturing and murdering his neighbor. Rox wouldn't be surprised to learn it was true. "That doesn't change the fact that it would take more than a highway robber to take down Gryert. You should have known we were being watched before he circled back."

More eyes on Rox. She crossed her arms over her chest, deadly from head to toe. "I wouldn't have been hired if I didn't know how to protect my perimeter. Whatever followed Gryert wasn't with us before he left and isn't with us now."

Calder stepped forward, keeping his voice low enough to hiss in Rox's ear unheard by others. "You're only safe here because you hold a contract with the Twins. If one of us dies, that contract is broken. And what good are you to us if you can't do your job? You may be fierce, but no one could take all of us. Least of all a woman." Calder ran his fingers through Rox's hair and Rox's stomach turned.

In a single motion, Rox drew a knife from her sleeve and leveled it at Calder's stomach, the blade pressing firmly against his leather tunic, piercing the top layer. It would only take two motions: the plunge, and then a twist. Two motions and his threat would be eradicated. But in those motions she would give up everything she'd been working for. "Touch me and you offend the Twins."

Calder sneered, his curved, hawk-like nose flaring. "Kill me and you won't get paid."

They stood in a lethal stalemate, eyes locked with warring motives and desires. Rox forced her breath to remain steady, her muscles taut, her eyes narrowed. If there was any doubt that the Twins would honor their contract, death would be the least of her worries. Especially at Calder's hand. But more than their respect of the Twins, many of the Circle respected her ferocity, her cunning. If the party attacked, she would take many of them down with her, and the dissolution of the party for any reason would enrage the tyrannical mage Twins of the Core. She couldn't appear weak.

Couldn't slip. Couldn't give them any reason to doubt her value to their masters.

The clatter of horses' hooves, riding fast, echoed through the forest. Another fraction of their party was returning. The sound broke the tension between Rox and Calder, drawing the Circle's attention. A dozen men, weary from riding hard to meet the rest of the Circle, rode into sight. Rox recognized Kasin, Calder's second in command, leading the group, his beard wild and tangled across his face, his eyes weary. Calder would need to check in with him quickly if either man hoped to rest before leaving again in a few hours.

Calder took a step back and Rox sheathed her dagger. "We leave at dawn," Rox called to be heard over the sounds of the new party dismounting. "Better sleep now if you want to sleep at all." She met Calder's eyes again. "I'm sure you and Kasin have plenty to talk about."

Calder glanced her over, evaluating her. Rox saw in Calder's eyes what she already knew: she was still too much of a threat to attack. Too dangerous. Too well connected. But he'd be watching.

He spun on his heel, turning to Kasin. "With me! We'll chart our next course."

Rox watched him leave, turning her back on him only when he greeted Kasin. No matter how tired she was, she needed to get out of the camp. She stomped into the forest after Fisk, searching for him in the brush, her gloved hands catching on thorns and briars. She wasn't trying to be silent. Twigs and dead plants crunched under her boots. She accidentally kicked a rock, sending it soaring into a nearby tree, then rebounding into a bramble bush where a bird exploded into the air in shock. She watched its wings, sparkling white in the darkness as it flew to safety.

She let out a heavy breath as she escaped the Circle's hearing range. Calder wanted her dead. She could see it in his eyes every time he looked at her. He would enjoy making her suffer first, but his main motive was to leave her corpse behind on the roadside. No one would recognize her. She didn't have family to look for her. Even if she was discovered by a nearby town, she'd just end up in an unmarked grave. If the Circle attacked her, Calder was the first she'd take down, and he knew it. Only fear kept her safe.

Her boots sank deep into the mud with a graceless *schloop* as she continued further into the forest. She could tell from the consistency of the soil and the musty, earthy scent that clung to her nose and mouth that there was a swamp nearby. She paused as she stepped again and sank to the middle of her calves. Fisk wouldn't have traveled much farther. He hated mud.

Rox stopped, resting her fists on her hips, her face twisted in a crooked, dark grimace. Fisk should have heard her coming. He was sulking. "Stop messing around, Fisk. Get out here, it's safe now."

Fisk scuttled toward her from beneath a nearby tree and raced up her arm to her neck, complaining loudly about his forced foray into the wet underbrush. She grunted as his wet, dirty paws clambered across her nape. "It wasn't my fault."

Fisk huffed in response.

Rox contemplated searching the perimeter once again, but decided against it. After the look in Calder's eyes, she wouldn't put it past him to try to find her away from the Circle. For once, there was safety in the ranks of the Circle.

She marched slowly back to camp, her jaw clenched tighter than her gloved fists. She didn't allow herself to feel bad about her position, to dwell on how disgusted she was by her charges. There were more important things to focus on: payment. No matter what she did, no matter where she led these marauders, it would all be worth it. She just had to do her job and survive. Still, she treasured her alone time, the hours she spent scouting and creating a perimeter. The longer she could be away from the Circle and their foul stench, fouler mouths and murderous impulses the better.

Most of the Circle were sleeping again when she returned. She spotted Calder, Kasin and a handful of other party leaders meeting on the far edge of camp. They'd lit two torches, the light glowing across a series of letters and maps laid out across a fallen tree. Calder held his chin in his hand, deep in thought.

Rox paused in the shadowy depths of the forest, watching with a single arched eyebrow. It would be wise for her to stay a step ahead of Calder.

She moved silently, staying deep enough in the forest not to attract attention until she was as close to Calder's meeting as possible. She crouched beside a thick, thorny bramble bush, focusing intently. She couldn't see them anymore, she was too close to stand without being betrayed by the light of the torches, but she could hear them just fine.

"We found the third piece has been returned to the Core, but the Twins say the second two are in the desert," Kasin reported. The sound of a finger striking parchment echoed. They were looking at a map.

Calder's voice was low and thoughtful as he plotted his next move. "There aren't a lot of villages in the desert."

"Initial scryings have placed one artifact buried in the sand and the other in the Great Market."

"We'll need a larger party if we're going to take on the Market."

"We may not be able to take it at all. It will require more subtlety than our usual ventures."

"Subtlety? From these brutes? By the time we get to the Market they'll be frothing at the mouth for a raid."

"We've been given clearance to pillage as we please. The Twins believe the random violence will disguise our true purpose."

Calder's voice was thick with pleasure. Rox didn't have to see him to know he was smiling. "Good. Then we head south. Perhaps we'll run across a merchant's caravan on our way into the desert."

Their voices faded as the meeting broke and they returned to the main camp. Rox waited for them to go silent and settle into their beds before standing. She drew a deep breath, steeling herself for the destruction and mayhem to come. She'd always known the Twins had a purpose for sending out the Circle, but she'd assumed it was to amass wealth, maybe sow fear. She had never involved herself in their raids, staying behind as they'd pillaged and plundered a half dozen villages, leaving behind only corpses and ash. She didn't realize they'd been searching for something.

The mention of artifacts was intriguing. She wondered exactly what they were, if she'd seen one of the artifacts in the loot bags constantly coming in and out of camp. Still, she decided not to dwell on the thought. Whatever the Twins were looking for was bound to be dangerous. She would do well not to research them any further. Her curiosity didn't matter. She didn't want to be involved in their plans. She wanted to finish the mission and earn her wage. The moment she was paid, she could break ties with them forever.

She circled back around in case any of the men were awake enough to be suspicious of where she re-entered camp. She slid onto her sleeping mat, pulling a light-weight wool blanket over her shoulders. She was small enough that the cheap lap-blanket she'd been given when she joined the party nearly covered her entire body. She wasn't going to be able to sleep. Still, resting in silence was a luxury she never took for granted.

Fisk slinked out of her jacket, curling in the crook of her arm and burying his head beneath her sleeve before promptly falling asleep. Rox stroked the top of his head with one finger, marveling again that despite everything they'd been through, he still trusted her so much.

"You're a fool," she whispered affectionately, laying a gentle kiss on his downy head and saying a silent prayer to the Mother for safety. "But it will all be over soon. One way or another."

Chapter Four

Wind and sand howled past the city gates, engulfing Oasis in it torrential wake. Jacquin crawled across the desert floor, her mouth and lungs filling with sand, the tiny grains drowning her as if she'd been plunged underwater. Her nails clawed at the shifting desert, searching desperately for something to hold onto as the storm ripped at her hair and skin, slicing her open then filling her bloody cuts with more sand.

Her hands reached out wildly, hoping to find a sanctuary, and found the front step of her wagon. She grabbed it with trembling hands and pulled herself up, flinging the tattered, weatherbeaten wooden door to her home open as she slid inside, closing the door behind herself.

She lay collapsed on the carpeted floor, gasping and coughing, trying to purge her lungs of the deadly sand. Finally, fresh air flooded her mouth and she breathed deep, closing her eyes as she clung to life. Oasis had never been hit like this before. She worried about Khalisa, about the rest of her Tribe. The storm had descended so suddenly: had they made it to safety? She imagined her sister, swallowed forever in the depths of the desert and trembled. She needed to find her, but she knew if she opened her front door she'd destroy her only safe haven.

She heard a scuffle across her carpet and felt silken fur brush her hand. When she didn't move, a quick, sharp sting, a bite, on her arm demanded her attention. She opened her eyes to meet gold eyes full of concern. Her brows knit in confusion. When had she acquired a waterferret? The creatures rarely journeyed beyond the coastal towns in the south.

She pushed herself up onto her hands and shouted with surprise as she realized she wasn't alone. A figure cloaked in silver, hidden from head to mid-calf sat on the far side of the cabin, a sword with a demonic red gem in the hilt resting blade-down before it. The figure turned to her, piercing eyes examining her from the depths of the hood. It spoke in a whisper, in a language Jacquin couldn't understand. Its voice was inhuman, distorted by magic and the pounding of the storm against the walls of the wagon.

"Who are you?" Jacquin's voice trembled as she realized she had to be dreaming. Her silver-cloaked guardian only appeared in visions and dreams, and the storm was too severe, too symbolic to be a vision of what was to come.

The figure sat in silence, one gauntlet-clad hand stroking the red jewel. In an instant, another figure, mirror-image of the first, appeared on the opposite side of the wagon. The waterferret let out a shrill cry of alarm and disappeared from existence, abandoning Jacquin to the strangers. Jacquin shrank back against the door to her wagon, the energy in the room growing heavy and malevolent. She knew in an instant that these two were not her protector. They were false copies.

They stood as one, crossing slowly toward her in perfect unison. The storm howled around her, raking at the wagon like a beast, but she suddenly found she trusted the chaotic, unbiased wrath of the storm over these malevolent creatures.

She reached up and threw the door open, instantly engulfing the wagon in sand, allowing herself to be swept outside. She was lost in the wind, gravity and physics disappearing into the science of the dream world. She couldn't breathe. Couldn't see. Everything was pain and confusion,

Finally, she relaxed, giving herself up to the storm. Like a rag doll tossed about in a heavy current, she flew, twisted and bent in time with the tempest. Just as she was about to loose consciousness, to release the last bits of her being to the ether, she felt strong hands grab her around the waist, pulling her back to her feet. The sand continued to howl, but for a moment everything directly around her was still. She was standing in the eye of the storm, no more sand in her throat, no grainy sensation in her hair of clothes. She'd been washed clean. Purified.

She looked up to see a third figure, still clad in silver, but radiating warmth. She reached up, hear hand disappearing into the darkness of the hood, her fingers touching smooth skin, a narrow jaw. The ferret rested on the figure's shoulder.

Jacquin pressed tight against the silver traveler, still trembling from the storm and the false copies I her wagon. "My protector."

Jacquin woke with a gasp, instantly surrounded by the dark safety of her wagon. The night was still and peaceful outside. A thin fog of incense, nearly dissipated out the small nooks and crannies in her wagon, tinted the air with jasmine and cinnamon. Her skin was damp with sweat and tears. She'd been crying in her sleep.

Memories returned slowly. She'd spent the night trying to meditate, to find answers in the depths of her visions, but nothing had come. The magic must have settled around her while she slept, weaving into her dreams.

Come.

The single word echoed in her mind, seeming to fill her room and vibrate out into the night air. She suddenly felt an overwhelming pull, spreading from her stomach to her chest, rooting in her heart and tugging her toward the front door. She crawled out from under her woven quilt, three different silk pillows scattering across the floor with the movement.

She pulled a silk sari around her waist, tossing the loose end over her shoulder to quickly cover her bare skin. She hesitated before the door, her hand on the latch, vivid memories of the storm haunting her mind.

Come.

She turned the latch and stepped out into the night.

Come... Come... Come...

The whisper became more urgent, more constant, the sound seeming to ring from her mind up to the stars. Jacquin knew even as she walked that there was something odd, inhuman about the call, but she couldn't resist it. Was she still dreaming? In a vision? She couldn't tell anymore.

Her bare feet seemed to float across the sand as she journeyed beyond the market, past the dance circle to the wall of Oasis. Still the call beckoned, urging her beyond the town's border.

She raced toward her sanctuary, to the pile of broken wagons and carts and leapt from axle to wheel to trembling roof until she could jump up and grab the edge of the city wall. Her fingers scrambled, searching for purchase, and finally she pulled herself up to the edge.

She stared out at the desert, stretching endlessly into the night. Rolling dunes of sand dotted with the occasional cactus and scrub brush. Oasis was named for the natural oasis in the center of the town proper, but just outside the walls any sign of water or shade disappeared. The only inhabitants able to survive in the harsh ocean of sand were vicious reptiles and sand worms.

Jacquin walked along the wall, traveling along its narrow ledge like a tight-rope walker until she reached a section where a camel-trader's barn met the wall. She scampered down the edge of the barn, her feet hitting the ground with a heavy thump. The camels in the barn rustled at the noise but quickly settled back down to sleep.

Jacquin raced out into the night, the pull in her chest warming and growing stronger with each step until it suddenly dissipated. She paused at the sudden loss, coming to her senses as the chill of the night sank into her skin and she realized where she was. She rarely traveled beyond the walls of Oasis, not out of fear, but common sense. All it would take was a misplaced foot and she could be bitten by a poisonous snake or sink into a sand-worm's tunnel, disappearing forever. And that was without the threat of highwaymen or drunken merchants.

As she turned to return home, she heard a shift in the sand. She whipped around and froze, her heart stopping in her chest, her breath catching in her throat.

A small, lithe creature covered head to toe in cat-like fur, her tabby-orange ears folded back against the top of her head approached. The creature sniffed the air, a green-glass curved sword glistening on her belt. A changling. The call had been a trap.

Jacquin had heard stories of changlings, vicious, primal creatures from the north once thought extinct. The history books were full of wars with the changlings, including the battle believed to have wiped the species from Aggar, but merchants swore they had returned, brought stories of changling tribes traveling south, desecrating villages and attacking travelers unfortunate enough to find themselves in their path. What were they doing in Oasis? Her recent visions flooded her mind, visions of people dying, slashed and shot with glass weapons. A changling attack.

Jacquin's hand twitched, wanting to reach for the knife she often wore at her hip but she hadn't brought it with her. She had nothing but the sari. She racked her mind, trying to remember how to escape a changling, nervous that any movement would be seen as an invitation to attack. Changlings were conniving, vicious and impossibly fast. She'd never escape.

She breathed deep, clenching her fists at her sides. So this is how she'd go, slashed and gored by a feral changling in the desert. Would anyone find her body? Know what happened to her? Would there be any warning before the changlings attacked Oasis in force?

She'd always thought she'd see her own death before it happened.

The changling prowled forward, her claws catching the moonlight until they glowed. Her hands were the perfect blend of cat and human, with long, slender fingers and wicked, curved claws. She wore a leather loincloth and little else, a belt at her waist holding her sword and a water skin. She seemed to be traveling alone. A scout.

The creature moved until she stood directly before Jacquin.

She was nearly two heads shorter, but she radiated lethal danger. The changling looked up into her eyes, gold irises meeting Jacquin's brown. Jacquin licked her lips, her mouth dry with fear. "Please. Don't."

The changling reached out, but instead of attacking, she touched Jacquin's waist, laying a hand on the exposed skin near her navel.

Jacquin was instantly submerged in a pool of vision and memory, the images spinning and spiraling together in an unintelligible blend. She could smell pine and snow, blood and sulfur. Her body radiated both heat and cold, her mouth coated with the taste of blood. She felt split between too many bodies, felt claws extend and retract in her hands, the feel of cold glass, both at her hip and thrust through her chest. She could hear people scream, the cries both human and pack, their unbearable cries threatening to split her head from the inside out. A fiery, opaline glow reflected off every surface, casting the visions of murder and mutilation with a crystalline haze.

To Jacquin's surprise, the creature immediately turned and ran away, fleeing gracefully back into darkness. Jacquin let out a heavy breath of disbelief, her body still paralyzed from the encounter. She'd never heard of a changling letting a human live. Still, she wouldn't question it.

She turned and ran back for Oasis, moving as swiftly as possible, adrenaline and fear pumping through her veins, urging her forward until she leapt up the camels' barn, over the wall and tumbled to the desert floor on the other side.

She landed hard, collapsing to the ground like she had in her dream. She gasped into the sand, her heart speeding in her chest and her breath coming in rapid shots as she came down from her near-death experience. Changlings were near Oasis. They never traveled alone. Chances were there was an entire party staking out the city.

She had to find her sister.

Jacquin pounded on Khalisa's door, hoping her sister had returned home for the night. She heard a scuffle within and Khalisa answered, her hair in disarray, tangled around her shoulders. Her weary eyes brightened with concern as she led Jacquin into her wagon.

Khalisa's wagon was larger than Jacquin's and less functional, a thick scent of spices and wax from candles and soap infused in every panel. While Jacquin's home had once traveled the desert when the Tribe was more nomadic, Khalisa's home had been built in Oasis and would never leave. Guests expected nomadic wagons when they visited the Tribe. They didn't realize more than half of them were as immovable and rooted to the earth as the buildings in the town proper.

Khalisa held Jacquin's shoulders, searching her face for the source of her obvious alarm. "What's wrong?"

"A changling. I saw a changling."

Khalisa's charcoal brow lifted in confusion. "Jacquin, you're not making any sense. Did you have a vision?"

Jacquin shook her head, taking a deep breath and forcing herself to be more clear. "No. It was real. A changling outside the walls."

Khalisa paled. "Could you have been seeing something else? A different creature?"

Jacquin shook her head, her hair trembling along the lines of her shoulders. "It walked right up to me!"

Khalisa gripped Jacquin's shoulders tighter, her full lips forming a hard, straight line. "You were outside the town walls alone? At night?"

"You have to tell the Council. Alert Oasis guards. Changlings don't travel alone."

Khalisa pulled back her hair with a quick twist of her wrists, spinning the ebony mass back into a bun secured with ridged hair sticks. It had always amazed Jacquin the difference a hairstyle could make in her sister. With a few swift movements she went from sultry dancer, impish lover, to one of the Tribe's most honored council members. The shift from flirt to n'Sappho.

Khalisa pulled a soft, quilted robe over her thin, woven nightgown and rushed out into the night, her long stride assured and self-confident. Jacquin followed close behind, hugging her arms to her chest. Khalisa knocked on a large, blonde-pine wagon in the center of the Tribe's caravan.

Khalisa's voice was steady and strong, her face still. "Aalim!"

The door opened and Aalim stepped out onto his front steps. The leader of the Tribe's council filled the doorway with his tall, well-muscled frame, his dark hair strung with quill feathers and beads falling to the middle of his back.

"Khalisa?"

"A changling has been spotted outside town walls."

Aalim's jaw clenched with apprehension, his muscles growing taut as he realized the full implications of Khalisa's warning. "Are we sure?"

"Jacquin saw it herself."

Aalim looked Jacquin over apprehensively, one thick eyebrow

raised. "Was she in her right mind?"

Jacquin felt her cheeks blush with frustration. "I know the difference between my visions and reality."

Aalim seemed unsure, his head tilted to one side as he considered the veracity of Jacquin's claims. Khalisa's eyes narrowed to dangerous slits, the steadiness and certainty in her expression finally swaying Aalim's opinion. "What can we do?"

"The Council needs to be on the lookout for an attack, and we need to alert the city proper. As long as they guard the gates, we won't be safe unless everyone in Oasis is on alert."

"Why would they trust us?"

"You have contacts with the desertmen of Oasis," Khalisa argued. "Let them present the information to their governor."

"Tell them a dancing seer known for her fake card readings has seen a changling in the desert? Almost an entire continent away from their raiding grounds?"

Khalisa's eyes darkened and she rose up to her full height, defending her younger sister without words. Aalim visibly shrank beneath her lethal presence. "You tell them a changling has been seen. You leave my sister out of it."

"They won't believe me."

"They will when they're gored by glass daggers," Jacquin hissed.

Aalim grunted, shifting uncomfortably, but finally nodding. Khalisa growled. "First thing in the morning."

Aalim nodded, the beads in his hair clacking together as he tried to distance himself from Khalisa. "Fine. First thing in the morning."

Aalim disappeared back into his cabin, closing and locking his door behind his back. Khalisa crossed her arms tight over her chest.

Jacquin took her arm, leading her away from the wagon, her body rigid with frustration. "Thank you. He wouldn't have listened to me without you," Jacquin muttered.

"He's a good man. Too good sometimes. But he had no right to question your abilities, Jacquin."

Jacquin shrugged gently. "I'm used to it."

"It's absurd. Seers built our Tribe. To talk about them like that..." Khalisa trembled in anger.

"It doesn't help that I fake visions to steal from merchants."

"Everyone steals from merchants. Aalim is prejudiced."

"But will he warn Oasis?"

"Yes. He gave his word."

"Good."

Khalisa slung her arm around Jacquin's shoulders, holding her possessively. "You deserve better, Jaci."

Jacquin leaned against her sister's shoulder, drawing warmth and comfort from the touch as they walked back to Khalisa's wagon. "Can I stay with you tonight?"

Khalisa kissed the top of her head. "Always."

They returned to Khalisa's cabin and Khalisa busied herself making tea, pouring her frustration into the preparation. Jacquin stood in the back of the wagon, running her fingers through a short curtain of Khalisa's necklaces, hanging from hooks off the wall. The cool metal, the weight of the chains, was oddly comforting. She paused on a carved wooden pendant of a scorpion, rocking her thumb over the tip of its spiked tail.

"This will help." Jacquin turned as Khalisa offered her a cup of amber-colored tea, a concoction designed to help her sleep.

Khalisa's voice was heavy with unanswered questions, but Jacquin carefully avoided giving her an easy way to broach them. After a long silence, Khalisa finally asked, "I've never seen you like this. What did you see tonight, Jaci? I can tell you had a vision. Something besides the changling has shaken you."

Jacquin sat slowly, taking a long sip of her sister's tea, letting the hot liquid slide down her throat and warm her belly. "Not just tonight. Every day for almost three tenmoons. I touch people – tribe, merchant, desertman – and I watch them die. And more than a few have been killed with glass swords and arrows. Changling weaponry. If we don't do something, the changlings will attack Oasis. It will be a massacre."

Khalisa's dark skin paled. "Three tenmoons? You've been suffering like this for three tenmoons and you never told me?"

Jacquin looked guiltily into the depths of her teacup, her eyes making shapes and designs out of the tea leaves at the bottom of the cup. "It's hard to talk about."

"You can trust me."

Jacquin pulled her sister into a tight hug, holding her close. The motion startled Khalisa, her muscles rippling tight for a moment beneath Jacquin's embrace before loosening in worry. "Thank you," Jacquin muttered against Khalisa's shoulder. "Thank you for always believing me."

Khalisa held Jacquin for a long moment, contemplating her answer. "Many have trouble believing a beautiful woman with an extraordinary gift."

Jacquin held her older sister tighter. "I'm glad you're here."

"Always, Jaci." Khalisa pulled away and smiled gently, the

expression full of love and concern. "Now come. Changlings or no, you need sleep if you're wandering into the desert alone at night."

Jacquin chuckled softly, leaning forward against Khalisa's shoulder. She had no doubt sleep would elude her, but perhaps with her sister near she'd find a moment's rest.

Chapter Five

Adrian slid down the peaked roof, her feet skimming over sleek tiles, her cloak billowing back behind her to cut her speed. She traveled by feel, judging weights and balances in the pads of her feet, moving through the darkness with ease despite being unfamiliar with her surroundings.

She hadn't learned the name of the town, a ramshackle mining settlement built up around a massive coal deposit deep in the brushland just north of the Great Desert. The brushlands were dotted with towns like these, thrown together and eventually abandoned when the mines had been depleted. The workers barely survived, living in the shadow of a wealthy foreman or handful of wealthy sponsors.

She glanced over the roof's ledge to the street below, lit by a series of covered lanterns and torches, casting deep shadows along ever corner. Her eyes narrowed as she watched two black-cloaked travelers pause before a run-down tavern. Circle members had been trickling into the town all day, coming in small parties to keep from arousing suspicion. Someone with moderate intelligence had to be leading them, but they couldn't fool Adrian. She would know anyone from the Core on sight.

Adrian's lips curled back in a snarl. Too many men had entered the town for the group to be a splinter of the Circle. She couldn't tell if they planned to attack the village or just rest on their way to their next destination. She clenched her jaw. There was a time she could have just looked at them and known their intention, but not anymore. She let out a deep breath. It was the only time she ever regretted giving up her empathic abilities.

Adrian crouched down, sitting along the edge of the roof, careful to remain in the shadows. There were too many of them to attack directly and she couldn't kill any of them publicly without drawing the attention of the others. She would have to be more subtle.

She pulled a small, wax paper bundle from a pouch at her waist. She unwrapped the paper, revealing a leaf-wrapped bundle, still soft from cooking earlier in the day. Without taking her eyes off the Circle's men, she nibbled at the *boko*, the stuffing, now chilled, made of a few rabbits she'd snared and a collection of root vegetables she collected while traveling.

The scent of her food attracted a raven, who fluttered to the roof and sat along the edge beside her. Adrian instinctively ripped a hunk of her meal free and placed it on the roof before the bird. She watched him tear at the meat paste with mild interest, lingering on the way his feathers ruffled and spasmed with each motion. There was something about the way he moved that betrayed his hunger. He wasn't particularly skinny or desperate, but there was a sense about him, an ache that made Adrian's stomach rumble, hollow and empty.

A bottle broke on the street below and the bird arched up in surprise, catching Adrian's eye. Adrian felt as if she'd been punched in the face, pain exploding behind her eyes and rippling down the muscles of her neck and spine. Her stomach rolled and burned, a mix of unstable, clashing magics warring for control over her heart and mind.

She scrambled backward, her palms scraping across rough tile and her leather boot sliding across shallow, standing water from recent storms. She forced her eyes closed, a gasp exploding from her chest as if coming up for air. She heard the bird flee, its wings wildly flipping through the air to get away from Adrian's gaze.

She slowly opened her eyes again as her stomach started to settle. Her hands spasmed and trembled. She balled her hands into tight fists, waiting to regain control. She glanced down, catching her own reflection in a small pool of rain water, the light of the torches from the streets casting her face in deep shadow. Even in the darkness she could make out shocking, ice-blue eyes.

She immediately turned away, clenching her jaw tight in frustration, a flash of hot anger and guilt burning just under her skin. She'd been so shaken by the forced connection with the raven even her most intricate illusions had been shattered. She knew better than to catch an innocent eye. She'd been able to eradicate her Blue Sight urges in most humans, but every now and then she'd look into the eyes of a truly innocent beast and the magic would overcome her.

She held her hand palm up before her face and focused on creating a dark flame. Her palm tingled, but she couldn't summon the destructive fire that normally came so naturally to her. She continued to focus with ruthless intensity, sweat sprouting across her brow, her muscles aching from the effort. Finally, a weak flame burst to life in her hand and the warmth, the connection she'd felt to the raven, disappeared.

She closed her hand, extinguishing the flame, and began working on a new illusion. Symbols and ruins formed in her mind, a carefully crafted spell she'd perfected as a child. She whispered ancient words of power under her breath, slipping the last of her magical energy into the spell and, when she opened her eyes a second time and cautiously glanced into the puddle, hazel irises reflected back at her.

She stood carefully, swaying momentarily on her feet before regaining her balance. She stretched, her ropey muscles lengthening and contracting with almost mechanical precision. The physicality of the movements helped recenter her, calming the wrath of the warring Blue Sight and destruction magics flooding her body. Soon all that was left was the ice-cold emptiness she'd developed in childhood.

She leaned her weight over one foot, looming over the street like a gargoyle guarding its perch. The men she'd been watching had disappeared, but it didn't matter. She knew where the Circle was now. She wouldn't lose sight of them again.

Her lips curled away from her teeth as anger replaced the empathy she'd felt for the raven. Her mind spun, plotting and strategizing as lightning-fast as a military general. She couldn't attack anyone outright, but she needed a kill tonight.

She waited for over an hour, weighing the risk of leasing a room for the night in the same inn as the Circle, when two of the Circle's men exited, stumbling drunkenly into the night.

With a flick of her cloak, Adrian ran for the edge of the shop and leapt to the ground, landing with a thud in a back alley and throwing her weight forward into a somersault to absorb the blow. She rolled to her feet in a single, swift movement. She fixed her hood over her silver hair and continued out onto the street.

She followed the drunken Circle raiders, staying far enough back not to catch their attention, waiting for them to turn down a dark alley or stumble outside city limits. She fingered the hilt of a dagger in her long sleeve, her hands arching to throw it. She grinned as the men tripped to the side, ducking between a closed bakery and a butcher's shop.

She raced forward, drawing her knife as she rounded the corner after them, keeping close against the wall, using her returning illusion magic to blend in with the shadows. She needed to move completely unseen, silence them before they could cry out,.

One man supported his friend as he vomited on the dirt path. Adrian stalked forward toward the standing marauder, a surge of excitement setting every nerve on fire with each step. She raised her knife, aiming to slit his throat, when the sharp thud of a boot striking stone echoed through the alley.

"You've strayed too far from the inn."

A sharp female voice dripping with disdain reverberated through the alley. Adrian immediately ducked back into the shadows. A small woman strode forward, her hood thrown back behind cropped dark gold curls. She crossed her arms over her chest, her body hugged neck to toe in traveler's leathers, revealing the lines of a half dozen weapons. Adrian arched a single silver brow, feeling a heat in her stomach she hadn't felt since beginning her travels.

"You're not our guardian in town, Rox," the sick marauder garbled.

"Calder's orders. Or do you have to be reminded of what happened to Gryert?"

"You said we're not being followed."

Rox's eyes narrowed into dangerous slits. "There are more threats than assassins."

The standing marauder helped his friend to his feet. "Like Gryert's ghost."

Rox growled low under her breath, the sound more animal than human. "There's no ghost haunting the Circle."

"Tell that to Gryert."

Adrian felt a rush of pleasure at the look of fear in the raider's eyes. A ghost. It wouldn't be the first time the comparison had been made, especially as Adrian stood shrouded in shadow. She liked the thought that the Circle was haunted enough by Gryert's death to fear her even when they were safe from her blade. It would certainly make killing them easier if the deaths were blamed on the supernatural.

Rox stood with her hands on her hips, every inch of her petite frame emanating frustration. "Just get back to the inn."

The men stumbled out of the alley, Rox traveling behind to guard their rear. Adrian watched them go, her stomach sinking. She wasn't likely to find more wandering Circle men with Rox keeping them in the inn.

Adrian grunted in frustration, her entire body aching for the kill, for movement, for action. Thinking of Rox, her taut curves hugged with leather, her eyes burning with confidence, only made the ache worse. Her wrist burned and she held it through her sleeve, her vice-like grip extinguishing the sensation.

Adrian swore under her breath and strode back onto to the main street through town, blending in with the handful of villagers still out for the night and the closed merchant stalls. Her head buzzed, the events of the night clouding her thoughts in a haze of desire and magic. She followed Rox and the Circle members back to the inn, careful to remain as unobtrusive and unremarkable as possible.

The inn was bustling with both locals and the Circle, the crowd so thick Adrian could slide into a corner seat near the kitchens without even the innkeeper noticing. The kitchen had been closed for the night, only tankards of ale flowed past the bar as patrons threw dice and told stories beside a small log fire.

The room was coated in grime, coal dust permanently infused in every plank of wood, every stone. It wasn't an issue of cleanliness. The inn could be scoured hourly and still garner a thick layer of soot within minutes. Adrian was thankful for the residue, which clung to her cloak and coated her gloves. It helped her blend in with the burly workers relaxing with a drink before heading back into the mines.

Adrian leaned back in her chair, her hood pulled up just far enough to hide her hair, and studied her prey. There were just over a dozen Circle members scattered throughout the inn, only a portion of the full party. They had likely splintered into different inns to avoid suspicion.

Adrian's eyes wandered to Rox, undoubtedly tied to the Circle but her distaste of the raiders obvious even without Blue Sight intuition. A water ferret scurried out of the folds of Rox's cloak, circling her arms and hands as Rox chased it with her fingers. Adrian couldn't help but look the smaller woman over and wonder what could bind such a women to the most vicious, deadly party to leave the Core since its inception.

"Anything to drink tonight, traveler?"

Adrian glanced up at a curvaceous blond waitress, her hair rippling past her bare shoulders. She had no connection or knowledge of the Circle or its activities. Adrian smiled slowly, taking in her slightly tanned skin, a permanent mark from the sun that betrayed a genetic connection to the Amazons.

Adrian leaned forward on her elbows, brazenly looking the woman over from head to toe, her face intentionally angled toward the light to reveal her features. She could sense the woman's interest as she cautiously scanned Adrian's narrow face, her ropey frame. Adrian grinned lightly. Perhaps there was more Amazon in this woman than just her skin.

"I'm not interested in drinks... what was your name?"

The woman blushed lightly, clasping her hands before her waist, her eyes flashing mischief. "Mary. And you are?"

"Only here for the night."

Adrian reached out, placing a single hand lightly on Mary's entwined fingers. Excitement sparked in her stomach, growing as quickly as her restlessness as the touch had no effect on her: no burning skin, no Blue Sight bonding. Mary would be the perfect distraction. "How late do you work tonight, *Min?*"

Mary glanced nervously over her shoulder, scanning the bar and kitchens for who Adrian assumed to be her father. With a swift, inconspicuous motion Mary slid a small key across the table. Adrian immediately rested her hand over it, hiding it from view. "My room's in the attic. I get off on the hour."

Mary strode away without another word, mingling with the other patrons in the common room. Adrian leaned back in her chair, her hood falling lower over her face, a triumphant smile turning the corners of her lips. Mary moved with a familiar confidence through the crowd, taking their drunken advances and unintelligible orders with ease. Adrian lingered over the lines of her body, the swells and curves so rare in the women of the north.

She ran her fingers over the lines of Mary's key, her attention wandering to other corners of the inn, counting every Circle member mingling and drinking around her, oblivious to her presence. She felt bloodlust, hot and all-consuming swelling beneath her skin as she imagined burying her knife in every one of the thugs from the Core. Her cheeks darkened as she imagined how enraged the Twins would be, losing their precious band of vandals and murderers.

Adrian felt a sharp pain at her shin and glanced down in surprise. A sleek water ferret had crawled under the table and nipped her leg just above the cuff of her boot. She scowled and nudged it away, its tiny claws skittering across the stone floor as it fought to stay under the table. Adrian snarled under her breath as she continued to ward off the creature, the tip of her boot bobbing and parrying like a sword as the creature savaged her leather shoe with tiny claws and teeth.

"Fisk!"

The terse command cut through the noise of the inn like a knife. The ferret instantly froze, rearing up onto its hind legs, revealing patches of luminous deep green and aqua scales along its belly. Adrian glanced up at Rox, sitting in the opposite corner with her feet propped on the table, her glare locked on the ferret. She snapped and the creature raced back toward her, scaling her leg, spiraling up her torso and ducking into the folds of her hood like a burrow.

Rox didn't acknowledge Adrian, simply returned to her drink. Adrian found herself, once again, captivated by the woman's presence. She wasn't Adrian's usual type, lean and rough around the edges, but she suddenly found herself wishing it was Rox's key clenched in her fist. Adrian wondered what she was doing with the Circle. She clearly detested the Circle she traveled with and the Twins rarely ever employed women, let alone women who were so physically unimposing. Still, no *mala'* would have such fire in her eyes or be as brazen as Rox had been with the drunk marauders before. She was likely a guide or a magician. Adrian wondered with a brief sinking feeling if she'd ever have to kill Rox.

Mary passed in front of Adrian's table as she stepped back into the kitchens, returning shortly without her apron or dishes.

"I'm going to bed, Da'," she called to the bar. The burly blond barkeep nodded to his daughter with an affectionate smile and Mary strolled up the stairs to the higher levels of the inn.

Adrian waited until the barkeep's attention had returned to his customers before standing and slowly following Mary up the worn wooden stairs. She passed a long hallway of hostel-style rooms lined with bunks and cots until she found a narrow, angled staircase leading up to the attic. She focused on a series of illusion spells, running her hands through her silver hair, darkening it to a pale gold before unlocking Mary's door and stepping inside.

The room was cloaked in darkness, heavy curtains drawn over the only windows, edged in moonlight leaking through the edges of the tattered material. She tensed, instinctively crouching into a fighting stance as she tuned her other senses on searching for a trap.

A single candle flared to life on the opposite end of the room, releasing a single, sharp scent of ash and flame, creating dark gold pools of light across a carved wooden night table and a narrow bed dressed with thick, hand-stitched quilts. Mary stood leaning back against the wall along the edge of the candle's light, her corset and overskirt already on the floor. The flames cast rippling shadows across her woven linen chemise and the bare skin of her collar, arms and legs. Her body was a textured map of peaks and deep valleys. Adrian ran her tongue over the inside of her lip, already hungry.

Mary looked Adrian over, her *amarin* whispering of lust, fear, and excitement. Adrian blinked, distancing herself from Mary's emotions. "I'm glad you came."

Adrian loosened her cloak, letting it fall to the floor. Mary made a soft sound of appreciation as Adrian's face and frame were revealed unhindered by the cloak.

Adrian didn't wait for further invitation. She pulled Mary close, kissing her rough and deep as Mary melted against her. Adrian lost herself in Mary's softness, her scent like cream and fresh bread, her hair like strands of silk. She hadn't had anything so warm, so sweet, since being banished from the Core. For a moment the energy she reserved for death shifted to passion, her restlessness sated with lust.

Mary gasped, the sound ragged with desire as Adrian nipped and kissed down the lines of her neck and collar toward the curve of her breasts, her hands tugging and shifting at linen in search of bare skin.

Mary wrapped a leg around her hips and an image of Rox suddenly flashed through Adrian's mind. She paused in shock, pushing the other woman from her thoughts.

Mary's lips trembled with desire, her skin like caramel under Adrian's hands, now dark with lust. "Who are you?"

Adrian led her to the bed, laying her back as her teeth tugged at the laces of Mary's chemise. "Does it matter?"

Mary pulled Adrian's shirt over her head and kissed her again. "No."

Adrian woke as dawn bled around Mary's curtains, leaking sunlight into the attic apartment. Mary slept beside her, tangled in quilts, a woven tapestry of skin and cloth, her hair fanned out across the pillows and Adrian's chest. Adrian sat up slowly, trying not to wake Mary as she climbed out of bed in search of her clothes.

"Going so soon?"

Adrian turned as she pulled her pants back over her hips and tied them close. Mary leaned up, resting on her elbows, her hair a tangled mass running down her shoulders and back. Adrian smirked appreciatively at the sight. Her restlessness was already returning, but for a few hours in the night she had been calm and centered, drowning in passion instead of death. "I have errands to run."

Mary pouted. Adrian grinned and rushed to her side, leaning over her and kissing her gently, the kiss deepening as Mary pulled her down toward the bed. Adrian grunted and pulled away, "I really do have to go."

Adrian searched for her shirt, spotting it beneath the end table. "I never noticed your tattoo before." Adrian froze, glancing down at the small outline of a stone on her inner arm. It wasn't a tattoo. "My cousin was a Blue Sight. She never understood why people tattoo a lifestone mark on their wrists. Do you think it's romantic?"

Adrian pulled her shirt over her head, hiding the mark. "It was a foolish mistake in my youth."

"She was always afraid of being bonded. Meeting a stranger

and suddenly being tied to them for life? It's terrifying."

"It keeps Blue Sights safe from the Plague. It's evolution."

"It's genetic slavery," Mary grunted.

Adrian held her arm through her sleeve. Her stomach twisted. "Only if a Blue Sight comes into contact with their bondmate." Adrian pulled her boots on and stood, grabbing her cloak and pulling it over her shoulders. "I have to go."

Mary climbed out of bed and pulled Adrian into her arms. "Did I offend you?"

Adrian kissed her, savoring the sensation. "No. You were just what I needed."

Adrian released her and left the room, descending the attic stairs back toward the common room. She glanced into the hostel rooms as she traveled, a knot untangling in her stomach as she spotted a half dozen unconscious Circle members draped over the cots and bunks.

In the last room before the stairs to the common room, Adrian spotted Rox asleep sitting up in the corner, cocooned in a wool blanket. Adrian paused, watching the older woman sleep, one hand over the lifestone mark on her wrist. She contemplated entering the room, studying her more closely when her blanket bounced and Fisk popped his head out, watching Adrian with bared teeth. Adrian scowled. She didn't need to be discovered by the Circle because of an angry ferret.

She headed back down the stairs toward the common room and with a few whispered phrases she was shrouded again in shadow.

Chapter Six

Rox stared at a bramble bush, watching a collection of bumble bees dance across the small white and pink blossoms. She lay on her bedmat, an arm propped under her head, the ground rough and sharp. Fisk rested in the cradle of her side, his head propped on her hip, his weight comforting. In the distance she could hear the screams, smell the smoke rising over the nearby hills. She focused more intensely on the bees, dancing and spinning over the flowers, oblivious to the nearby destruction. She willed her mind to join them, leaping from plant to plant, nothing weighing on her mind but pollen and honey.

A woman's piercing, strangled scream shattered through the noise of the raid to be immediately silenced. Rox clenched her jaw, her fists curled into hard fists. She refused to take part in the Circle's raids, but she was no less accountable for their actions. She protected them, even guided them when their maps proved inaccurate. It might as well be her dagger that had silenced the woman's cries. But there was no other option. No choice. She needed to be paid.

The pound of hooves echoed through the brush, sending a cloud of dust into the air. Circle members had been traveling back and forth between town and the camp all day to offload plunder. Rox didn't move as a band of a half dozen men returned, their horses weighed down with money, antiques and other valuables.

"We don't have time to drag them along."

"We have more than enough men to send a party back to the Core. No use wasting such hardy stock."

Another dozen men returned, the sounds of their party interspersed with whimpers and muffled moans. Rox sat up and spun toward the returning marauders. Each raider pulled a soot-covered, bound and gagged women behind their horses, their bruised and raw hands tied to long leashes attached to the raiders' saddles.

Rox leapt to her feet, her eyes blazing rage. "No slaves." She charged forward, confronting the band of marauders.

"You have no authority here." Calder rode up fast, circling around the rest of his men. Rox's breath caught in her throat. A young girl, no older than 4 tenmoons, was bound and draped over the back of Calder's saddle. Her blond curls hung limp with dirt and sweat around her panicked green eyes. Her skin was covered in ash, smelling of fire and blood. Long streams of tears left filthy streaks down her cheeks. "We loot as we please."

"You're a monster," Rox hissed between her teeth. Calder smirked back at her, his eyes full of malicious glee. Calder had never shown an affinity for children before and Rox knew he usually didn't keep slaves. He had brought the girl to torment Rox.

Calder slid off his saddle, landing on the ground with a heavy thud. He pulled the girl off the saddle, dropping her on the ground and crouching before her. He grabbed the child's face, forcing her to look at him as she wept. "Such a fragile little thing, isn't she? And so very familiar."

Rox felt her heart break, her breath heavy in her chest. She could so clearly see another little girl, willowy and wild, her long gold girls whipping through the wind, tangled with leaves and twigs. She could see the child in the young slave's eyes, imagine the other child covered in ash and soot and blood.

Calder ran his fingers through the child's hair. "Golden curls. Green eyes." Calder looked Rox in the eye. "I think I'll call her Serena."

Rox drew a green glass dagger off her back and charged, Calder meeting her blow with his sword, expecting her attack. He laughed aloud and pushed her back. "Kill me and you'll never get your daughter back from the Core, Rox. You willing to trade this one's life for your girl's?"

Rox charged again, her mind a blank chasm of rage. Calder blocked a few of her blows, but in minutes she tackled him to the ground. Without hesitating she drove her knife through his hand, pinning him to the ground.

He screamed in pain, blood pooling out of his hand, staining the green glass blade a sickly brown. "You bitch! You're never getting paid!"

Rox grabbed him by the face, holding him still. Her eyes danced with insane, chaotic light, her lips curled back in a snarl. "You're still alive. You're not vitally wounded. And Helos has the magic to seal your hand. Raids come with risks."

"You're dead."

"Not yet. The Twins will never forgive you if you kill me after being healed."

"Accidents happen."

Rox grabbed him by the throat, sensitive and fragile organs and veins pounding chaotically under her hands. "Give me the girl."

Rox felt rough hands grab her under the arms, pulling her slender frame off the ground. She grabbed her knife, ripping it from Calder's hand as a burly thug pulled her toward her bedmat. Another man knocked it from her hand again.

Rox struggled against her captor, biting and clawing to get to the young girl. The child watched Rox with desperate eyes, running to reach her when another marauder scooped her under one arm and started carrying her away with the other slaves. The child cried, the sounds muffled through the strip of cloth tied over her mouth as a gag.

Rox shrieked, her voice primal and wild. "Give me the girl!"

Calder stood, his healer already rushing to his aid. "She's mine by right of plunder."

"And mine by duel!"

The marauder held Rox down and tied her hands and feet, leaving her bound on her bedmat.

Calder, now healed, strode toward her and kicked her hard in the ribs. He sneered, the expression full of embarrassment at letting her stab him and fury. "Perhaps it will be easier for you to wait out the raid here."

He continued on toward the stash of loot collected deeper in the brush. A marauder known for his clashes with Calder lingered behind the rest of the party and, when no one was looking, grabbed Rox's dagger and tossed it closer.

"Wanted to stab 'im for ages."

"Let me go and I'll do a lot more than stab him," Rox swore.

The man considered, then shook his head. "Nah. I don't have a contract with the Twins. Calder'd kill me. And everyone knows yer rages, Rox. Don't want ya wild in the camp until ya calm down." Rox's eyes darkened and the man took another step back. "Still, there's yer knife. I never see ya without it, so I figure it means somethin' to ya."

Rox closed her eyes, forcing herself to calm. The knife was important to her. A family heirloom. But it didn't mean anything to her while a little girl cried, bound and gagged, not far away. When she opened her eyes again, the man had disappeared.

Rox waited, not moving a muscle as she listened to the Circle unload their plunder and prepare to return to town. She became calmer, more focused as she waited, the raging storms of her mind dissipating into a deadly quiet. She'd kill Calder. After she was paid, after her daughter, Serena, was free. She would watch the light go out in his maniacal eyes and feel his heart stop. Every slave he took to the Core, every man, woman and child he killed, would find justice through her blade.

Less than an hour later Calder led the remaining Circle members back into town. "Fisk!" she called into the nearby brush. Fisk, who had fled during the attack, raced back to join her. She motioned to her knife and he ran to it, propping it carefully up by the hilt.

Rox rolled, scurrying like a caterpillar against her bonds, until she reached her knife. She grabbed the hilt, projecting from the ground, and angled it toward the ropes binding her wrists. The thin, sharp blade, still covered in Calder's blood, sliced easily through the bonds, freeing her hands. She quickly cut the ties around her feet and threw them aside, standing and stretching her arms and legs as she wiped her knife with a cloth from her pack and resheathed it at her back.

She raced through the brush toward a small copse of trees hiding the marauder's loot. As she pushed through the brush into the copse, however, she paused. The slaves were guarded by half a dozen new marauders. There was no way she could take them all. Not in broad daylight, and not without severing her deal with the Twins.

The young girl spotted Rox, her face pleading for escape. Rox locked eyes with her and nodded, hoping the child could read every intention in her heart. *I'll save you. You'll survive. You won't end up like my daughter.*

Dusk had fallen and the raid had turned into a celebration. The flames still rose high into the burnt-orange sky, but the screams were gone, replaced with wild slurs and drunken cheers. Rox listened, sick to her stomach. The only good thing about the party was the absence of raiders at the camp.

Rox knocked Fisk away from a bubbling metal bowl suspended over the small fire she'd built hours before. "That will kill you."

Fisk skulked back a few steps, staring at the hunter-green brew. She pulled the last pinch of white powder, a blend of herbs and blessed dust from her hometown, from a leather bag at her waist and added it to the broth. The broth steamed, blowing a flash of earthy, musty hot air into her face, whipping at her warm, pink cheeks.

Despite the fact that she had been hired as a protector and occasional assassin by the Twins, the Circle rarely realized the arsenal of supplies she kept in her small pack. The powder was the base for a powerful tranquilizer poison, the last she had. But it was worth it.

She grabbed her glass dagger from the belt at her waist and

dipped the blade in the brew, waiting until the hilt in her hand grew warm to the touch. When she pulled the blade from the brew, it was coated in a pale, sticky paste that was already hardening, infusing along the edge of the edge of the blade.

"Get my darts."

Fisk scuttled to the edge of the small clearing Rox had turned into a makeshift pharmacy half a league from the Circle's camp and rooted through her bag, dragging back a small, bound leather pack. Rox untied it, revealing a series of darts and needles. There was no need to waste what was left of the poison.

She was able to dip six darts and 15 needles before the brew turned a sickly brown. She used a clean knife to make small notches in the sides of the poisoned darts and rewrapped them, handing them to Fisk to put back in her bag. She carefully tipped the remnants of the poison into a shallow hole she'd dug earlier in the day and she mixed it with the dirt she'd removed from the hole, making a thick mud.

She doused her fire, carefully sheathing her blade at her hip and stood. The sky was red as the last light of day clung to the clouds. It would be dark before she reached the Circle's camp and if the sounds from the destroyed village were any indication, nearly every member of the Circle was in town.

Rox glanced back at Fisk, her eyes already beginning to glow as her eyes began to shift to her night vision. "Stay with the pack."

Fisk hummed low in his throat and circled her pack before settling down on the bag like a nest. Rox huffed. Even with her bedmat laid out beside the bag, Fisk chose to leave his fur embedded in her only good travel pack.

"Be here when I get back."

Fisk huffed. He knew what to do. It wasn't the first time she'd left him in charge of guarding her gear.

Rox turned and jogged back to the Circle's camp, heading for the copse of trees where the loot had been kept. She crept forward, weaving through the copse until she could assess the situation. The women and child were tied to trees, secured tight enough that all but three raiders returned to the city to celebrate. The three remaining were already drunk enough not to be a threat. Rox grinned, feral and wild.

She slipped along around the copse, circling behind the guards and moving silently in front of the slaves. She turned to the women, holding a single finger to her lips. They nodded, their muscles tense with fear and hope, their dirty faces streaked with tears and sweat.

Rox pulled her glass dagger from her belt and moved swiftly toward the drunk guards. She struck in three lightning-fast movements, leaving shallow cuts along their necks, instantly knocking them out, leaving them sprawled across the ground. She stood over each and used the hilt of her knife to bludgeon their heads, not enough to kill them, but enough to blame their unconsciousness on an escaped slave beating them from behind.

The women let out a collective groan of panic and relief at their imminent freedom, each struggling against their bonds as a surge of adrenaline shot through their veins. Rox ran to each, cutting them free of their bonds. As she reached the child, the young girl collapsed off the tree and buried herself in Rox's arms. Rox froze in shock, the feel of tiny hands gripping her waist, soft gold curls under her chin, a tiny child trembling in her arms tore at her heart. She was suddenly back in time, Serena crawling into her arms in the middle of the night, trembling from a thunder storm. Her daughter being dragged away as Rox screamed from behind the bars of a Core prison cell.

Rox held the child, her grip tight and possessive. She looked up at one of the lingering women. "You know this child?" The woman was still too shocked to speak, but she nodded. Rox pulled away just enough to angle the child's face to the woman. "You know her?" The child reached for the woman, who scooped her into a tight embrace.

Rox grabbed a knife out of the nearest guard's belt and handed it to the woman. "You worked free of your bonds. You knocked out the guards and cut everyone free, do you understand?"

The woman nodded again and took the knife. "Thank you." Her voice was raspy and soft, weighed down with grief and pain.

Rox's eyes burned as she looked at the child, worried about the burns on her arms and legs from her bonds, the injuries weaker than the irreparable mental pain that would follow her for the rest of her life. "You take care of her, do you understand me? You give her a good life. You owe me yours, now it belongs to that child."

The woman held the girl closer and nodded again. Rox clenched her jaw tight and nodded back, trying to hope that the woman would keep her word. "Now get out of here before they return."

Without any more prompting, the woman raced out into the night, the rest of the women following close behind. Rox said a prayer to the goddess for their safety, then immediately turned in the opposite direction and ran for her makeshift camp.

As the copse disappeared from view, Rox froze. Standing ahead of her, unmoving, was a cloaked figure. She crouched into a fighting stance. No one in the Circle wore a cloak so low over his face or traveled alone.

The figure moved forward and Rox blinked. Despite seeing everything around it clearly, the figure had no form, like a mass of living shadow. She felt an icy-cold stone form in the pit of her stomach as she remembered Tyrius' talk of demons stalking the camp. She felt a sudden surge of fear for the slaves she'd just released into the night. She wouldn't let anything, supernatural or otherwise, hurt them.

"I see you," Rox growled. The figure paused again, glancing over its shoulders. "Yes. You. Why are you following me?"

The figure took another step forward and Rox drew her knife. "I don't care if you're a demon. Demons can be killed."

The creature drew a long, curved sword, the silver blade glowing pale blue in the moonlight. Rox's lips curled back in a wild grin. Finally. Something she could kill without offending the Twins.

Rox charged with a wild snarl, her dagger raised. The figure dodged her blow, unsteady as if in shock. Rox laughed, the sound almost a bark. Seemed the Circle Ghost wasn't used to being challenged.

She swiped again, dodging a thrust by the shadow before circling to strike again, her knife an extension of her arm. She moved low to the ground, crouched and springing like a cat. The shadow recovered from its shock and sank down into its heels, thrusting and parrying with more skill than Rox expected.

Rox shifted and swayed, using her momentum to avoid her enemy's sword. The shadow was taller and heavier than she was, but Rox was more agile, negating any advantage the shadow had by using a longer weapon.

Rox avoided downward strike, shifting to the side just as the figure struck, catching her off guard. She narrowly avoided being gored, the blade instead slicing through her shirt, drawing a line of blood across her waist.

Rox felt blood rush to her face, her skin hot as she bared her teeth. Thoughts disappeared, swallowed in a black abyss of rage. She launched another attack, moving like a cornered animal. She growled and snarled, taking the edge off a half dozen attacks, leaving her marked with ribbons of blood as the shadow fell back beneath her relentless blows.

Rox reached out and grabbed the demon by the neck, barely noticing how solid it was in her gloved fist. The shadow let out a cry of shock, the sound only feeding Rox's rage as she pulled the shadow to the ground, kicking its sword out of its grasp.

The shadow fought back, kicking and punching as Rox pinned it down. In a move of desperation, the shadow grabbed Rox around the waist and shifted its weight, throwing Rox back. Rox grunted as she hit the ground, clawing and biting at her larger attacker until her teeth met what tasted like linen.

The shadow shouted in shock as Rox ripped through the material with her teeth, tearing free a chunk of cloth. Rox took advantage of the creature's surprise and threw it back, wrapping her hands around its neck again. The shadow reached up, grabbing her shoulders, trying to push Rox off, but Rox couldn't be moved.

Suddenly, the shadow's hands glowed bright white and a shock of light exploded through the clearing with a deafening boom. Rox screamed in surprise as the light blinded her, the flash searing through her retinas as she instinctively covered her eyes with her hands. The shadow knocked her back and disappeared.

Rox rolled on the ground, holding her face in shock and terror a her ears rung from the blast and her vision went from blinding white to black. She groped along the ground, chunks of dirt and rocks sliding beneath her as she tried to crawl away, to escape her magical attacker, but no attack came. The shadow creature had fled, leaving Rox blind and deaf in the heart of the Aggar brushlands.

Dawn came slowly, the light warming Rox's eyelids. She could hear a soft breeze in the brambles around her, the soft scratches of a mockingbird searching for insects. Rox shifted at the sounds, grunting as she woke slowly, her body stiff from cold and the shallow cuts healing across her body.

She pushed herself up on her hands and her eyes fluttered open. She gasped with relief as the world swam into focus. The effects of the shadow's spell had worn off, her senses returned.

Rox pushed herself off the ground. The clearing was broken and disheveled from the fight the night before. Rox ran her fingers over a crushed patch of tall grass. With a clear mind, she could tell that the shadow had to be more solid than a ghost to leave such marks. She'd felt skin when she strangled the creature, tasted cloth when she bit it. Rox's hands balled into fists. Tyrius was a fool. Their demon was a mage.

She grabbed her dagger out of the dirt and ran to retrieve Fisk and her pack and change clothing before heading back to the Circle's camp.

Calder stood waiting for her as she returned, his arms crossed, his jaw tight with rage. "Where were you last night?"

"Not tied up waiting for you," Rox groused. "I camped on my own."

"You sure you didn't return in the night to free our slaves?"

Rox glared at him. "If you couldn't keep your slaves secure, that's your problem."

She tried to pass and Calder grabbed her arm. "Where did you get that cut over your eye?"

"Hit my head on a rock."

"I know you freed them."

"Really? What do your guards say?" Rox ripped her arm out of his grip. "You have nothing to put me here last night." Calder's eyes burned with rage and Rox knew she had him. He had no proof.

"Let her go, Calder. We have to plan our course into the desert."

Calder shot her one last glare, a clear warning that he'd be watching her more carefully, and turned to his fellow lead, joining him at a map laid across the ground. "We have a few injured from last night and we have to send a party of at least twelve back to the Core with the bounty. We can't attack the Great Market like this."

Calder scanned the map. "We send a party of our healthiest back to the Core while we continue toward the Market. We'll stop nearby, somewhere inconspicuous, and let the injured heal while we wait for the party from the Core to return."

"The closest village is here. A small town called Oasis."

Calder nodded. "Then we go to Oasis."

PART TWO

BONDING

Chapter One

Jacquin tossed in bed, turning to stare at the ceiling of her wagon, her hands clasped behind her head. She couldn't sleep. There was something in the air, something still and tense, like the calm before a storm.

She'd felt a steadily-climbing sense of uneasiness the last few days. Khalisa had presented Jacquin's information about the changling in the desert, but next to nothing had been done in the Tribe or in Oasis to strengthen defenses. No one else had seen a changling and, despite the merchant's stories, most still believed they were extinct. No one believed her. Her warnings were the ramblings of a lying seer.

Jacquin ran a hand over her bare stomach, the pull she'd felt the night she'd met the changling had never quite dissipated. She felt it tugging at her navel, like a silver chain guiding her past Oasis' walls deep into the desert. She'd taken to shutting herself in her wagon, even avoiding dancing for the last few days to ensure she wasn't drawn back over the walls. More than once she'd found herself wandering to the city gates before she realized where she was going.

She closed her eyes and the visions ran through the back of her mind, gentler than the others, but constant. Pine needles and ice, stalagmites made of rainbows and clawed fingers slashing through skin wove an unintelligible tapestry seen through eyes, filtered through languages and rooted in experiences that weren't quite human. Changling visions.

Jacquin had never had a vision from another species before. Something was changing, not just in Jacquin but in all magic in Oasis. Jacquin wished there was another legitimate seer closer than the Great Market who could shed light on her predicament.

A trembling thud pounded along the top of her wagon like a sudden rainstorm. Jacquin arched a single brow as she sat up, staring at the ceiling of her wagon. After a long moment of silence another staggered beat rapped across her roof and Jacquin could make out the distinct strike of footsteps. Someone was running along the top of her wagon.

In the distance a shriek pierced the air, shattering the silence.

Jacquin leapt out of bed, throwing aside her quilt as she bolted out the front door, her skirt whipping and tangling around her legs. She only paused long enough to grab a slender, sharp knife from her desk.

The night had erupted in chaos. Hundreds of changlings flooded over the lower city walls, racing across the wagons' rooftops, leaping from home to home throwing open doors and rushing into the main town. The moon cast pale blue shadows across the changlings' cat-like fur, their small, slender frames and wickedly curved claws. Each carried a glass weapon – razor-sharp daggers and swords, glass arrows fletched with feathers from the icy northern regions of Aggar. Their eyes, bright and glowing like their Eitteh ancestors, burned with all-consuming rage as they berserked.

Jacquin stood frozen at the sight. Her head swam, emotions and visions from humans and changlings alike warred in her mind, creating a sharp, searing ache just behind her eyes.

She heard another cry and spun around as a member of her Tribe, a young man named Starin who had been one of Jacquin's fire dancers for years, doubled over, a long glass arrow in his stomach. Jacquin had forseen his death nearly a monarc ago. Every vision she'd had, every death she'd forseen for the last few monarcs raced through her thoughts. Glass weapons. Shadowy invaders. She'd been seeing this attack.

Jacquin raced toward the dancers' circle, searching for her friends, but the town was a swirling confusion of changlings, Tribe and desertmen. The sand was muddy with blood, the air thick with shrieks of pain and grief. Jacquin couldn't focus on the people around her, couldn't make out anyone she knew in the chaos.

"Down!"

Jacquin threw herself to the ground as a crossbow bolt embedded itself in a sleek, grey changling who had been about to gore a desert woman behind Jacquin.

Jacquin looked up as a small woman dressed in leather with short, blond curls reloaded her bow and shot another changling, this time saving a sword dancer from Khalisa's troupe from being stabbed.

Jacquin locked onto the woman, the only still thing in the vortex of battle. There was an intensity in her eyes Jacquin had never seen before, an intense focus as clear and sharp as Jacquin was confused. She moved as gracefully as the changlings, her travel leathers hugging her body in a way that outlined her muscles, showcasing even the smallest movement. Jacquin wondered if she was a dancer.

The woman walked to Jacquin and extended a gloved hand, helping her to her feet. Her grip was strong and confident. "You should hide," she recommended, her eyes flitting back and forth, continually assessing the battle. Jacquin grabbed her shoulder, using her strength for support as her head swam once again.

The woman grabbed Jacquin around the waist, pulling her close and twisting her to the side as a changling attacked, its claws extended like curved knives. With a flick of her wrist, the woman sent a crossbow bolt between the changling's eyes, dropping it mid-strike.

Jacquin gasped, holding tighter to the shorter woman's shoulder, shocked back to her senses by the direct threat. The woman released her, loading her bow again. "Get somewhere covered, out of the way."

Jacquin took a deep breath, shaking off the debilitating visions, her ebony hair rippling across her back with the movement. "I'll be fine," Jacquin assured her. "This is my home."

The woman looked her over quickly, assessing her physic, the way she held her knife. After a long moment she nodded. "Fine."

The woman lingered a moment longer, her eyes dancing over Jacquin once more, then she disappeared back into the battle. Jacquin let out a breath she hadn't realized she'd been holding.

"Jacquin!" The desperate scream split the night air, cutting through the sounds of the raid. Jacquin spun around. Khalisa.

Jacquin raced through the market, her nerves on edge as she dodged debris and fleeing friends. She held her dagger tight in her hand, ready to defend herself, but no changling charged her.

She raced toward Khalisa's wagon, rounding the corner to see two changlings circle her sister, knives at the ready. Jacquin leapt into the fray, her knife flying, stabbing one in the stomach then the other in the throat. Khalisa grabbed her arm as the changlings fell, bleeding out into the desert sand.

"What do we do?"

Jacquin bent and grabbed a solid glass short sword from one of the dead changling's hands. The weight was perfectly balanced. "Stay in your wagon. Bar the door. I'll keep you safe."

"You're not a fighter, Jaci!"

"I'm more of a fighter than you are. Please."

"Jaci..."

Jacquin pushed her sister into her wagon, shutting the door behind her and holding it closed as Khalisa fought to escape. After a long moment Khalisa finally relented and locked the door. "I won't leave you," Jacquin swore through the wood and crouched into a fighting stance before Khalisa's home.

Changlings continued to stream past, but none of them even glanced at her. She tensed, holding her knife tighter. Something was going on. Why weren't they attacking her? Still, she wouldn't question it if it kept Khalisa safe.

A sharp hiss of pain caught Jacquin's attention and she turned to the noise. Her breath caught in her throat. Her heart froze. A silver-cloaked figure, identical to the protector in her visions, fought a mob of changlings nearby. A changling grabbed what Jacquin could now see clearly was a woman by the throat and threw her to the ground, knocking her hood aside. Jacquin watched in rapt attention as the woman fought back, leaping to her feet and dodging two swords at once. Jacquin had never seen her guardian without her hood. The woman's features were instantly etched into memory: her short, asymmetrical hair a shocking pale silver, her features sharp and elegant. Jacquin could make out a ropey, muscular frame beneath her loose travel clothes, her skill with the sword exceptional in one no older than fifteen tenmoons.

The woman stabbed one of her attackers and dodged another when she locked eyes with Jacquin. She paused for a moment, almost as if in recognition, the distraction long enough for one of her changling attackers to cut a long gash down her back, slicing through cloak and shirt.

The woman screamed, falling to her knees from the wound and Jacquin charged forward. She attacked in a series or kicks and twists, a deadly whirlwind of grace and ferocity. Each attack was a blend of movement and basic swordplay, her motions unique and unpredictable, like a freestyled dance.

The woman struggled to her feet, clenching her jaw against her pain and easing her back against Jacquin's. They fought back-to-back, dodging and thrusting in time, moving as if they'd fought together for years. There was something about the way the woman moved, the way she fought back against her own pain to survive, the way her body fit with Jacquin's no matter what angle they met that was instantly familiar. Within minutes Jacquin was convinced that her guardian in her dreams hadn't been a manifestation of her mind: she had been a vision.

With their skills combined, Jacquin and the figure quickly dispatched the small band of changlings, their feline bodies lying in a crumpled heap on the desert floor. In the distance, Jacquin could finally hear the heavy stomp of Oasis guards. They must be overtaking the changling bandits.

The woman in silver collapsed to the ground, her energy

vanishing with her adrenaline as the immediate threat was resolved. Jacquin wrapped her arms beneath the woman's shoulders and pulled her back to her feet. The woman clung to her waist, using her for support as Jacquin dragged her to Khalisa's wagon.

Jacquin pounded on the door and Khalisa instantly pulled her inside, locking the door behind them. The woman's sword clattered to the floor of the wagon as she went limp in Jacquin's arms.

Jacquin laid the woman face-down on Khalisa's bed, peeling away the dirty, damaged cloak and cutting away the back of her shirt. "She's hurt." Jacquin's voice was heavy with grief and desperation. Every moment of peace she'd felt because of her protector's presence, every deadly vision her protector had guided her out of ran through her mind. The woman was no stranger. She was Jacquin's dearest friend.

Khalisa grabbed a wet rag and began cleaning the woman's wounds. The woman drifted in and out of unconsciousness, waking just long enough to panic and try to escape before passing out again from the wild movements. The scent of her blood filled the wagon, sharp and metallic as it ran down her back every time she tried to stand.

Jacquin crouched over the bedmat, angling herself to be at eye level with her guardian as she woke again and fought to stand.

Jacquin grabbed her shoulders, her face twisted with concern and fear. "You need to stop fighting. You'll bleed to death."

The woman paused as she saw Jacquin, looking deep into Jacquin's eyes. Once again Jacquin felt the woman recognized her. "Who are you?" The woman's voice was rich and deep, husky with pain. Jacquin's heart jumped. Her guardian had never spoken before.

"Jacquin n'Huitaca of the *Dey Sorormin* Tribe. Who are you?"

Khalisa paused her cleaning in surprise. "You don't know her?"

The woman fought to stand again and failed. Jacquin's face fell, her lips falling into a hard, straight line. "I saved your life. At least tell me your name."

The woman hesitated. "Adrian," she finally admitted.

Khalisa glanced over Adrian at her sister. Jacquin reached out and took Adrian's shoulders as she nodded and Khalisa poured a bottle of brandy over Adrian's back. Adrian screamed in pain as the alcohol worked to disinfect her wounds. Jacquin leapt up and held Adrian's shoulders down as Khalisa pinned her hips. Adrian arched, too strong for Jacquin to pin, grabbed Jacquin around the waist and tackled her to the floor. The motion pulled at Adrian's wound and she shouted in pain, tears streaming down her face as she passed out, her head falling on Jacquin's waist.

Jacquin felt every muscle in her body spasm and tremble. She was hypersensitive to the weight of Adrian's limp form draped across her waist. The places where Adrian's face and shoulders, bare from struggling in a destroyed shirt, pressed against Jacquin's stomach burned. Jacquin clenched and unclenched her fists, her arms aching and stinging.

Khalisa eased Adrian off her sister and back to the floor. "Did she hurt you?"

"No," Jacquin assured her, her voice soft and breathless.

"Then here." Khalisa handed Jacquin her wet rag, now stained with Adrian's blood. She rushed to her desk, pulling out a sewing needle and holding it over a candle.

Jacquin turned her attention to Adrian, mopping up the fresh blood that had welled from her wound. She ran her fingers lightly over Adrian's bare skin, soft and warm despite her injury. The lines of her shoulder blades rose sharply from her back, the lines of muscle and bone betraying a hard life of constant travel. Jacquin's hands found Adrian's hair and she marveled at how soft it was despite its metallic appearance. Jacquin had never seen hair so strikingly silver on someone so young. She wondered if it was magic or more common in people from the north.

"Hold her down. She might wake," Khalisa ordered as she knelt beside Adrian, sterilized needle in hand.

Jacquin looked down at Adrian and couldn't find the desire to pin her. Instead, she moved out of Khalisa's way and positioned Adrian's head comfortably on her lap. She soothed the woman with gentle strokes through her hair and over her shoulders as Khalisa stitched her wound closed, the white thread quickly turning scarlet with blood.

Adrian began to stir against Jacquin and she instinctually bent and kissed the top of Adrian's head. Khalisa paused, looking up at her sister in surprise and Jacquin's breath caught in her lungs in surprise.

"You sure you don't know her?" Khalisa questioned.

Jacquin shook her head. "I don't know."

Adrian stirred again and Khalisa quickly finished her stitching, tying a knot at Adrian's hip to secure the sutures. Adrian grunted in pain and tried pressing off the floor. Jacquin shushed her, petting her hair and shoulders like a sick child. "Don't move. You'll pull a stitch."

Adrian slowly grabbed Jacquin's knees, assessing her surroundings while forcing herself to remain calm. She looked up, meeting Jacquin's eyes with her hazel ones, the color of her irises seeming to swim and flash in time with Adrian's exhaustion.

Adrian's face twisted in confusion and pain, her silver-white brows knitting over wide eyes. "You helped me?"

"You fought for our Tribe."

A calm seemed to settle between Adrian and Jacquin, a familiarity and comfort that blocked out the rest of the world and encircled them in peace. Jacquin moved to brush her fingers through Adrian's hair again and Adrian caught her hand, entwining their fingers. Her grip was solid, protective. Jacquin's heart trembled in her chest.

Suddenly, Adrian winced as if she'd torn a stitch, but her wound remained sealed. She pulled her hand violently away from Jacquin's and struggled to get away. Jacquin felt a sharp ache as Adrian broke away from her, leaping to her feet in concern.

"You have to stay still!"

Adrian struggled to her feet, her face twisted with too many emotions for Jacquin to comprehend. Khalisa reached out to her and Adrian pushed her away and threw open the wagon door, letting the scents and sounds of battle flood the wagon again.

"Adrian!" Jacquin shouted, the woman's name tearing from her throat.

Adrian hesitated a moment in the doorway, every muscle in her body tense, sand brushing past her from the desert beyond. Instead of turning back, Adrian charged back into Oasis, fleeing into the chaos of battle.

Jacquin ran out after her, but Adrian had already disappeared. The pathways of the Tribe were littered with bodies, the scent of death and corpses frying in the desert sun was overwhelming. Jacquin refused to linger over the bodies of her Tribe. She didn't know who had died, but she knew she had grown up with every one of them, had shared warm summer days dancing with them, cold winter nights curled with them beside a fire. If she let herself see them now, she'd be overcome with grief.

The fighting had died down. There were more wounded being carried to healers than warriors battling changlings. Oasis guards in their burnt orange uniforms charged through the settlement, rounding up surviving marauders.

A loud bang boomed through the air, shaking the ground hard enough to knock Jacquin to her knees. A glowing, swirling dome rose high over the walls of Oasis, sealing the entire town beneath a protective force field. Jacquin looked around in shock and spotted dozens of mages standing atop the town walls, their arms raised high into the air. Jacquin felt a deep ache in her chest as if she'd been suddenly cut off from the rest of the world.

Jacquin reached out for an Oasis guard, his skin dark enough to betray a blood connection to the Tribe. "What's going on?"

"Another band of changlings was spotted on the horizon. We've sealed Oasis. Nothing can get in or out. Return home. We'll find the rest of the changlings. When we're sure the town and our perimeter outside the force field are safe, we'll lift the spell."

"We're trapped?"

"For our own good."

The guard continued on and Jacquin let him go. She held a clenched fist over her heart. If the town was sealed, Adrian wouldn't be able to leave Oasis.

Khalisa pulled Jacquin to her feet and led her inside the wagon, locking the door behind them.

Jacquin glanced around in shock, trying to adapt to the sudden feeling of isolation brought on by the magical barrier. She spotted Adrian's curved sword, kicked under Khalisa's table. She slowly reached out and grabbed it by the hilt, weighing the blade in her hands. There were faint grooves in the handle, smooth curves formed from years of constant use. Jacquin could feel the shape of Adrian's fingers, slightly larger than Jacquin's. Jacquin closed her eyes and wondered where the woman had gone, why she'd fled.

"Jacquin, what's going on? Who was that?" Khalisa's voice was soft with concern.

"I don't know. But I've seen her before. In my visions."

"Visions? More than one?"

"Dozens. Maybe hundreds. Since I was a child."

Jacquin looked up from the blade to her sister, her eyes inexplicably filling with tears. She'd only touched Adrian for a few minutes, but she already missed her touch, the weight of her, the way she smelled and moved. She had seen Adrian's face for the first time not an hour ago and she felt like she'd lost her dearest friend.

Khalisa touched Adrian's sword with a small smile turning the corners of her full lips. "It's a fine blade. Beautifully crafted. She'll want it back."

Jacquin wiped the tears from her eyes, taking a deep, ragged breath. "I hope so."

Khalisa slowly took the blade from Jacquin's hands and sat it on the table. She pulled her sister into a tight embrace. "I don't know what you saw about this woman, or how deeply you feel for her. But I saw the way she looked at you. There's a connection between the two of you. And I've seen you do more with a connection and a fine sword than find a mysterious woman."

Jacquin chuckled and grinned, tossing her hair back over her shoulder. "You're right."

A grief-stricken wail echoed on the wind, twisting through the cracks in Khalisa's wagon and both women froze. Jacquin recognized the voice of Aalim's niece. Jacquin closed her eyes, wondering what dear one she'd lost.

Reality closed in around the sisters, a reminder that their Tribe was significantly smaller, that their dear friends were sprawled dead just outside their home. Khalisa's grip on Jacquin's shoulders tightened, neither woman knowing what to say.

Finally, Khalisa spoke, her voice barely a whisper. "I'm glad you found me."

"I'm glad you're safe." Jacquin buried her face in her older sister's shoulder and closed her eyes. She hoped with all her heart Adrian was safe, too.

Chapter Two

Adrian stumbled through Oasis, falling back against a rough, adobe wall as her back burned like shards of glass embedded just under her skin. Her illusion, hiding her from sight, flickered as she was distracted by her wounds. She'd used some of her healing magic to seal the cut, but her healing abilities had become harder to control over the last couple years. Only the first few layers of skin had sealed, and she'd only managed that because of Jacquin's sister's skill with a needle.

The walls of Oasis loomed over her, the buildings taller and more reminiscent of the Ramains towns further north. Where the wagons of the Tribe had been freeing, the buildings of Oasis were protective. Here there were shadows she could meld into, where in the Tribe she'd had to use a much more powerful invisibility spell to escape Jacquin.

Jacquin. Adrian closed her eyes, her face twisting with rage, desire and fear. Even as far from the Tribe as she could be without crossing the force field she could sense the woman near. The Fates had a cruel sense of humor, bringing her to Jacquin this way.

Night had already fallen, the cold setting in, chilling her to the bone. She'd stolen a shirt and cloak from an abandoned house but it wasn't warm enough to ward off a night in the desert. She'd need to find a different source of heat.

Adrian slowly sat, the ground of Oasis proper damp from the humid heat of the living oasis at its center, a garden of tropical plants and trees surrounding a large pool of water. In the distance she could hear the wailing cries of families mourning their loved ones and, even further, the sound of drums and flutes, the pound of dancing feet. She could see flames licking high at the sky. The Tribe was burning their dead, celebrating their lives.

Adrian grabbed her right wrist, her skin still throbbing from touching Jacquin. She peeled back her sleeve and clenched her jaw. The lines of her lifestone birthmark were inflamed, her skin swelling and growing hard as a real lifestone, lying dormant beneath her skin her entire life, rose to the surface. She'd been avoiding finding her bondmate since she'd realized what lifebonding entailed, running fast and far in the hopes that she'd never find her heart so entwined with another she would literally die if she wandered too far from her bondmate's side.

Now here, in the middle of the desert, nearly as far from her birthplace as she could possibly be, a strange desert woman had triggered her lifestone in the heat of battle. Adrian clenched her fists with rage. If she'd just been fighting in a different part of town. If she'd been a day later following the Circle to Oasis or if she'd never left the Grey Exiles in the first place she never would have met Jacquin. But the Fates had intervened, guiding her down the exact path she needed to follow to find herself enslaved to a woman she barely knew.

Still, as she thought of Jacquin, her gentleness, her softness, the dark curves of her body and obvious skill with a short sword, she knew she could have been bonded to far worse. If their paths had crossed differently, Adrian might have pursued her. She grinned slowly, remembering the feel of her cheek resting on Jacquin's thighs as Jacquin's sister stitched Adrian's back closed.

Adrian shook her head hard, her cheeks growing dark with rage. The fond thoughts weren't her own, they were because of the bonding. Evolution was dragging her to Jacquin and she refused to be its pawn. She had more important things to do than fawn over a beautiful woman. The lifestone wouldn't control her.

Then why are you hiding in the cold?

The thought whispered through her mind, cutting through the tangled knots of her emotions. She pounded her fist rhythmically against the wall, locked in a battle of wills with her own mind. The Tribe's bonfire was more than warm enough to keep her safe through the night, and there was no need for her to stay close to the Circle; they were nursing their own wounds and just as trapped as anyone else. If it wasn't for Jacquin, she'd be at the fire already. Her bonding was controlling her, turning her into a scared child. Still, she knew there were other reasons she wanted to venture back to the Tribe. Reasons that could find her locked to the Tribe forever.

If she's your bondmate, you should know more about her.

Adrian scowled. It was a sound strategy, and the Mother knew she wanted to know more about the mysterious Tribeswoman.

She has your sword.

Adrian huffed, loud and deep like an angry horse. *Fine.*

She eased back to her feet, making sure not to break the tender healing flesh over her wound, and dug her hands in her pockets as she shrouded herself in shadow and headed toward the Tribe bonfire.

Smoke rose in waves into the air, drifting high into the sky. Adrian watched it fly, hampered only briefly by the magical barrier over the town. It seemed the force field didn't affect weather.

Adrian skirted along the outside of the Tribe's bonfire, avoiding the massive gathering of dancers and performers. The fire rose at least a head taller than anyone moving around it, waves of heat blanketing dancer's circle almost to the edge of the main town. Buried deep in the fire were the wrapped bodies of those who had died in the raid, Tribe and desert man alike. While many of the desertmen chose to bury their dead, those with blood ties to the Tribe seemed to have turned out en force to honor their heritage.

The wood had obviously been treated with oils and herbs, casting a sharp, spiced scent into the air to subdue the smell of burning flesh. The precious commodities had to be delivered from the north expressly for use in funeral pyres. The Tribe must have used their entire stock to honor their dead.

The Tribe moved around the fire, dancing and singing, celebrating the lives of those who had passed. The only mourners weeping seemed to be desertmen. Still, if Adrian looked close enough, she could see the tears sparkling in the eyes of the musicians, whipping off the cheeks of the dancers as they spun and rolled.

Adrian silently searched for Jacquin, keeping to the shadows, her eyes flitting across the performers. She didn't know Jacquin's profession, but she could guess from her physique, the intensity in her eyes, the way she'd fought that she was one of the Tribe's performers. Adrian could tell she wasn't a sword dancer – Jacquin handled a sword differently. Still, Jacquin wasn't among the dancers or fire twirlers, but Adrian could feel her near. Adrian wondered if she had stayed home, mourning a loved one.

Adrian wandered deeper into the settlement, moving toward a small marketplace formed from rows of wagons and carts. Herbal remedies and spiced soaps scented the air, silks and candles sold next to dried fruit and magical charms. Adrian grinned wryly at the charms, more talismans than genuine magical symbols.

The shopkeep, an elderly woman wrapped in colorful, patched robes, her dark grey hair threaded with beads and feathers, circled around to her. The woman was obviously playing on merchant superstitions about desert witches. "See anything you like, wanderer?"

Adrian pulled back her hood far enough to reveal her face. "I'm looking for Jacquin n'Huitaca."

The woman smiled, mischief sparkling in her eyes. "Ah. You seek a different kind of magic, then."

Adrian's brows lifted in surprise. "She's a mage?"

The woman laid a dark, wrinkled hand on a smooth crystal ball. "Seer. One of the most gifted outside the Great Market. She's doing card readings tonight one row over."

Jacquin snorted. "Between you and me, *Min*, do you mean an actress?"

The woman lifted her hands, stacks of bangles clinking like wind chimes as they shifted around her thin wrists. "You will have to decide for yourself, wanderer."

Jacquin dropped a small gemstone on the woman's table for her information and continued deeper into the market.

"You've traveled a long way to find yourself here."

Adrian froze, Jacquin's voice drifting through the sounds of haggling and the pound of drums. Adrian instantly spotted her sitting at a booth outside an old, worn wagon, a deck of ancient tarot cards resting in her hands.

She was obviously a dancer, dressed only in layers of thin, scarlet ribbons knotted and tied like intricate embroidery over her chest and hips and strung in her long, raven hair. The fabric hugged her body, every line and curve on full display, the loose ends of the ribbons swaying, adding rippling movement to every motion. Adrian's heart pounded in her chest, a deep ache spreading through her stomach and hips. She couldn't help but imagine Jacquin dancing near the bonfire, encircled by flame and desert sand.

Adrian popped her jaw, trying to relieve tension, and fought the urge to move closer, resting against the side of an empty cart, her arms crossed over her chest. Her wrist burned. Her heart ached. *This was a mistake.*

"You're a messenger of the Mother," a merchant wept as she hugged Jacquin close, finding whatever answers she needed in Jacquin's obviously faked predictions. She dropped a few coins on Jacquin's table and left, traveling back to the fire.

Jacquin collected the money with a sweep of her hand and for a brief moment her face fell. She wiped a tear from her eye before it could fall down her cheek and Adrian stood straighter. There was a haunted sorrow in her eyes as she glanced at the woman walking away, a look Adrian knew too well. The look of a mage.... Adrian studied her face, painfully open and honest for less than a breath. Perhaps the seer of Oasis wasn't completely fake.

Before Adrian realized it, she was standing before Jacquin's cart. She couldn't fight it. Jacquin looked up, her eyes wide in surprise, and Adrian suddenly forgot why she'd ever wanted to stay away.

Jacquin's voice was full of surprise, her eyes softening from sultry fortune-teller to genuine concern. "Adrian?"

"You have my sword." The words spilled from Adrian's lips unbidden. She silently cursed herself for being so tactless.

Jacquin nodded and stepped into her wagon, returning shortly with Adrian's sword, now cleaned and polished.

"It's a beautiful weapon," Jacquin observed as Adrian sheathed her sword. "Did the stitches hold?"

Adrian tossed her cloak over one shoulder, turned and lifted the back of her shirt to show Jacquin the sealed skin. Jacquin gasped, instinctively reaching out to touch Adrian's wound. A swell of heat spread from Jacquin's fingers across Adrian's back, making her heart pound in her throat. "Do you always heal so quickly?"

Adrian turned, readjusting her clothing. "Healing magic. It would never have sealed so well without your sister's help."

Jacquin smiled, the expression genuine and sparkling. "Khalisa will be pleased to know it."

"Is she safe?"

Jacquin nodded. "She's angry. She tried to warn the Council about the attack and they wouldn't listen to her."

Adrian sat at Jacquin's table, her brow rising in confusion. "She knew about the attack beforehand?"

"I saw a changling in the desert. They never travel alone."

Adrian's face hardened, her eyes squinting with a sudden sense of protection and frustration. "Why didn't they believe you?"

"I'm a seer and a false fortune teller. The Council doesn't see me as particularly reliable."

"You really are a seer then?"

Jacquin looked her over carefully, her eyes intense, studying Adrian, searching her face for something unspoken. Adrian studied her eyes, trying to read her thoughts. "How much do you really know about me, Adrian?"

Adrian sat back in surprise. "Nothing," she admitted. "Nothing but what you've told me."

"You've never dreamed..." Jacquin's words broke off mid-sentence, her eyes edged with pain. Adrian's heart ached as she realized she'd somehow hurt Jacquin already.

Adrian laid a deep red gem on Jacquin's table. "Read my cards."

Jacquin looked up in shock. "What?"

"Tell me my future."

Jacquin grinned wryly. "I just told you I make a living fabricating predictions."

"Then tell me a story."

Adrian placed her hand on the cards and Jacquin covered it with her own. "No. Not the cards. There's no magic in them but memories. Come with me."

Jacquin grabbed Adrian's hand and led her into her wagon, pulling her card-reading table inside after them. Adrian stood in the middle of the wagon, the structure only large enough to house a small eating area and a pile of pillows and blankets Adrian assumed to be Jacquin's bed. Adrian stared up in awe at the worn, child-like carvings along the ceiling, the marks soft with the passage of time. The wagon rocked lightly as she walked, lighter and more mobile than Khalisa's wagon had been. Jacquin's home was obviously older than many of the other wagons in the Tribe caravan, built for travel.

Jacquin was infused into every grain, every beam. Her colors reflected off the pillows, the curtains, the dark browns, scarlets and oranges dancing as the light slid off silks and hand-made lace. Her scent was heavy in the air, a mix of perfumes and natural musk infused in the pillows, the workbench, the open trunk full of dance costumes.

Her eyes wandered to Jacquin's bed and her thoughts started to wander to soft curves draped in crimson lace, skin like silk and hot breath on warm, wet skin.

Adrian tore her eyes from the bed and clenched her fists. She had told herself she would only look for Jacquin. Now she was in her home. She was losing control. Adrian redirected her attention to the sketches along the wooden beams, her fingers finding a rough carving of a family, a husband, wife, and two daughters.

"This was my family's home for many years. Back when the Tribe traveled every winter to the Great Market." Jacquin crouched on the far side of the wagon, crouching down to light a long, deep green branch of incense. The flame sparked a light plume of smoke that faintly reminded Adrian of the silverpines of home, the scent standing out in sharp contrast with the more exotic spices that permeated the air of Oasis. Adrian lifted a single brow. How did Jacquin know to light such a scent?

"You don't travel anymore?"

Jacquin lit a scarlet candle inside a stained-glass lantern, its light casting a fractured sunset across the wagon's walls and the lines of Jacquin's bare skin. "Business is good here, and the trip can be dangerous. The Tribe has stayed here permanently since I was five tenmoons."

"And your parents?"

Jacquin's face fell and she turned from Adrian as she fetched two silk pillows from her bed. "As I said. The trip can be dangerous."

Adrian clenched her jaw. "I'm sorry."

Jacquin squeezed her hand in answer and sat on one of the pillows. "Please, sit."

Adrian cautiously obeyed, spreading her cloak out around her as she sat cross-legged on the offered cushion, her knees touching Jacquin's. Jacquin closed her eyes and breathed deeply, the scents of pine and ice drifting once again past the warm herbs and spices of the desert. Adrian took a deep breath through her mouth, almost tasting home along her tongue.

Jacquin reached out and took Adrian's hands, her skin warm and her grip gentle. "Just breathe with me."

Jacquin's words seemed distant, as if whispered from far away. Adrian's eyes slowly closed as she was enveloped in Jacquin's presence, the weaving scents of burning incense and the touch of Jacquin's hands, her closeness soothing the pain in her developing lifestone. Adrian's breath caught and followed Jacquin's until they were breathing as one, the dull thud of Jacquin's pulse in her hands soothing and synching with Adrian's heartbeat pounding in her chest and echoing behind her ears.

"You're a mage." Jacquin's words were a statement of fact, her voice even low.

"Yes." Adrian couldn't tell if Jacquin could even hear her, but she felt an overwhelming urge to answer, to be honest.

"A warmage. But not as you should be."

Adrian's brow furrowed. "I am as I've always been."

"You're confused. Tainted. Tied in knots no sword can sever."

Adrian felt a cold sweat bead along her neck and hairline. How far could Jacquin delve into her life?

Jacquin rocked back slightly, a physical manifestation of an action in a dream. "You're a Blue Sight."

Adrian gasped in shame, instinctively trying to pull away, but Jacquin's grip tightened and the wagon disappeared. Adrian opened her eyes in shock and her heart stopped. She was no longer in the desert, but deep in the ice fields of the Core, wrapped in the leathers and furs of her childhood.

She pulled herself off the ground, brushing feather-soft snow off her shoulders with thickly-gloved hands. She spun around, her long, silver braid flying behind her with the movement. She felt her cheeks and hair, her breath coming in short, desperate gasps. She was young again, barely an adolescent.

She looked up at the sky, the low-hanging, stark white clouds like a false ceiling over the entire plane. In the distance she could see the fortress of the Core, rising up like the tip of a massive, stone iceberg. The sky over the Core glowed with red smoke, rising up like a spiraling serpent.

"You remember this day."

Adrian turned. Jacquin, still dressed in her dancer's garb, stood in the middle of the snow like a desert goddess. Her feet left no mark in the ice as she walked.

"Yes." Adrian's voice was that of a woman, not the young girl she'd been, but it was still just as tainted with fear, breathless with pain. "You were supposed to read my future."

"Your future is bound to this day."

"You don't think I know that?" Adrian growled through gritted teeth.

"Your vengeance will be your downfall."

Adrian ran to Jacquin, but she always seemed a step further away. "Vengeance is all I have."

Jacquin's eyes filled with sorrow. "As long as you say it, it will be so."

Fires lit around the base of the Core, a thousand tiny torches flaring to life. Panic blossomed to life in Adrian's chest. "I want to go now."

"The vision isn't done."

"This is my past! You have no right!"

"Jacquin can't hear you. She is seeing your truth, but is not with you."

"Who are you?"

"A manifestation of your connection."

A deep purple plum swirled and evaporated, two tall, identical cloaked figures leading the mob of torches. *Adrian...*

Adrian's skin went numb with fear, her eyes locked on Jacquin. She couldn't see. She couldn't know the truth.

Adrian ground her teeth balled her hands into fists, white balls of rippling lightning forming around her hands.

The manifestation of Jacquin was instantly before her, grabbing her arm in a crippling-tight grip. Adrian's lifestone birthmark flared to life, burning deep, ember-red lines into her skin as the stone broke through her skin. "Blue Sights do not destroy."

Adrian growled and threw the ball of lightning at the manifestation of Jacquin, instantly shattering the vision. Adrian's eyes flew open and she scrambled to her feet. The wagon spun and twisted as she fought to regain balance. Her heart and blood flipped and twisted beneath her skin, her magic a violent torrent of opposites, refusing to calm or blend.

Jacquin held her head in her hands, screaming as she covered her eyes, her fingers digging into scalp as she violently trembled.

"Adrian?!" Jacquin screamed. She slowly lowered her arms, a flame-red outline of Adrian's lifestone tattoo rising to the surface of her right wrist like the welts of a brand. She turned to Adrian in terror and pain. "What's happening?"

A primal panic gripped Adrian's heart. This wasn't right. Jacquin's pain. The bonding. Jacquin had almost seen too much. If she had delved any further, they'd all be in danger.

"I'm sorry," Adrian moaned, the words tearing from the depths of her heart as she fled the wagon.

"Adrian!" Jacquin screamed as she tried to crawl after her new bondmate, the name tearing from her throat as Adrian raced into the depths of the caravan.

Adrian didn't turn, didn't answer. She couldn't. She had to keep Jacquin safe. She needed to hide until the barrier around Oasis was lifted, then she needed to leave. She'd find a way to break the bonding later.

Through sheer force of will, she cloaked herself in an illusion of shadow. For now, she had to stay away from Jacquin, no matter how much it hurt either of them.

Chapter Three

Rox glared out the window at the light shimmer of the magical force field doming Oasis. The new light of day glanced off the magical glow, creating tiny, rippling rainbows as the sunlight caught and refracted off the crystalline magical structure. It was quiet in the inn. The Circle and inn staff were still sleeping, resting and healing after fighting the changlings. They had nowhere to go until the barrier lifted anyway.

Fisk ran toward her, an apple clenched in his front paws. He offered it to her and she let out a soft breath of disappointment between her teeth. "We don't steal unless it's necessary, Fisk."

The water ferret groused, racing up to sit beside her and bit into the apple himself. Rox grunted disapprovingly and made a mental note to pay the innkeeper for the piece of fruit later.

Rox sat draped across an empty window seat, bouncing her fingers off the wooden window frame. She was tense, every muscle in her body jumping and rebelling against the sudden feeling of entrapment.

"Feeling caged?"

Rox jumped at the sound of Calder's voice as he sat at the table beside her. "Go back to bed, Calder."

"And miss the chance at a private chat?"

"We've had enough of those lately."

"The Twins won't like this delay."

"And that's my concern why?"

"You led us here."

"Any guide would have led you here."

"Before or after distracting the Circle from the fact that they set an entire bounty of slaves free?"

Rox turned to Calder, fixing him with an even, lethal glare. "No loyal guide would set your slaves free."

"Can we please stop lying to each other, Rox?"

Rox stood from the window seat, snapping her fingers for Fisk, who instantly dropped the remains of his breakfast to race up her arm to hide in her cloak. "I don't think we ever started, Calder. I think we've both been perfectly clear about our intentions. And quite frankly, I find it exhausting. Excuse me." Without another word, she turned on her heel, her boots striking sharply against the stone and tile floors as she strode out the front door of the inn and out into Oasis.

The rest of the town was just waking, preparing for a day not of trading and selling, but repairing damaged property and rebuilding lives. Teams of children were gathering around the oasis, gathering shredded leaves and downed trees clogging the pool. Men and women already sweating in the early-morning heat worked together to rebuild market stalls and doorways, piles of destroyed furniture shattered pottery sitting before every doorway. Much of it was still stained with blood.

Rox avoided their eyes, haunted and full of grief. She knew that look too well. She'd been keeping it from her own face for many monarcs.

In the distance she heard the steady beat of drum song, flutes and whistles being tuned and readied for song. The Tribe was preparing to greet the new day and the sounds drew Rox away from the solemn desert man town and the inn full of Circle raiders.

She jogged through the narrow streets of Oasis out toward the open sands that stretched between the town and the Tribe. She could see a dancers' circle building around the remnants of the funeral bonfire from the night before, still smoldering low, burning until there was nothing left to set ablaze.

She turned the last corner until the edge of Oasis and grunted as she slammed into another person. She fell to the ground in shock. She couldn't see anyone, but she was certain she'd felt a human frame. Her eyes narrowed and she saw a shift in the shadows down a nearby alley and her tension turned to a primal thrill of the hunt. She saw the shadowy figure of the Circle Ghost, the mage in the desert, in the back of her mind. She sprang to her feet, drawing her knife. It must have followed them through the desert.

She pressed against the alley walls, staying a few steps behind the figure, stalking it through a series of alley ways deeper into Oasis. She carefully watched the mage move, its steps unsure and uneven. Something was obviously wrong. Rox wondered if it had been wounded during the Changling battle. It was certainly far from the confident mage who had pulled a sword on her in the desert.

The mage wove around to the back of Oasis, finally coming to a stop in a small, gated courtyard lined on two sides by the tall, stone Oasis walls and the south side of a large, stone warehouse, casting the courtyard in deep shadow. The courtyard had been recently swept, the debris of broken leaves from the nearby oasis and shattered stone laying in short piles on the courtyard tiles.

The mage paused in the center of the courtyard, digging through its cloak and producing a loaf of bread. Fisk peeked out of Rox's hood, his nose pointing knowingly at the food. Rox glowered at him and tapped his nose, sending him skulking around her neck and deep into her pocket.

"I can see you. Even in the dark." Rox hissed as she moved into the shadows of the courtyard, her eyes instantly adjusting to the dimmer light, betraying her prey. "You would have been safer in the light." The mage spun, instantly crouching, unsheathing its sword. "I saw you walk. You're hurt." The mage silently raised its hand, a ball of fire consuming its fist. "And alert everyone in town of your presence? When you can't escape?"

The mage's hand lowered, but the flames burned as brightly as before. "What do you want?" The mage's voice was distorted, rippling in pitch and tone, switching from male to female, masked by illusion magic.

Rox grinned. The mage was nervous; so different than the first time they'd met. "I protect the Circle. I don't appreciate my perimeter being crossed."

"You defend murderers and bandits?"

"For a fee."

The mage snarled. "Mercenary."

Rox gripped her knife harder. "You don't have the right to judge me. You have no idea who I am."

"You set the Circle slaves free."

Rox hesitated, a cold heat in her chest. "You saw?"

"What kind of mercenary is willing to defend the Circle, then risks her job for a kidnapped child?"

"That's none of your concern."

"You fought with a glass weapon before the changlings attacked."

Rox rose up, her brow furrowing. She suddenly felt exposed, laid bare before the inquisitive, perceptive mage. "Can you read minds?"

The mage laughed, the dark sound reverberating and swelling through the courtyard. "Nervous?"

Rox fell back into her fighting stance, her knife drawn. "No."

"Do the Twins know how little your loyalties lie with the Core?"

"Is there anything the Twins don't know?"

"And you still think they'll pay you?"

Rox's stomach clenched as the mage spoke one of her greatest fears aloud. They had to honor their contract. Rox didn't have any other options. "I protect the Circle."

"You lost one already."

Rox strode forward, anger burning through her veins, replacing every other emotion. "Come near them again and I'll kill you."

The mage glowed a faint red, its voice growing more primal. "The Circle is mine. Just like Gryert. Just like the Twins."

Rox swung, her knife flying low, slicing for the mage's waist. The mage dodged, the flame in its hand going out as it used both hands to swing its sword down at the smaller Rox. Rox twisted aside and grinned with teeth. The mage never fought with both hands in the desert.

"You're injured. Do you really want to do this?"

The mage thrust again, her sword coming fast and changing directions in the last second, nearly catching Rox off guard. "I don't need to be whole to deal with a Core thug."

Rox blocked with her knife, absorbing the impact of the mage's blow while deflecting the blade. "I'm not from the Core."

They exchanged blows, Rox's swift dagger strikes raining down on the mage, looking for any opening in the mage's defense, while the mage's strong, calculated strikes sent the small mercenary to her knees.

Rox drew a second, tiny dagger as slim as a finger from her boot and held the blade between her index and middle fingers as she punched, aiming up for the mage's gut. The mage spotted her attack just in time, using her foot to kick Rox's fist aside, stomping on her hand until the dagger fell free. The mage kicked the dagger away her foot flew again, striking Rox in the face, knocking her to her side.

The mage whipped its cloak, shrouding Rox momentarily in shadow. Rox dove, narrowly avoiding the concealed attack of the mage's sword, and grabbing the mage's ankles and sweeping its legs out from under it.

The mage fell back into a pile of debris, dust and leaves shifting and blowing aside as it landed, its sword flying to the side, crashing against the town wall. The mage hit the ground hard, landing on its back with an audible crash. It let out a moan of pain, the sound momentarily devoid of illusion and magic. The voice of an injured woman. Rox hesitated, the sound unexpectedly human.

The mage pushed hard off the ground, snarling in a desperate frenzy, its hand flying as a shock of lightning flew from its hand at Rox. Rox dodged, the lightning grazing her arm, sending a sharp jolt through her body, momentarily stopping her heart as she seized, her arm jumping involuntarily.

Rox charged, her knife hitting the floor in her frenzy as she attacked instead with her hands, straddling the mage, punching and clawing at the shadowed figure, her fists bursting with a satisfying bloom of pain and pressure as she connected with skin and bones. Her knuckles blossomed with bruises as her bare hands connected with loose traveler's linens and skin, betraying the mage beneath the illusion.

She reached down and grabbed a sturdy piece of wood, raising it like a bludgeon, but the mage threw a wild punch at her stomach, knocking the air from her lungs and collapsing her waist, stunning her long enough for the mage to knock the wood from her hands.

The mage grabbed at her arms and legs, trying to throw her, but Rox was wild, out of her mind with bloodlust and growing with strength as her adrenaline rose. She grabbed wildly, her hands finding the mage's neck, and she wrapped her hands like ropes around the mage's throat.

Suddenly, a searing pain ripped through Rox's hands, spreading up her arms and tearing through her entire frame. She shouted in surprise and pain, her hands burning as if on fire. She clenched her teeth in rage. A mage's spell wouldn't get the better of her. She squeezed harder, but her hands began to spasm out of her control, losing their grip on the mage's throat.

To her shock, the mage arched back in pain beneath Rox, nearly bucking the mercenary to the courtyard ground, its head tipping back in a howl of pain. The shadow illusion shattered like glass, revealing a young woman nearly eight tenmoons younger than Rox, her cloak thrown back as she continued to writhe and scream, her fingers and heels digging into the courtyard stones, her striking silver hair splayed across the stones, framing her head in a mane of moonlight.

The courtyard smelled of burned flesh. A thin stream of blood trickled down the mage's hand from beneath her sleeve, staining the courtyard stones.

Rox scrambled off the mage, every muscle cramping and trembling. "What's happening?" Rox demanded.

The mage only wept and seized, her fingers tearing and scratching at her left wrist. Rox fought her own contractions as she grabbed for the mage's shirt, tearing the sleeve free from the shoulder. She gasped in horror. The skin of the mage's forearm was crimson and raw as if from a deep burn, a lump rising to the surface, splitting and tearing at her skin.

The mage lifted both of her arms and as the sleeve fell back on her right arm, Rox noticed a small, pale stone already embedded in her right wrist. The mage looked in horror between both arms, tears running down her cheeks, outlining her lips twisted in disgust.

Rox loosened the ties at her wrist and pulled back her leather sleeve. She fell back in shock. The pattern of a small stone, the same size as the one rising to the surface on the mage's arm, was burning into her skin as well, leaving raised welts over darkened skin. She trembled. Rox knew nothing of magic, she had purposefully avoided crossing paths with it until she first met the Twins. Still, she recognized it when she saw it.

"What did you do?!" Rox screamed, grabbing the mage by the face, raising her arm before her. "What does this mean? Is it a curse?"

The mage grunted through clenched teeth, her skin damp with sweat, her eyes burning with rage. Rox slapped her, demanding her attention. "What is this?!"

The mage rolled hard, pushing Rox away. Stumbled to her feet, barely able to stand up straight as she groped for her sword along the city wall. Rox pushed herself to her feet as well, blocking the mage against the wall. "What did you do?"

"Don't touch me!" the mage screamed, her voice desperate and terrified, the change in tone startling Rox to her senses. Rox subconsciously stumbled backward, her hands falling non-threateningly to her sides.

Rox heard the same sound, the same tone, in hundreds of men and women in the Circle raids and slave cells of the core. In an instant she knew the marks weren't the work of the mage. The mage felt more violated and disgusted than Rox did.

The mage fled and Rox let her go, the woman flying away from the courtyard and back into Oasis. Rox fell back against the wall, stunned and numb from the fight and magical imprint on her arm. She raised her arm, running her fingers over the mark. Her skin was beginning to cool, the pain subsiding, but the marks were melting into smooth lines, like a magical tattoo.

She ran to the entrance of the courtyard and caught sight of the mage turning down an alley. As her adrenaline calmed, so did her rage and she found, instead of anger, a growing fascination with the Circle Ghost. She hadn't expected a woman; she'd barely expected a human. But it was the look in her face, the horror and vulnerability, that caught Rox's attention. There was something more to her than an assassin. Something off-balance and frightened.

You'd hunt the Circle if they weren't paying you, too.

The realization Rox had been burying in the back of her mind since beginning her work for the Twins rose to the surface. It didn't matter. She couldn't let anyone near the Circle if she wanted to buy back her daughter's freedom, but perhaps the mage wasn't the rightful target for her rage. Part of her hoped she'd run into the woman again someday, and not just to find out what the mark on her wrist meant.

Rox returned to the courtyard and grabbed her knife, resheathing it behind her back beneath her jacket. It unnerved her that the mage had made the connection between the blade and the changling weapons. It was a family weapon, passed down to her from her grandmother, but not that changlings were a real threat again, it might be wise not to use the weapon so visibly.

Fisk raced back to her from the far corner of the courtyard, a chunk of the mage's bread in his hands. Rox couldn't help but grunt a laugh at the absurdity of the sight. "All that and you were still fixated on her food?"

Fisk took a bite of the loaf, ignoring his master's tone. Rox reached out to him with her right arm and he paused, dropping the bread to grab her open sleeve and sniff at the new mark on her wrist. He looked up at her questioningly. "I have no idea."

Fisk scurried up her arm and settled on her shoulder. She scratched his back. She looked down at her wrist, studying the design. There was something familiar about it, but she couldn't place where she'd seen it before. "Do you think there are any desert witches in the Tribe? They might know what this is."

Rox had grown up hearing about the desert witches, fortune tellers, seers and charm weavers who wandered the sands of the southern continent. While many desertmen had come to Rox's seaside village to trade, she'd never seen nomads until coming to Oasis.

Fisk only curled into a ball to sleep. Rox drew a deep breath and retied her sleeve. Her old tension, her restlessness, was already returning despite the battle, her thoughts now locked on the silver mage who'd fled to the depths of Oasis. She could use a walk, desert witches or no. It couldn't hurt to check.

Chapter Four

Jacquin crouched beside the dancing flames of the funeral pyre, the fire allowed to burn lower as the sun rose, blanketing Oasis in a heavy, stifling heat that seemed more oppressive beneath the shifting magic of the dome barrier. Jacquin shifted her weight from foot to foot in time with the pounding of drums and whistle of flutes, the movements nearly hidden beneath the rippling layers of her silk skirt, her bare feet digging into the sand for balance.

She extended her hands toward the fire, the leather and silk bands stacked half-way up each arm shifted and slid around her forearms. She tugged at a particularly tight ribbon knotted over the stone tattoo that had formed on her arm after her vision with Adrian. Her hair draped heavy and full over her back and shoulders, brushing along the edges of the thick silk band tied around her chest. She lifted the mane off the back of her neck, a rush of air licking at her nape and upper back.

Jacquin let out a heavy sigh, her jaw clenched, every muscle in her body tense and electric. She wanted to run, to move, to dance, but it was only a symptom of a deeper need. She closed her eyes and Adrian was instantly in her mind's eye, every line and angle of her face memorized, the sound of her voice a clear echo in her ears. She could visualize with perfect clarity the snowy plains of Adrian's memory, the young, frightened girl watching an approaching mob with wild eyes, the same wild eyes that had met Jacquin's as they were suddenly thrown from the vision and Adrian fled into the depths of Oasis.

Jacquin imagined Adrian's hand in hers, the way they'd fit together while fighting changlings, the feel of Adrian's head in her lap. Her heart pounded in her chest and she subconsciously held her wrist right over the mark Adrian's vision had left on her wrist. There would be no relief in dancing today.

"You aren't performing today?" Jacquin turned. Khalisa approached, dressed in a simple, woven robe, her hair pulled up as if returning from a Council meeting.

Jacquin shook her head, rising to her feet. Khalisa looked her over with a sad, knowing expression. "Still thinking of Adrian?"

Jacquin's narrow chin twitched. She had told Khalisa that Adrian had returned and run away again, though she hadn't mentioned the vision or the mark on her arm. She didn't know how her protective sister would respond to seeing a magical brand on Jacquin's arm. "I can't stop."

"She's obviously dealing with a lot of her own issues, but she wouldn't have come back to you if she wasn't drawn to you, too. Give her time."

Jacquin remembered Adrian's haunted eyes after the vision. Jacquin had scared her. "If the barrier lifts, she'll leave."

"Don't be so sure. Not many can resist the seer of the *Dey Sorormin* Tribe." Khalisa's smile was kind, hinting at their more flippant teasings before the raid. Jacquin, however, couldn't find enough humor in the situation to play along.

Jacquin hugged her arms close to her chest. "I'm coming out of my skin, Khalisa."

"Then dance. Sometimes it's better than a bedmate." Khalisa winked.

Jacquin's eyes fell, briefly betraying the desire burning in her stomach, dancing beneath her skin. "Not today."

Khalisa rolled her shoulders with a shrug. "Then perhaps there's no better way to attract a substitution. Adrian isn't available. Perhaps there's another in the crowd just as lonely as you are."

Jacquin glanced back at the gathered crowd of Tribe and mourning desertmen watching a fire juggler in rapt attention. There was certainly a surplus of people looking for distraction, mourning for others.

"Perhaps."

Khalisa pulled her sister into a tight hug. "And Jaci... if there's more to this, more worrying you than Adrian, know I'm here."

Jacquin didn't need Khalisa to say more to know what she was thinking. She was thinking about their parents. The deaths during the raids had shaken Khalisa, reminding her of the death of their parents and her promise to keep Jacquin safe.

"You did your best to warn them. They wouldn't listen to you."

Khalisa pulled back slightly, shaking her head. "You always see through me even before I do."

Jacquin smiled softly. "We're both alive. That's what matters."

Khalisa hugged her again, then nodded toward the dance circle. "You deserve some comfort."

Jacquin parted with her sister, strolling toward the dance

circle, skirting along the edges so as not to distract from the performers. She wove through the audience, her eyes flitting over friends and regular customers. Most of the merchants and temporary visitors in Oasis were still holed up in their inns, afraid to venture far after the raid. Still, there were a few faces she didn't recognize, but none that captured her interest. She rolled her shoulders and sighed as she realized she was still searching for Adrian.

As she approached the far end of the crowd she paused. A small woman, her hood thrown back, revealing short, gold curls stood among the crowd, the same woman who had saved her during the raid. A water ferret sat on her shoulder, leaning back on his haunches to sit up straight and see the drummers. Jacquin felt a memory pull at the back of her mind, remind her of a vision she'd had before the raid of the false Adrians and the sandstorm. A waterferret had saved her. How strange to see both the intriguing warrior woman and the waterferret from her vision together.

Jacquin approached faster, easily moving over the sand to catch a better view of the woman's face. She didn't get ten steps away from the woman before she turned, spotting Jacquin approach. Recognition flashed in her eyes and Jacquin felt the desire roiling through her blood spike at the look in the woman's eyes. There was something just as intense, just as deliberate and primal in the warrior as in Jacquin. Something that momentarily made Jacquin forget Adrian.

A sly grin spread across Jacquin's face and she nodded to herself, breaking free of the warrior's gaze and moving quickly around the circle, greeting the sword dancer preparing to go on. She slipped the woman a gold coin.

"One dance. Please."

The dancer pocketed the coin and nodded, retreating back toward the caravan to continue stretching.

As the next song began, Jacquin stepped slowly into the center of the circle, the audience watching her curiously. She wasn't dressed to dance, eschewing a performer's face paint and body-revealing ties and bands for a full skirt and wrap. But Jacquin didn't need the trappings of a performer to win her prize.

Jacquin danced, using her hips, hands and hair to express the emotions, the tension and lust eating away at her core. She used her feet to skim and kick the sand into swirling patterns, adding movement to the long skirt slipping and sliding along her feet and thighs.

She closed her eyes, forgetting the audience, losing herself in movement and need. She flipped and arched, each movement exaggerated and extended as far as her body could handle, a feat of athleticism as much as art.

As the music started to slow, approaching the final chorus, Jacquin's eyes fluttered open, locked immediately on the warrior woman. Jacquin's eyes glowed with obvious victory. The woman's attention was locked on her every move, her mouth slightly parted with obvious attraction. Jacquin moved toward the smaller woman, dancing slower, more focused, until they were close enough to touch. The woman remained respectful, restrained and unmoving even as Jacquin reached out to her, pressing against her, her hips still moving in time to the music. She ran her fingers through the golden curls, tipping the woman's head back with a silent request.

The woman needed nothing more than Jacquin's permission. In an instant she wrapped her arms tight around Jacquin's waist, her grip stronger than Jacquin expected, and claimed Jacquin's mouth in a hard, deep kiss. The audience gasped, some even applauded. It wasn't unusual for Tribe dancers to kiss or seduce lovers out of the audience, but Jacquin was known for keeping her dalliances out of her performances. Jacquin's regulars were in shock, but Jacquin could barely hear them. She was instantly lost in the embrace of the warrior, her hands and mouth hungry for relief from the tension that had been building for days, the woman's grip almost animalistic as they kissed.

Jacquin broke the embrace, taking a deep breath of air, the song already ended. "Come with me." It wasn't a question.

She ran through the Tribe, her warrior close behind, and led her lover to her wagon, locking the door behind them as they embraced again, their hands more bold, more desperate as cloak and silk were left in piles on the floor.

"What's your name?" Jacquin gasped as her lover kissed and nipped a sharp line down her neck, Jacquin's fingers pulling desperately at the knotted cords binding together the warrior's travel leathers.

"Rox."

"Jacquin."

Rox peeled her own shirt and pants off, her fingers more nimble with the light armor, and the women fell in a tangle across Jacquin's soft nest of pillows and furs. Pillows skittered across the wooden wagon floor as Rox and Jacquin tumbled, Fisk racing wildly from his impassioned owner, growling with frustration as he climbed to the top of a wooden shelf and curled into a ball.

Within moments Jacquin had Rox pinned gently to the ground, a heated smile lighting her face with amusement.

Jacquin nuzzled the side of her neck, licking and kissing the ridges of Rox's ear. "For a warrior who had no problem taking charge in battle, you didn't take long to get on your back."

Rox wrapped her arms around Jacquin's waist, pulling her closer as Jacquin's body sank between her knees. Rox's voice was rasped with wild hunger, yet softer than Jacquin thought possible. "Sometimes I get tired of being in charge."

Jacquin smiled wider at the response and abandoned herself to exploring Rox's body. She reveled in the silken feel of the woman's skin beneath her own, her body solid and strong, the lines of her muscles defined and toned creating peaks and valleys across her skin as Jacquin's mouth danced across her body.

Rox's hands skimmed along Jacquin's back and twisted in Jacquin's hair, her fingers desperate and clinging, her nails biting into Jacquin's skin as she gasped arched with desire as Jacquin sought every sensitive place.

Jacquin closed her eyes as she kissed a narrow, precise line across Rox's small breasts, running her tongue over the swell, finding a hard, taut nipple. Rox was warm, tasting mildly of salt. Her body was more used to the heat of the desert than Jacquin had expected from a woman who smelled of the north.

Jacquin drew Rox's nipple deep in her mouth and felt a shock of amusement and desire as Rox groaned with delight, sending a flash of truth into the back of Jacquin's mind: a vision of a small village by the sea, the scent of seaweed and the taste of the desert in the back of Jacquin's mouth. Jacquin glanced up at Rox in surprise. She hailed from the south, too.

Jacquin's embrace became more curious, more urgent as she tasted visions and snippets of memories buried in the lines of Rox's body. Sorrow. Loneliness. Fear. In the lines of her shoulders she saw visions of Fisk, her ferret, hiding in her hair and cloak from a sea-soaked, half-dead kit she'd found in a dockyard to the adult hob rebelliously munching stolen food on her shoulder, his belly scales sparkling in the sunlight, his fur soft as down.

Rox's chest and arms were hot as flame, leaving a burning, electric buzz against Jacquin's lips. She saw battles and midnight assassinations, the fights always close-range and frenzied. She could tell Rox favored daggers and her hands, weapons that allowed her physical contact with her enemies. There was something about learning the tiny, petite warrior had a propensity to berserk, to be brutal and fierce, that made her all the more delicious and mysterious to Jacquin.

Jacquin's head clouded the more she explored Rox's body,

thought disappearing in a sudden primal desire that spread to her lover. She could see pine trees flying as if she were running through the forest, her body more limber and loose than it had ever been, even while dancing. She felt the chill of snow flying around her, a brisk tickle along her body as she realized she was covered in soft fur. The visions didn't belong to Rox. They were older, buried deep in her genes.

Rox arched and growled beneath her, wrapping her body around Jacquin, biting at her arms and collar, demanding more. Jacquin laughed aloud, Rox's wildness intoxicating.

Jacquin's hands skimmed across Rox's hips, her fingers finding damp, hot curls and Rox pushed into her hand, obvious in her desires. Jacquin indulged her, their lips meeting in a frenzied battle of lips, teeth and tongues. Rox's breath came in quick, breathy gasps as Jacquin worked her toward climax, her body jumping and trembling as Jacquin brought her to climax. Finally, Rox groaned deep in her throat, her body tensing and opening beneath Jacquin's hand and she collapsed back against the pillows, satiated into a listless daze.

Jacquin kissed her lips once more, gently, and continued her exploration, her touch more gentle. As she skimmed down her torso she tasted lines of pine, snow, tears and pain. She could feel an oppressive presence in Rox's life, an immediate threat to her safety that left her hard, isolated. A heavy darkness spread across Jacquin's skin, skimming along her body like smoke. Tears welled in Jacquin's eyes, leaving cold trails down her warm cheeks.

As she reached a long, thin scar spanning across Rox's hips, lined with silver, spider-web thin scars she saw a flash of a small child, a young, wild girl with curly blond hair rippling over her shoulders, her head thrown back in delighted laughter. As she spanned the scar she felt the weight of an infant in her arms, a tiny finger wrapped around her own. The weight of the babe growing in her womb. The warm, fresh smell of the infant's head and the curl of her first smile. Rox was a mother.

Rox's hands left Jacquin's hair. Jacquin pushed up on her hands, barely bringing her lips off Rox's body, suddenly uncomfortable looking deeper into Rox's mind. There was such heartache, so much tragedy Jacquin was sure Rox's daughter had died. She looked up as Rox wept, her arm over her eyes.

Jacquin slid up her body, holding her tight. Rox wrapped her arms around the young woman's shoulders, burying her face in Jacquin's hair, her body trembling as she fought to dry her tears. "I'm sorry."

Jacquin shook her head, kissing along her shoulders. "Cry. Your secrets are always safe with me."

Rox's hands moved to Jacquin's shoulders and Jacquin took her right hand, kissing gently along her palm and wrist. Jacquin started to melt, relaxing as her weeping stilled and slowly stopped. Jacquin paused, frozen in surprise as her lips skimmed across a small, warm mark on her wrist. A black-outline tattoo of a stone.

Jacquin pulled away just enough to meet Rox's eyes. "Where did you get this?"

Rox looked down at her wrist in Jacquin's hand and her eyebrows raised. "You recognize it? It was left on me by a mage."

Jacquin sat up, guiding Rox to sit with her. She untied the leather and silk bands from her wrist and revealed her own mark, identical to Rox's. Rox reached out in shock, touching Jacquin's mark. "What does it mean?"

"It means you had a run in with Adrian."

Rox tensed, her face falling, her lips tight. "Is it a curse?"

Jacquin shook her head slowly, running her thumb over the design. She couldn't forget the horror in Adrian's eyes when she saw the mark on Jacquin's wrist, the way she'd fled as if for her life. "If it is, it's her curse, not ours."

"Do you know her?"

Jacquin let out a soft breath, running her hand through her hair. How did Rox know Adrian? "Not well. How do you know her?"

"She's been following my charges. We fought. I grabbed her throat and the mark burned into my skin. I thought she cast a spell on me. I was hoping one of the Tribe mages could tell me what it meant."

Jacquin's brow furrowed, her stomach twisting at the thought that Adrian and Rox might be enemies.

A light scratching echoed along the floor of the wagon and Rox's head instantly snapped to the side, searching for Fisk. The waterferret was still resting on the shelf. "What was that?"

The sound of wood shattering split the air as a dark blue glass knife split through the floor boards. Jacquin screamed in surprise and leapt to her feet. Rox instantly grabbed her knife from Jacquin's floor and raced out the door. Jacquin grabbed a robe, throwing it around her shoulders as she followed.

Rox dragged a changling out from under Jacquin's wagon, using her fist and knife in close-range combat. The changling, a sleek, ebony black feline with thinning fur revealing human-like musculature, fought back just as fiercely. The changling twisted out of Rox's grasp and raced away from the Tribe, toward the outskirts of

Oasis. Rox instantly pursued and Jacquin, followed, chasing the changling to an open stretch of sand between the caravan and the city walls. Rox tackled the attacker, sending them rolling and wrestling across the ground.

Jacquin stood back, both fighters were too flexible, fierce and agile for Jacquin to intervene. Their skills were so evenly matched Jacquin couldn't help but notice how similarly they approached the battle, as if they'd been trained by the same masters.

Rox shifted, digging in her heels and flipping her attacker, pinning the changling on its back, her knife raised, ready to strike the creature's neck when both fighters froze. Jacquin gasped as her mind exploded, consumed with a vision. She was standing in the dark, cool air skimming past her skin, a trickle of water running in the distance. She knew without seeing that she was standing in a cave. In the distance a red stone glowed, filling Jacquin with an overwhelming sense of dread.

In the distance she could hear a whisper, words cutting in and out, stilted and pained. *Please... Help... Die...*

She blinked and was back in the desert. The fighters were still frozen, Rox's knife raised. She was blinking rapidly, squinting down at the changling, who laid still, breathing heavily, a look of fierce determination in his eyes.

"I don't understand you, your words don't make any sense," Rox hissed. "Magic in my head won't win you mercy."

"He's not pleading for his life," Jacquin announced. "He's pleading for his people."

The changling turned to Jacquin, his eyes suddenly soft with gratitude before turning back to Rox, relaxing, ready to die.

Jacquin locked eyes with Rox, the fighter's breath catching in her throat. Jacquin spoke softly. "And he doesn't have magic."

Jacquin took a few steps forward, wanting to try communicating with the changling again, but Rox suddenly threw the creature aside, the changling instantly fleeing, Rox chasing him away, her knife raised, until he moved out of sight.

"What did you do?!" Jacquin gasped. "I was connected to him. I could have communicated with him!"

"I heard him just fine," Rox growled as she stalked back toward the Tribe. Her nude frame was tense, covered in scratches and nicks from the changling's knife. She looked wild, almost inhuman.

Jacquin raced after her. "Do you have visions, too? How did he try to communicate?"

Rox turned and glared, the expression piercing Jacquin to her heart. "I don't like magic, Jacquin. Especially in my mind."

"He was pleading for more than his life. There might be a reason the changlings are here."

"He noticed my mark." Rox interrupted, lifting her arm to show the mark Adrian had left on her wrist. "He recognized it."

Jacquin glanced at the stone print on her own skin in confusion. "How would he know?"

"I don't know. But we're going to find Adrian and find out."

Chapter Five

Arian curled in a ball, buried deep in the furthest corner of Oasis. After wandering and hiding from both the town and the caravan she'd been drawn to an abandoned junkyard just past the Tribe's caravan, a pile of destroyed wagons and wagon parts, furniture and merchant carts. The deeper she'd crawled through the sand under the skeletons of the caravan's homes, relishing the shaded relief from the sun, the safer she'd felt. She reached a small wagon, sunk to the door in the sand, buried beneath larger structures. The inside was decorated with a worn rug, pillows and a table with candles and incense. It seemed she wasn't the only one to find the wagon a welcome relief from the sun and residents of Oasis.

She dragged herself into the pile of pillows and allowed herself to lie still for the first time since fighting Rox. Her back had opened again in places, blood staining the back of her shirt, the wounds stinging from the sand and sun. Her arms ached and burned, though the skin had closed hours before. A hard, pale stone streaked with veins of color adorned each wrist.

Adrian held out both hands, staring at the stones, tears slipping silently from her eyes. She'd spent her entire life avoiding lifebonding, and now she had somehow bonded to two very different women. She'd never heard of a Blue Sight bonding with more than one partner. Bondmates were physically incapable of living without the other for long. Adrian couldn't imagine how she'd manage to stay close enough to both a wandering mercenary and a desert dancer to keep breathing.

She eased back, grinding her teeth and wincing with pain. She reached back, trying to ease some healing magic into her wounds but her head instantly spun and her stomach turned. Her magic was bound, warring against itself, destroying her from the inside out, a torrent of destruction and Blue Sight that refused to manifest past her hands.

Her illusion had been destroyed the instant she'd bonded with Adrian. She couldn't even hide her hair, let alone cloak herself in shadow. She covered her face with her hands and felt a warm buzz over her eyes. Even when she had no voluntary control over her powers, the illusion that hid her eyes remained.

She took a deep breath and tried to find the missteps, the miscalculations that had led her to this place, hiding in the heart of a junkyard, magicless, lifebonded and near death. She could hear her war tutors from her childhood listing every error in her strategies. She'd lost focus, misjudged her enemy, assumed that as she pursued the Circle older threats would fall by the wayside. She should have seen it coming. Her fascination with both Rox and Jacquin should have made her wary, should have kept her away. She should have killed Rox in the brushlands, not just blinded her temporarily. She should have fled Jacquin when she'd felt so natural fighting at her side.

It was the Blue Sight. In her childhood, for every strategy that had been drilled into her head by a slew of generals and war heroes there had been two lessons on magical control. Her skin still burned with the memory of her mage mentors, constantly correcting and burning out every empathic, healing instinct infused in her blood from birth. The Blue Sight was the real enemy, older than the Circle and even older than the rise of the Twins. It was her weakness. Her core flaw. And now it was threatening to consume her again.

Adrian had always known she was inherently flawed. She had failed her parents, her destiny, at birth. She was a liability. Female. Blue Sighted. Empathic. It had lost her everything – her home, her family. Now it would cost her life and freedom.

She lay still, wallowing in pain and memory. She could hear the drums pick up in the distance and she knew night had fallen. A deep chill began to seep through the walls of the wagon, clinging to her destroyed clothing and working through her skin. She shivered once and moaned, the motion irritating her wounds. She closed her eyes, letting out a deep breath as if it were her last. She'd have an infection within hours. Probably a fever by the end of the night. If she stayed very still, if she did nothing to stop it, she could be dead in a day. In the depths of her despair, she wondered if it wouldn't be for the best. It would certainly break the chains of her bondings.

Adrian shifted in and out of restless dreams, moving from the desert to the icy, endless tundras of the Core, swapping the low wood ceilings of the dilapidated wagon for the towering, lonely, dark stone fortress walls of her childhood. She saw her brothers in the distance, sparring with swords and magic, perfectly synced. They were vicious, brilliant, noble, full of promise. They were everything they were supposed to be. Everything Adrian should have been. Everything she could never attain.

The sounds of shifting sand and wood echoed through the

wagon and the door opened, sending a burst of icy air over Adrian's battered frame. A lantern lit the interior of the wagon and a soft, feminine gasp made Adrian shift, her eyes opening to slits. A shallow breath passed her lips. She knew that voice.

Jacquin raced toward her, falling to her knees beside Adrian, cautiously reaching out to touch her shoulder. Adrian winced, torn between never wanting to see Jacquin again and an undeniable need to be closer to her. *Don't save me. Please. You don't know what you're binding yourself to.*

"Adrian? Adrian, can you hear me?" Jacquin's voice was full of sorrow and fear, her hands insistent.

"How did you know she'd be here?"

Adrian's breath caught in the back of her throat and her eyes widened with fear as she recognized Rox's voice. She instinctively shifted, fighting against her pain and magical paralysis to escape, expecting to feel a glass knife in her back at any moment.

Jacquin reached out to her, trying to calm her as she attempted to scramble away. "No, no Adrian, you're safe. You're going to hurt yourself. Please."

Adrian pulled away from Jacquin, her lifestones buzzing with both her bondmates near, her mind a swirl of confusion. Her heart yearned to find peace in Jacquin's arms, but her instincts screamed that there was nothing safe about Jacquin and Rox together. Bondmate or no, Rox would sooner see her dead than help her heal.

Jacquin reached out to her again and their eyes met, every chaotic, desperate, lonely feeling in Adrian's heart latching onto the visionary, paralyzing them both. Adrian's Blue Sight abilities flared, making her acutely aware of Jacquin's emotions as she was flooded with Adrian's pain, her past and her fear.

Jacquin trembled under Adrian's gaze, tears streaming down her cheeks as she tried to make sense of the mental assault of Adrian's heart. Her eyes glazed with vision, her lips moving in a silent scream. Adrian could feel her heart racing, her breathing shallow and labored as if it was Adrian's own body. Adrian tried to look away, to release Jacquin, but she couldn't move, her magic just as focused and intent on Jacquin's *amarin* as Jacquin was on Adrian's past.

"Jacquin?" Rox raced across the wagon, grabbing Jacquin and pulling her away from Adrian's stare. Jacquin collapsed across the sandy carpet, gasping aloud as her vision broke.

Rox met Adrian's eyes instead, her glare steady and steely. Adrian locked onto her, but instead of overwhelming the small woman, Adrian began to feel her passion, her ferocity, her presence like an icy taste of pine and sea water in the back of Adrian's throat. Rox didn't flinch as her heart and presence were opened to Adrian's Sight, her face steady, her muscles tight as her will slowly started to overcome Adrian's wild power.

Stop it.

Adrian could hear Rox's words in her mind, traveling over their shared connection. Adrian's brow furrowed in confusion. She'd never been able to telepathically connect with someone. She couldn't tell if the words were really Rox's thoughts, or her Blue Sight interpreting Rox's *amarin*, translating her feelings into words in an attempt to make sense of them.

You don't know what I've been through.

Instead of wilting beneath Adrian's past, Rox's eyes burned, her shoulders squaring with pride and rage. *You're not the only one in pain.*

Adrian's past flickered through her thoughts again, releasing old memories and insecurities. *You don't know anything.*

I know the Twins.

Not like I do.

They continued to magically square off, locked in a battle of wills and pain, but as Adrian's strength began to fade, Rox was unwavering. Within moments Adrian started to lean on Rox, her steadiness, seemingly unaffected by Adrian's chaotic instability, calmed Adrian's heart, slowly bringing her back to her senses.

"Are you done?" Rox snarled as Adrian let out a heavy breath and collapsed heavier against the pillows, breaking eye contact and covering her face with her hands.   Jacquin let out a soft whimper, still lying across the wagon floor, Rox's ferret curled against her chest. Rox moved to her, pulling her into her arms and holding her tight. Adrian glared, trying to understand where the two vastly different women could have met, let alone become so close.

Adrian felt a subtle warmth spread just beneath her skin as her Blue Sight calmed, mingling with her magic in ways that sapped her destructive magic instead of stiffling it. Adrian reached back and touched the base of her back. Her magic swelled from her hands in tiny waves, lapping at her injuries and resealing her wound while washing away various minor cuts and bruises.

She slowly sat up as Jacquin left Rox, turning to light the candles on the small table near the front door. "Did I hurt you?" Adrian whispered, afraid of the answer.

Jacquin hesitated, but slowly shook her head. "No. I'm fine." Jacquin was so distant, almost aloof, that Adrian didn't believe her. She'd hurt her bondmate already. Things would only get worse if

Jacquin stayed.

Jacquin paused, her mouth slightly open, unsure of whether to speak or not. Finally, "You're fighting your nature, Adrian. That's why you can't control it. Why it tries to feed off others."

Adrian grit her teeth. "It's not my nature. I can stop it."

"What do these mean?" Rox interrupted, holding out her bare arm, her sleeve pulled back to the elbow. Adrian's eyes immediately went to the stone tattoo on her wrist.

Adrian shook her head and looked away. "I don't know."

"You're a liar.

Jacquin took Rox's hand. "Leave her alone. She's hurt."

"I don't care. She cursed us."

Adrian glared, her blue eyes flashing. "I didn't do anything to you."

"You're dangerous."

Adrian's voice was sharp and ragged as she tried to stand and confront Rox. "Says the mercenary guarding the Circle."

Rox's skin darkened with rage as she took a step forward toward Adrian before Jacquin stood between the two women, her hands outstretched, her lips curled back in determination. "Stop it. Both of you." Jacquin's voice was unquestionable and firm, shocking both women into silence. Fisk sat on Jacquin's shoulder, trilling angrily.

Rox scowled at her pet. "Traitor."

Jacquin knelt before Adrian, taking her hands. "We didn't come here to attack you. We're just scared. If you didn't do this to us, what did?" Jacquin turned Adrian's arms, revealing the two lifestones embedded in her wrists. "What happened to you?"

Rox gasped and fell to her knees beside Adrian, the anger vanishing from her face, replaced with fear. "I never saw them clearly."

Adrian's cheeks burned to chocolate brown with embarrassment. Jacquin turned to Rox. "I don't understand."

Rox grit her teeth. "She's a Blue Sight. Those are lifestones."

Jacquin's mouth twitched in recognition. "But that... The stories say lifestones are chosen?"

Adrian pulled her arms away from Jacquin, holding them close to her chest. "Lifestones haven't been voluntary in millennia. Not since the Purge."

Rox ran her fingers through her short mane of curls. "Blue Sights are so rare. I've never met one, but I grew up with a boy whose cousin was one. He said the bonding is biological."

"We don't have Blue Sights in the desert," Jacquin admitted.

"At least not that I've ever heard."

"It's a disease," Adrian hissed, catching both women off guard. "A warped mutation. The Terrans dumped nanobots into our atmosphere and the only Blue Sights who survived were bonded. The lifestones changed their genetic makeup enough to keep them safe from the disease. A few hundred years of evolution and adaptation later and now they're a part of us. Any Blue Sight born without a lifestone dies at birth. Purged. But the rest of us?" Adrian held out her wrist again, the light of the lanterns catching the smooth angles of the lifestone, the iridescent veins of color dancing in the faint light. "They lie dormant under our skin, triggered by deep, emotional contact with our bondmates. We don't choose who we bond to. We can't escape them. One touch and we're no longer our own."

"Bondmates?" Jacquin ran her fingers over Adrian's lifestone, the sensation warm and electric across Adrian's skin. She stared down at it in shock. She hadn't realized how sensitive the stone was, connected so tightly to her nervous system Jacquin might as well have been touching her skin. "Like in the old stories of the Council?"

Adrian nodded. "Permanently bonded – mind, body and spirit – to a stranger."

"That's terrible," Jacquin whispered. "I'm so sorry."

Adrian looked up, staring at Jacquin's lips, refusing to meet her eyes again. Her voice was fragile, trembling with fear and unanswered questions. "I didn't mean to bond with you."

Jacquin held her hand tightly, the security in her grip comforting. "I'm honored."

"You bonded with me?" Rox voice was cautious and tense. Adrian looked her over, unsure if she was angry, confused or both. "I understand Jacquin, but me? I was trying to kill you, and you tied yourself to me for the rest of your life?"

"It wasn't my choice," Adrian argued. "And I intend to find someone who can break the bond. There are mages all over the Great Market. Someone has to know how to reverse this."

Rox was becoming more agitated, shifting from foot to foot, her eyes moving back and forth as her mind spun with unspoken thoughts. "You think so? Most don't know anything about Blue Sights, let alone bonding. And I've never heard of a bond between more than two people, have you?"

Adrian shook her head. "Never."

"Then what makes you think even the mages in the Great Market will know what to do?"

Adrian slammed her fist on her knee. "Because they have to! What other choice do we have?"

"We can ignore it," Rox grunted with a shrug.

"We won't survive being separated for long," Jacquin remarked, her chin resting in her hand as she thought, her other hand still holding Adrian's. "There are a few stories of bondmates being separated. They never last long."

Rox shook her head. "They must be stories. And even if they're not, those bondmates were in love or joined by choice. We don't even know each other."

Jacquin cocked her head to one side, her eyes focusing and unfocusing as if she were seeing worlds Adrian and Rox couldn't comprehend. "You have to admit we all feel drawn to each other."

Adrian and Rox regarded each other with wary snarls. Rox crossed her arms over her chest. "Drawn to kill each other."

Jacquin shook her head, her ebony hair rippling like a waterfall. "You know that's not true."

"She hunts my charges," Rox groused.

"Your charges are a roving band of thugs and murderers," Adrian challenged.

Rox glared. "A job's a job."

"Not when it involves decimating entire villages."

Jacquin turned to Rox in shock, her face scrunched with hurt and horror. "What is she talking about, Rox? Are these men in Oasis?"

Rox took a step back, clenching her fists. "I have my reasons."

"There are no good reasons for helping the Circle," Adrian snarled.

"Not everyone has the privilege of following their heart. Some of us are just trying to survive."

"The Twins are looking for something, Rox. Something they need the Circle's help to find. Once they have it, they'll try to move beyond the Core. You're helping start a war that could threaten all of Aggar. This isn't just following your heart. This is about the entire planet. What could possibly be worth sacrificing the world?"

Rox hesitated, her mouth opening as if to say something, but she clenched her jaw, thinking better of it. She snapped and Fisk raced from Jacquin's shoulder to Rox's pocket. "I don't have to stay here and be judged by you two. The Fates take your lifebonding. I'm done with it."

She turned and reached for the wagon door. The moment her hand touched the door handle a loud, blaring siren sounded from the Oasis walls, metal bells clanging deeper in the city and a lone horn call rising from the nearby Tribe. Jacquin paled, her naturally dark skin falling a shade lighter. "Don't open the door!"

Rox pulled her hand away from the door just as the junkyard around the wagon shifted and rocked in a sudden gust of wind. "What does that siren mean?"

"Sand storm," Jacquin whispered. "We can't leave. Not until they sound the all-clear."

Adrian and Rox turned to her as one, their eyes wide and incredulous. Adrian looked Rox over, eyeing the dagger at her hip. "You mean we're trapped here?"

"Unless you want to suffocate on a sea of sand," Jacquin rebutted. "This is the safest place to be in Oasis right now. We're protected by the wall and the old wagons as well as our four walls. We'll be fine."

"If we don't kill each other first," Rox hissed.

Jacquin shot her a disapproving glare. "Then we'll just have to get along. Even opening the door could flood the wagon, depending on which direction the sand is blowing."

Rox slowly sat back down, leaning her back against the wagon's door, her eyes never leaving Adrian.

"Fine. But when this is over, I'm leaving."

Adrian laid back against the pillows again, easing the ache of her healing wounds. "Fine with me. I'd rather die from an exacerbated lifebond than become tied to you."

Jacquin held her head in her hands, the heightened emotions and intensity of Adrian's and Rox's clashing opinions tugging at her psychic energy, giving her a headache. "Could you both please stop fighting, then? Just for now? The room is so small."

Rox and Adrian both turned to Jacquin, their eyes instantly softening as they shared the one productive thing they had in common: a care for Jacquin.

"We're sorry," Adrian whispered as Fisk raced out of Rox's pocket and ran to Jacquin, standing on his hind legs to look into her eyes with as much concern as Rox.

"I'm fine," Jacquin argued, waving her hands in front of her face. "It's just that you're both very strong. You're very much alike: full of pain, loneliness. Perhaps if you got to know each other better you might find how alike you are."

"We're polar opposites," Adrian argued. "I could never work for the Circle."

"You don't know what you'd do in her situation," Jacquin rebutted.

"What situation?"

"Exactly," Jacquin countered. "You're both assuming. And, though I can't tell what lies in your pasts, I do know neither of your assumptions are completely true. Like it or not, we've all been bonded to each other and magic may not be able to sever those ties. Perhaps you should get to know each other better."

Adrian and Rox glanced from Jacquin to each other, their muscles instantly tensing. Adrian shook her head. "This storm is Fates' Jest."

Jacquin spread her hands wide, trying to create some form of peace between the hot-headed women. "Or perhaps the Mother knew it was the only way to make you two talk."

"There is nothing of the Mother in this forced bonding," Rox growled, crossing her ankles and leaning back, her hands behind her head.

Jacquin frowned. "That doesn't make it any less our reality."

Rox's voice was defiant and stubborn. "Fine."

Jacquin nodded, smiling encouragingly. "Good. Now let's try to learn something about each other." The wind shook the wagon again, beating and pounding against the more exposed wood like a mob knocking at the wagon. Jacquin looked up at the ceiling as if studying the sky and the wind shook again. "We're going to be here for a long time."

Chapter Six

Rox leaned back against the wagon door, one arm crossed over her chest, the other flipping her knife up at the ceiling, watching it catch lightly in the wood, then catching it as it fell. The candles were burning low, the wagon and junkyard trembling as the vicious sandstorm ripped and clawed at Oasis. Rox consoled herself with the thought that a sandstorm so violent would drive away the rest of the changlings outside Oasis walls and the force field would be retracted when the storm lifted.

"You're going to shatter the roof," Adrian groused from the other end of the wagon, the corner heavy with shadows as the light continued to fade. Only Adrian's eyes and silver hair flashed through the darkness, catching the candlelight like stars.

Rox regarded the mage with narrowed eyes, her mind spinning with strategy and suspicion. Adrian was the greatest threat to her mission, bonded or not, and it was clear the mage was at her weakest. She was hardly intimidating without her shadowy illusion and her injuries making it next to impossible for her to stand up straight. She was gaunt, lean from infection and heat exposure, her skin a sickly pale.

Rox continued to flip her dagger, the glass temporarily passing between Rox's eyes and Adrian, bathing the mage in a dark green filter. If Rox was any kind of protector, she'd kill Adrian now, remove the threat before she could heal and regain her strength. Still, she knew it would be impossible with Jacquin near and, despite her instincts, Rox questioned if she'd be able to go through with it. Enemy or not, there was something infuriating and complex about Adrian, something Rox found fascinating. It would be a shame to kill her now.

"I'm not throwing that hard," Rox rebutted.

"Please stop fighting." Jacquin's voice was tired, heavy with annoyance and frustration at having to constantly intervene in Rox's and Adrian's arguments. They had all slept for a few hours, but as dawn broke the storm was still going strong, leaving the three hungry women to sit in uncomfortable silence for hours at a time.

A gentle grin tugged at the corners of Rox's mouth. "You

sound like a mother."

Jacquin scowled, a spark of amusement in her eyes. "I feel like a mother."

Rox sat cross-legged beside Jacquin, resting her knife on her knee. "I'm sorry to be a bother."

Jacquin shifted and Fisk stretched tiredly across her lap like a lazy cat. Rox pursed her lips at the fickle beast, running her fingers over his soft neck. "You're not a bother. Neither of you. But if we're going to be here, if we're going to face the reality of our bonding, we need to get to know each other better."

"I'm still dedicated to taking down the Circle," Adrian interrupted. "That's more important than bonding. And she's the enemy. I don't need her knowing any more about me."

Rox felt her temperature rise, the tone of Adrian's voice quick to bring out her fiercest anger. "I didn't start this," Rox countered.

Jacquin growled in frustration. "Then don't get to know each other. Talk to me."

Both women froze, looking to Jacquin. It was clear they both cared about the dancer. Rox looked Adrian over cautiously, wondering what kind of past she and Jacquin shared.

Adrian crawled forward into the light, leaning back against the wagon wall, resting her arms on her raised knees, carefully avoiding her injuries. Her head cocked to the side, her lips pressed together as she thought. "You do seem to be the link that binds the three of us together, Jacquin."

Jacquin shrugged. "And yet you two have a history I know nothing about."

Rox fingered the hilt of her dagger. "It's a history you're better left out of."

Jacquin's eyes narrowed at Rox's attempt to brush her aside. "It seems fate has decided otherwise."

"I work to fight the tyrannical Twins of the Core in the north and Rox helps the Twins' main thugs."

Rox's face twisted with disgust. "I don't help them. I protect them. It's a job. I hate the Circle as much as you do."

"Then why do you work for them?"

Rox lifted her chin with pride and defiance. Adrian wouldn't pull her truths from her so easily.

"Perhaps this was the wrong way to start," Jacquin interrupted, resting her hand on Rox's knee. "Rox, your knife is beautiful. Where did you get it?"

Adrian snorted. "Pick it off a changling?"

"It's a family heirloom," Rox growled. "From my

grandmother. It's been in my family for centuries."

Jacquin reached out and Rox handed her the knife. The seer examined it, weighing it in her hands and running her fingers over the blade. "It's very like the changlings' weapons."

"It's an old changling knife. My grandmother says it belonged to her thrice great-grandmother. My family once hailed from the north, not far from the Core, where the old Clan settlement was before the Purge. My ancestor claimed to have been visited by the ancient ghost of a changling, who left this knife."

Jacquin leaned forward, resting her chin on her hand. "Fascinating."

Rox chuckled, remembering her mother scoffing at her grandmother's dramatic retelling of the supernatural encounter. "Not really. She was pretty insane. She caused so much trouble her children moved the family south until they settled along the coast. But the knife stayed in the family and became an interesting bedtime story. It's a good knife."

"That's why you smell of pine and the desert," Jacquin mused. Rox lifted a single eyebrow in response and Jacquin laughed. "I'm a seer, Rox. Scent is very important in my visions."

"You've had visions of me?"

Jacquin nodded hesitantly, her eyes flicking between Rox and Adrian. "I've had visions of both of you."

Adrian sat up straighter, her loose-fitting shirt swaying around her sickly frame. "Is that how you knew me before we met? You recognized me. I saw it in your eyes while your sister was healing me."

Jacquin chewed her bottom lip indecisively, then met Adrian's eyes with determination. "I've been having visions of you since I was a child."

The revelation hung heavy and cold in the air, Adrian's eyes wide with shock. "What kind of visions? What do you know about me?"

"I never even saw your face, just your frame. You were always cloaked, glowing silver. You protected me. Pulled me out of my darkest visions and nightmares. I thought I'd created you as a defense mechanism until we met during the raid."

Rox looked between the two women in surprise as they both processed Jacquin's revelation. Rox's eyes lingered on Jacquin and she felt her heart sink. It was clear fate had bound the two women together. Her bonding to Adrian had obviously been a mistake: bonding didn't happen between three people and Rox was the last woman Adrian would want as a bondmate. Still, the connection Rox had shared with Jacquin had felt real. Important after so long trapped among the Circle.

Rox's voice was cautious, almost nervous as she whispered, "Did you ever have a vision of me?"

Jacquin met her eyes, her expression sad. "No. But I did see Fisk a few times."

Rox glared down at her pet. "I hope you'll be very happy together."

Jacquin grabbed Rox's hand tightly in her own, her eyes insistent, her voice sure. "I haven't had visions about a lot of people that are important to me. I decide who I let into my life, Rox. And our connection is real."

Rox felt a flash of the passion she and Jacquin had shared and she couldn't deny that it had been real, at least on her side. Jacquin shook her head, her eyes amused as if she could read Rox's thoughts, and kissed her hand.

"What exactly are you to each other?" Rox and Jacquin turned to Adrian, eyeing them warily. "Rox and I are connected through the Circle. Jacquin and I met during the raid. How do you two know each other?"

Rox felt her skin darken, suddenly unsure of herself. "We just met yesterday."

"We're lovers," Jacquin announced, her voice steady, her eyes daring Adrian to comment.

Adrian's eyes widened in surprise. "You bedded a Circle merc?"

Rox shifted to stand, suddenly done with Adrian's brash tongue, but Jacquin's grip on her arm was like a vice. "Apparently so. I said we were lovers, not that we knew each other well. But I know Rox has a pure heart. I've seen it."

Rox snorted. "You don't have to lie to defend me."

"I'm not lying. You have good intentions, no matter what you've done. I would have sensed otherwise."

Rox didn't know how to respond or even if she liked knowing that Jacquin had seen into her intentions and possibly even her mind. "My mind is a dangerous place, Jacquin. Stay out of it. For your own sake."

Jacquin sighed sadly. "I never tried to enter it."

Adrian shifted again. "This is insane."

Rox's lips pulled back from her teeth as she hissed at Adrian. "I won't take your precious bondmate, warmage. You think I don't understand you're fated for each other?"

Jacquin reared back in shock at the outburst. "What do you

mean?"

"You don't think I recognize an epic pairing when I see it? A pairing that will be written about in history books and sung about by bards across Aggar? You're powerful mages, rebellious and visionary. Adrian fights what may be the worst threat to the Ramains since the Purge. Jacquin, you're beautiful and magical. You've been having visions of her for your entire life. You lifebonded immediately. I'm just a magicless merc on the wrong side of history. If there was a mistake it was me, not the bonding."

Adrian and Jacquin stared back at Rox in shocked silence, even Adrian's eyes momentarily growing soft at Rox's outburst.

"You don't see how powerful you are, do you?" Rox was surprised that it was Adrian who spoke, her voice soft and aggressive, almost angry. "Irresponsible."

"Powerful?"

Adrian struggled to sit up, to lean closer to Rox, her jaw clenched in frustration. "I knew the moment I first saw you. Which wasn't in the brushlands. I couldn't take my eyes off you. Your will is the strongest I've ever seen. You praise me for my abilities? Do you forget that you've bested me every time we've fought?" Rox couldn't respond, her tongue frozen beneath the possessive, furious glare in Adrian's eyes. "You are a force like nothing I've ever seen. If our positions were reversed, the Circle wouldn't be standing anymore. So don't wallow in your own sense of worthlessness. It's wasteful."

The tension between Rox and Adrian was palpable, an electric bond that held Rox paralyzed, warming her cheeks and quickening her breath. She could feel her heard pound hard against her ribs.

"Rox... why do you fight for the Circle?" Jacquin broached the question again, her voice soft and cautious. Rox's hand instinctively went to her heart as it constricted in pain at the memory of her daughter. A memory she couldn't trust to these women. Not yet.

"I don't want to talk about it."

Adrian moved closer. "Are you a prisoner?"

Rox felt tears in her eyes and she snarled, holding them back with pure force of will and false rage. "I'm no Core prisoner. Why do *you* fight them?"

"Because the Twins stole my family." Adrian's voice wols icy in its precision. "And my home. And I'll do anything to keep them from getting a single thing they want."

Rox felt sick at the thought that she and Adrian had a shared past. She couldn't tell if it was because she had something in common with her enemy or because Adrian was fighting where Rox was aiding the Twins in an attempt to get what she wanted.

"I don't have the luxury of rebellion."

Adrian's eyes became more possessive and protective than ever. "Are you magically controlled? I can break their spell."

"I'm acting of my own free will," Rox rebutted. "And I stand by my decisions."

"You're so lonely." Jacquin's voice rose, reaching through Adrian and Rox's bond like a gentle breeze.

"Stay out of my mind, Jacquin," Rox warned, but her voice was losing its strength. She couldn't tell these women why she helped the Circle, but a deep, welling shame in her stomach wanted nothing more than to explain herself to these powerful women. To show them she didn't support the Twins. She had no choice. Perhaps she did want Jacquin in her mind.

The three women sat in silence, so close now their knees almost touched. A heavy, warm stillness settled around them, an undeniable connection weaving them together. The anger was gone, replaced with a deep, unsettling sense that something was about to change.

Outside, the storm rose, howling louder and faster than ever, the sounds like the shriek of a wild beast. Adrian hugged her arms close to her waist, her hands clenching and unclenching. Her face was stiff with suppressed pain.

Jacquin turned to her, placing a hand on her thigh. "Adrian?"

Adrian shrugged, "The lifestones. They grow more... insistent the closer I get to you."

Jacquin removed her hand cautiously. "I'm sorry."

Adrian caught Jacquin's hand, holding it tightly. "No. Please. I think your presence – both your presences – is keeping me alive."

"I wish we had a warmer fire. We could cauterize any new wounds," Rox added.

Adrian shook her head. "I'll be fine. I was able to release enough healing magic after we made contact to seal the injuries. It will just take a long time to heal."

"When the storm dies we'll take you to a healer. The tribal healers are folk healers, but there's a trained mage in town. A Doctor," Jacquin offered.

Adrian shook her head, adamant. "Doctors are expensive. I'll be fine."

Jacquin grinned, her full lips parting slightly, her eyes heavy-lidded in her mischief. "I have the money. And the doctor is a long-time admirer of my dancing. He'll help us."

"Then I definitely don't want you to entreat him for me," Adrian groused. "You don't need to owe any favors to men."

Jacquin flinched slightly, her brow furrowing. "I'm not ashamed of using attraction for help. He's been a courteous sponsor for a long time."

"I don't trust those kinds of motives," Adrian pressed.

Jacquin's voice was sharp and fierce, her gentle demeanor disappearing in a hot blaze of certainty. "I'm a dancer, Adrian. I'm not a child. My livelihood depends on a delicate balance of lust and respect, a balance I control, and I like it that way. I'm not one of your slave women in the north. Don't try to save me before you know me."

Adrian sat back, confusion and new respect etched across her features. "I'm sorry."

Jacquin shook her head. "It's fine. It's a common misconception from northern travelers."

Fisk raced across Jacquin's lap, leaning back on his hind legs to stretch out tall and touch Jacquin's cheek with his nose. Her face split in a smile, as radiant as the stream of stars in the desert sky, and kissed the top of Fisk's head. Rox felt a mild surge of jealousy in her stomach and sighed at her own foolishness. She spotted Adrian squirming in the corner of her eye and she knew the other woman felt the same.

"This is ridiculous," Rox grumbled, sheathing her knife along her back with a sharp click. Jacquin and Adrian turned to her in confusion. "There's obviously something here between us. You all feel it. I know you do."

Adrian shook her head. "It's the bonding."

"It's not the bonding. We all felt something, even before the bond. Jacquin has been seeing Adrian her entire life. Adrian, you said you noticed me before we ever fought." Rox swallowed hard, forcing herself to continue. "And I couldn't stop thinking about you after our fight. I never saw a line of your body, you never spoke to me, but I could feel you. And I didn't want to kill you. Can you honestly say you wanted to kill me?"

Adrian's lips pressed together hard and she let out a sharp breath. "No. I hoped we'd never meet again."

"You were the only thing I could see during the raid," Jacquin whispered, her eyes locked on Rox. "I would have died if you hadn't saved me. Focused me. You're a touchstone. For Adrian, too it seems."

Adrian growled. "It's the bonding. You think it only affects us after we touch? It messes with fate. Draws us together when we'd never come together otherwise. Loving each other under these circumstances is like being intoxicated. It's not real."

"Whose to say the fates only affect those with lifestones?"

Jacquin rebutted. "I have been dealing with fate and the soul since childhood. A stone in your wrist that saves you from plague and binds you to people who will love and balance you means nothing to fate. It's just the way fate chooses to work through you."

"I'd rather have a choice," Adrian snarled. "Not be trapped."

"Would you choose someone else?" Jacquin insisted.

Adrian squared her shoulders. "I would choose no one."

Rox snorted. "Because your choices have served you so well in the past."

Adrian's eyes widened incredulously, her cheeks coloring with anger. Rox was surprised by the jolt of pleasure in her stomach at the look. She grinned. Adrian was more fun when she was angry.

Adrian leaned forward, ready to fight. "You're going to talk to me about choices, merc?"

"This merc bested you with a single look not yesterday, warmage. You think I couldn't feel you when you force-bonded me? You're a mess. Are your destruction abilities even natural?"

"Rox!" Jacquin chided, eyeing Adrian warily as the mage's rage continued to build. Rox didn't know what Jacquin had seen of Adrian's past, but she could tell from the look on Adrian's face and the fear in Jacquin's eyes that her words were hitting home. "Enough!"

Rox shook her head with a smug grin. "You're not free, Adrian. You're controlled by shame."

Adrian charge, lunging forward and tackling Rox back to the floor, her back striking sand and fragile wood with a heavy thud. After hours of sitting still, the rush, even the pain, made Rox laugh with delight, the sound only seeming to enrage Adrian more.

"Stop! You'll break the wagon!" Jacquin shouted as Rox and Adrian rolled, each fighting for dominance, wrestling and kicking, a tangle of limbs and aggression. "Adrian, you'll hurt yourself!"

Rox reached out, grabbing for Adrian's neck, but she reared back. "You think I'm going to let you strangle me again?"

Rox pressed heavily into the floor, allowing Adrian to pin her down. "I'm not even trying."

Adrian paused, a sneer etched into her face. "Neither am I."

Rox defiantly locked eyes with Adrian, charging into her Blue Sight so brazenly Adrian lost her grip on Rox's wrists in surprise. Rox felt a rush of Adrian's suppressed desire in their momentary connection. Rox grinned a vicious, teasing smirk. "You don't scare me, Adrian."

Adrian's defiance broke and she wrapped her hands through Rox hair and kissed her, an attack of lips and teeth as fierce as any of their battles. Rox grabbed the front of her shirt, holding her close while being careful to avoid her injuries, her kiss just as fierce and fiery as Adrian's.

"You're infuriating," Adrian hissed, shaking Rox, her grip like steel. "I shouldn't want you."

"Blame the lifestones," Rox growled and they kissed again, their hands searching for ties and loose clothing, layers peeling and torn away.

Adrian instantly assumed control, knocking Rox's hands away and pinning her again, her grip loosening as Rox relaxed into their power dynamic. Adrian slowed, her actions less violent without losing her intensity. Her eyes flickered like the scorching blue flames of a bonfire, her movements precise and smooth like a jungle cat hunting her prey. Rox admired her control, her skin flushing dark brown. Rox could smell the warm, pine and earth scent natural to Adrian. She couldn't help but notice that Adrian smelled of the Core.

Adrian looked up, releasing one of Rox's arms to reach out across the wagon to Jacquin. Jacquin watched the brawl, her Amazon genetics flushing her skin more red than brown, her eyes wide with desire. She didn't hesitate. She stood slowly and stripped away her silks, standing nude in the last breaths of the candle light, her tanned skin reflecting back glowing hues of caramel and sunlight.

Rox and Adrian froze, drinking in the sight of her, their bodies growing almost unbearably hot where they pressed together. Adrian trembled, her thighs squeezing tight around Rox's hips where she straddled her. Rox groaned deep in her throat, memories of Jacquin's touch, her skin, her body pressed tight against hers casting waves of pleasure across her skin.

Jacquin crossed the wagon, kneeling beside Rox to kiss Adrian, wrapping one arm around the mage with a hunger born from a lifetime of desire and fascination with her magical protector. Her other arm caressed Rox, her fingers trailing along the sensitive lines of her neck and jaw where her mouth had been the day before.

Rox reached out, running her fingers over the lines of Jacquin's hips and thigh, her skin softer than any of her silks, her eyes locked on Adrian and Jacquin's kiss. Jacquin pulled back slightly, locking eyes briefly with Adrian, communicating without words their desires.

An instant later Adrian slid down Rox's body, making room for Jacquin to turn, sliding atop Rox, a knee on either side of Rox's hips. Their lips meeting with gentleness and passion, Jacquin immediately finding a rhythm of softness, nips and licks Rox had responded to before.

Rox felt Adrian near her knees and she reached out with her legs, wrapping them around Adrian's hips in silent invitation. She dug her bare feet into the floor with pleasure as she felt Adrian's hands respond, exploring her hips and more sensitive areas with a slow urgency. Jacquin arched her back as if dancing, pressing her chest tighter against Rox, tipping her hips for Adrian who immediately found her with her mouth.

Rox and Jaquin kissed and caressed, each trembling and gasping beneath Adrian's touch, their skin pressing, sliding and grinding against each other, their kisses growing deeper and more insistent as they sped toward climax together. Rox felt the rough press of her legs holding Adrian near, her thighs pinned tight against Adrian's hips, the weight and security of both women a divine distraction, condensing her world down to touch, sensation, passion.

Rox felt her entire body explode, her muscles jumping and melting as Jacquin arched, gasping quick shots of breath against Rox's mouth, her hair falling loose and wild around them, Adrian's hands and mouth seeming to slide across both their bodies with abandon.

Jacquin came down first, collapsing against Rox as Rox still reveled in the electric waves of pleasure. Jacquin's eyes were soft, unfocused, her breathing gentle, her muscles loose. Tears ran down her cheeks and Rox reached up to wipe them away. Jacquin caught her hand, laying soft, feathery kisses along the lines of her hand. She whispered against Rox's skin, more to herself than anyone else. "Nothing. There's nothing in my mind. No visions. No chaos. Finally, nothing."

Rox could feel the heat and tenderness of Jacquin's bliss. Adrian leaned forward over the calming women and laid gentle kisses across Jacquin's back as her eyes met Rox's, tying them together once more.

Never stop looking at me. Please.

The words entered Rox's mind as if Adrian had whispered them against her ear, too real, too infused in Adrian, to be the whispers of her mind.

"You don't scare me, Adrian," Rox repeated gently. Adrian blinked away a tear. Rox grinned wider, breaking the sad, gentle tension in the room. Adrian grinned wolfishly, already knowing what Rox would say. "Now take me again."

Rox lay limp and warm among her lovers, Jacquin's arms wrapped tightly around her waist, Adrian's arms encircling Jacquin to rest on Rox's arms, her legs wrapped tight enough around the dancer to entangle with Rox's thighs. It had taken an entire day for them to tire, resting in spurts between love making, the howl of the storm a primal backdrop when the candles finally died and everything went dark.

The wind had died nearly an hour before. Adrian and Jacquin were still sleeping heavily but Rox hadn't been able to rest. As the passion of bonding had died down, her reality had settled around her once more, along with a heavy weight of guilt. She had let herself forget. In the throes of passion she'd buried herself in her lovers, escaping the Circle and the Twins but in the moment she'd also let go of Serena.

Love wasn't a part of the plan. She was growing weaker, allowing herself to think beyond the mission and her child and that was unacceptable. As much as she'd been drawn to Jacquin and Adrian, they were dangerous. Too dangerous.

She slowly pulled free from her lovers, moving so as not to wake them. She dressed quickly and wiped tears from her eyes as she silently commanded Fisk into her pocket and cautiously opened the wagon door. The sand was heavy and thick, the grains wearing away at the junkyard around them, but the storm had ended and she'd be able to crawl through the debris.

Horns blared in the distance and Rox looked up through the holes in the wagon parts above them. The force field was falling away. The Circle would want to leave as soon as possible.

Rox looked back at the wagon, her heart breaking at the thought of leaving, but she clenched her jaw and pushed her sadness aside. This wasn't about romance or bondmates. This was about Serena. And to Rox, her daughter was everything.

It was time to leave.

PART THREE

TRIAD

Chapter One

Jacquin coughed, the pressure tearing at her throat, burning in her lungs. Adrian bent to lift her up, clearing her airways as she took a deep, gasping breath.

Adrian let out a tense breath, clicking her tongue against her teeth. She'd stopped asking Jacquin if she was okay days ago. She obviously wasn't. Since Rox had disappeared, a mysterious illness had fallen over Jacquin, starting as a lack of appetite and fatigue and quickly turning to a fever and cough. The day before, Jacquin had lost the ability to speak.

Khalisa blended a sharp, bitter tea just outside Jacquin's wagon, the rancid odor reaching Jacquin through the haze of her fever and she curled her nose, moving to cover her mouth with her arm like an obstinate child. Adrian caught her wrist, shaking her head.

"You have to, Love. Medicine never tastes good."

Khalisa ran the brew in to her sister and Adrian held Jacquin's arms as Khalisa ran the broth past Jacquin's lips. "This isn't helping her," Khalisa muttered. "This is the best remedy available in Oasis and it's not even keeping her stable."

Jacquin lay back, Adrian and Khalisa's discussion coming in snippets as her mind shifted in and out of reality. The ceiling seemed to spin, the wooden beams warping and twisting as the etchings along the ceiling came to life and danced through the air. Jacquin knew, even in her fevered delirium, that the images weren't real. They weren't even premonitions. She was losing her mind.

She closed her eyes and the chaos of images continued in her mind, pulling her out of herself. She stalked through the rubble of a shattered stone building, angry voices and the pound of boots behind her. She dodged and wove around silverpines, leaping up into a tree with low-hanging branches, her muscles shifting and moving in perfect unison, pulling her high enough to avoid the mob that passed below.

She looked out through the trees at the ruins, her heart heavy with grief. She could barely recognize the shape anymore: the ruins of the Council's Keep. She dropped to the ground, her old-fashioned wool cloak billowing out behind of her. She made her way back to the ruins, pausing once in the front courtyard. Flashes of gunfire reflecting off swords flashed through her mind, the memory of the trees of Valley Bay going up in flames.

She looked up at the sky, heavy with white clouds like a ceiling over the world. It was a sky she knew well. A sky that didn't seem to be right without her beloved, buried too deeply beneath the sprawling rubble for her body to be found. There would never be a funeral pyre for Antonia n'Athena. She would forever rest on her last battlefield.

Jacquin felt herself separate from the Amazon of her vision and she watched the woman whisper a prayer over the ruins and flee in the opposite direction of the mob. Jacquin could taste sand and sunlight in the woman's intentions. She was heading for the desert.

Jacquin woke again in her wagon. She took a deep breath and could smell sea water and pine. Rox. Her eyes flew open, but it was only Adrian and Khalisa, their faces pale with worry. It wasn't Rox. It never was. Just her ghost.

"Thank you for staying with her, Adrian."

"There's nothing more important than Jacquin. Nothing."

Jacquin's eyes locked on her lover. Adrian's pallor wasn't just from worry. Her eyes were ringed in dark circles, her skin tinted a light green. Jacquin had paid to have her back healed when the storm passed. She couldn't pretend her weakness, her exhaustion, was due to injuries. It was Rox. Their bond was breaking, pulling apart, fraying at the seams and Adrian felt it, too. If Rox didn't return soon, Adrian would quickly fall ill as well.

Adrian turned as she felt Jacquin's gaze and her eyes, hidden once again behind a hazel illusion, narrowed. "I don't think we should give her the medicine anymore. She doesn't want it."

"She hates the taste," Khalisa pressed.

Adrian shook her head. "No."

The tea Khalisa had given her started to work its way through her body, easing her to sleep, forcing her body to conserve energy. Jacquin closed her eyes, trying to fight the effects. The tea would ease any other sick person, but for Jacquin it was a descent into madness, her visions enveloping her as the medicine robbed her of her strength to control what she saw.

Jacquin held to her vision of Rox as she drifted into unconsciousness, her lips moving slowly, forming Rox's name in a soundless whisper.

Jacquin descended into a vision, waking in the middle of a dark, ancient forest, her bare feet cold and sore against the rough forest floor. The trees, swathed in inky shadow, rose high above her, almost blocking out the deep blue night sky. An icy chill clung to her skin, chilling her to the bone. In the distance she could smell smoke rising above the scents of wet pine and cedar.

She heard a mournful yowl and turned, a orange and ginger eitteh stalking toward her, its sandy cream wings folded tight against its back like a rigid cloak. It looked up at Jacquin with sad eyes. As it stalked toward her, it grew, shifting and rising into a changling, its body expanding to reveal taut muscles and a masculine frame a bit shorter and more muscular than the changlings that had attacked Oasis. The changling's eyes echoed the same sadness as the eitteh.

Somewhere in the back of her mind she remembered that the winged cats were all female, but there was no mistaking the changling before her was male. Instead of a knife, a woman's shawl was strung through the loop on his belt, his pants tattered and torn from running through the forest.

In the distance, melding with the sent of smoke, was a loud, hoarse, feminine scream of pain. Jacquin jumped in surprise but knew in an instant the woman wasn't in trouble; she was giving birth. The changling turned to the sound, emitting a wild yowl that echoed through the trees to the sky as mournfully and viciously as any wolf's howl.

Jacquin wandered forward, catching the changling's eye. She instinctively flinched, waiting for an attack, but the changling was still, the sharp, feline angles of his face a frozen expression of pride and acceptance. They locked eyes and Jacquin gasped, instantly recognizing the creature's truth in a series of images and emotions. A woman bathed in moonlight, standing in the forest. A feather-light touch. A kiss. A sigh.

"She wasn't crazy, was she? And you weren't a ghost."

The woman screamed again in the distance, her voice joined with the squeal of a child, the infant's voice too strong, to pitched to be a fully human infant cry. Jacquin saw another flash of images. A child, as changling as human. A torch. A cry. Her heart sped with panic, her legs ached from running.

"And her family didn't move south voluntarily."

The changling turned from the sound, stalking deeper into the forest. Jacquin chased after him, pressing through the tangle of brambles and low-hanging tree branches, but he ran faster, blurring together with the forest. As Jacquin suddenly stepped outside the forest, her feet meeting familiar warm sand, the changling stood before her, no longer a man, but a woman, more catlike than human, her fur a perfect match for the winged eitteh from before. She carried a wooden, carved staff, her eyes narrow and intense.

Jacquin was consumed with vision, running through the forest, stones beneath her feet, claws and fur and the sharp edge of glass blades piercing her skin. She heard a rising, purred song echoing in the distance to be shattered with the hissed, screaming war cries of changling warriors. The scents of blood on snow, minerals strung through an underground river, sulfur and fire filled her nose and mouth all at once. A deeply rooted fear settled in her stomach. The sensations bombarded her, too much for her to comprehend or separate, a swirling storm of aggression and misery and fear choking her like the sandstorm, filling her lungs until she could no longer breathe.

Jacquin woke with a silent scream, arching out of bed and nearly tumbling to the floor. Adrian caught her, laying her back in bed with a distraught look on her face. Jacquin saw her lips move, felt the tightness in her hands, but she couldn't hear anything. She was loosing her senses to her visions and she grabbed Adrian's shirt in shaking, damp fists as she realized that she would soon lose her vision, and with it all connection to reality.

Adrian's lips urgently formed Jacquin's name, her breath coming too quickly for her to be doing anything but yelling. Jacquin tried to respond, but she was frozen, her body slowly rebelling against her desires.

She felt darkness closing in again and she held Adrian tighter, their eyes meeting as she plead with whatever God would hear her not to slip away again. Adrian kissed her, held her close, her hands desperate to protect her lover but they both knew there was nothing Adrian could do. She had stayed. She was all that was keeping Jacquin alive.

Darkness fell again and Jacquin was once again far from home, standing in the dark, her feet on cold stone and her hands bound. She wasn't in her own skin. The body was different, slighter, smaller. Her wrists burned from her bonds, the skin wearing away beneath the metal manacles. Her feet were numb from the cold, every movement sending shocks of electric pain up her legs. She felt thin linen around her haggard frame, her stomach nauseous with hunger, her tongue dry and heavy in her mouth.

All she could smell was the cold, the damp, the dirt, sweat and tears of the other prisoners. There was no light, but somehow Jacquin could still see the other cells – the other prisoners – in the darkness. Her eyes were locked on a small child across the stony aisle, her face covered with her hands, her knees tucked tight against her waist as she curled into a tiny ball on the cave floor as close to the prison bars as possible. She was too dehydrated to cry, all her tears spilt days before.

Jacquin reached out through the bars of her cell as far as the manacles would allow, attempting hopelessly to be closer to the child. She sang softly, wordlessly, her mouth too sore and broken with thirst to easily form words, but she could still hum, could still vocalize the child's favorite songs. She refused to let the girl – Serena – be alone for even a second in the dark.

A light echoed deeper in the prison, the sound of boots stomped forward. Jacquin turned to the sound, a cold fear rippling through her stomach, her eyes flickering back and forth between the child and the sound. A small contingent of guards began opening the cells, pulling prisoners seemingly at random until she noticed the mark on the guards' clubs. They were slave merchants.

A man stopped before Serena's door and unlocked it as another entered Rox's cell. The man didn't hesitate with Serena, throwing the limp child over his shoulder.

"Stop!" Jacquin shouted with all her strength, the sound ripping from her heart as she pushed her way toward her cell door. Jacquin hesitated, recognizing the voice. Rox. The man blocking her door pushed her back, the motion instantly igniting a fire in her stomach that eased away her pain, pushing everything but getting to her daughter to the back of her mind.

She charged, catching the man off guard as the frail prisoner who had been effortless to push away barreled into him, her hands flying like claws, her voice a crazed animal's howl. She didn't hesitate, didn't think, her nails and teeth finding every bit of exposed skin, her fingers warm with his blood before more men charged her. She flailed and slashed, catching another man by the throat and snapping his neck with her arms before another caught her from behind.

Everything became a blur of blood and screams. She didn't feel their fists as they punched her, only their weight as they fell limp to the floor. Serena screamed, both at the sight of her mother covered in blood and the man carrying her away.

Jacquin lunged, reaching out for Rox's child when she was grabbed by the neck and an icy blast encircled her, knocking her instantly unconscious, consuming Jacquin in darkness.

Jacquin gasped, her voice echoing in her vision, her own once more. She wept, Rox's grief over the loss of her daughter still a physical weight beneath her skin. She could still feel Rox near and she ran through the darkness in search of her lover, the ground beneath her feet turning cold and hard, high marble walls running to peaked vaulted ceilings shifted into view until she stood in the center of a great hall, walls and floors of slick, smooth, mottled black and white marble. A council of warriors and mages sat along the walls.

Sitting at the front of the room on a short dais were identical twins, young men in matching black travelers' leathers, the only sign of their nobility scarlet cloaks wrapped around their shoulders and over their heads like hoods. Jacquin walked up to them, unseen in the vision, and studied the Twins who Adrian and Rox so feared.

They were perfectly identical in all respects but their eyes. The twin on the right had green eyes, while the other had brown. She crossed her arms over her chest. Their identical appearance was a farce. They weren't identical, they were fraternal, using illusion to erase their differences.

Soft, shuffling footsteps and sounds of alarm echoed through the hall and Jacquin turned as Rox stumbled into view. She was manacled at her hands and feet, her dirty linen dress ragged and torn, dried blood in her hair, beneath her nails, down her chin and neck. She stood at the center of the wide hall, a lone pinpoint under full scrutiny of the council and the Twins.

Rox, ever defiant, seemed not to notice the men along the walls, her full attention on the Twins, her eyes wild, her stance low and aggressive, her mind spinning, trying to find a way to run, to attack, with bound hands and feet.

"Give me back my daughter."

The brown-eyed twin leaned forward, seemingly unfazed by Rox's wild, gory appearance. "Rox, is it?" Rox regarded him warily without answering. "You've been held prisoner for two weeks, picked up during our raids down the coast of the southern continent?"

Rox was single-minded, her voice hoarse and vicious. "I want my daughter back."

The twin continued on, "And yet somehow, despite limited food, water and exercise, you were able to escape your cell and kill four armed guards with your bare hands."

A murmur of approval and awe echoed between the courtiers and councilors, but Rox didn't even glance away from her captors. She took two shaky steps forward, soldiers in the crowd instantly moving forward to stop her, but the green-eyed twin waved them away.

Rox made it to the base of the dais, close enough that Jacquin could smell the old blood on her skin, the dirt and sour filth on her skin from weeks of imprisonment.

"Give me my daughter or I'll kill you," Rox hissed.

"We did some research on you, Rox," the green-eyed twin

whispered, unconcerned with his council hearing what he said. "You're a tracker and guide, yes? Leading merchants through the desert to southern ports."

"We want to offer you a deal. We have a contingent of soldiers in need of protection and guidance. Someone with your skills and ferocity." Rox bared her teeth in response and the brown-eyed twin laughed. "You will be paid, of course. Handsomely. Enough to ransom your daughter from captivity and purchase a small settlement for the two of you."

The green-eyed twin leaned in. "And to prove our good intentions, we will keep your daughter in holding until you return. If you are successful, no harm will befall her. If you fight us or try to escape, of course our offer would be forfeit and your daughter's fate would be at the hands of the highest bidder."

Rox paused for the first time, some of her ferocity falling. "I don't trust you."

The brown-eyed twin frowned, his eyes flashing red for a moment in his intensity. "We never break a contract. Anyone who harms your daughter or threatens to harm you would be instantly killed."

"You will take Serena's word if she says she's been hurt?"

Both twins smiled, the expression disturbingly identical. "Why would we question a child?"

Rox fell back, logic and reality working its way into her primal conscious. She had already decided to accept their offer. "I want to see her first."

The brown-eyed twin, who seemed to be the more dominant of the two, shook his head. "You could imagine, with your reputation for killing guards, that we can't trust you not to try to escape with your daughter. You will have her again when you return."

Rox pressed her lips tight together and shook her head. "I know you. You have eyes everywhere. You find a way for me to speak to Serena or I won't help you."

The green-eyed twin clapped his hands together, slowly pulling them apart, and a crystalline glass spread between his palms, creating a small mirror, revealing a small, stone room, Rox's daughter sitting in the corner, her knees curled to her chest, hiding her face. "Will this do?"

Rox paled, tears streaming down her cheeks, carving wet lines through the dirt and blood on her face. "Serena? Baby?"

The girl looked up, searching the darkness for her mother. Her voice was soft and strained. "Mama?"

"Serena, listen to me. You're going to be alright. I'm going to save you."

"Mama, I can't see you."

"I know, baby, but please listen to me. It's going to take me a while to get to you, but you're going to be safe. No one will hurt you. You remember when mama has to go on a job and you stay with grandma? It's like that, baby. I'll always come back for you."

"I'll be a good girl."

Rox shook her head, her hands twitching, grabbing at her manacles in a desperate urge to hold her daughter. Jacquin reached out, trying to touch Rox, to give her some comfort, but she knew she was walking through memory. There was nothing she could do.

"No, baby. Not a good girl. You be a brave girl. A strong girl. If someone hurts you, you tell someone. You don't have to be polite. You don't have to be quiet. You be loud. You be smart. You be my warrior girl like I know you can. Do you understand?"

"Yes, Mama."

"I love you, Serena."

"I love you, Mama."

The twin closed his hands and the mirror disappeared. Rox stepped back, her eyes determined and settled. The brown-eyed twin nodded. "That's that, then. You'll be taken to your quarters where you can bathe and eat. Your orders will come by morning."

The sounds of the vision faded, enveloping Jacquin in complete silence as she watched Rox walk away, led out of the hall by a team of armed guards. All confusion and pain at Rox leaving evaporated, replaced with a heavy emptiness. Rox didn't abandon her. She chose her daughter.

A soft padding sound echoed in the darkness and Jacquin turned as the ginger eitteh crept forward again, ruffling her wings in silent invitation. Jacquin didn't hesitate as she followed the feline, walking side-by-side with the eitteh back into the desert.

The warm sand and cool night air was familiar and comforting, soothing her heart after the trauma of Rox's past. The sound of dustings of sand catching in the night air, dancing in small clouds of spray was like a lover's sigh, the streaming waves of stars in the night sky singing across galaxies to heal Jacquin's soul. Jacquin thought if she were to die of her sickness in the real world, this is where she'd want to stay.

Jacquin glanced down at the eitteh and smiled gently. "Thank you for bringing me here."

The eitteh sat, seemingly weightless on the sand, its eyes still sad, beckoning. Jacquin spread her skirts like a blanket and sat before the creature, resting her arms on her knees and looking into the creature's eyes. "What do you need?"

In a blink of her eyes, the eitteh was once again the changling woman, sitting cross-legged before Jacquin, her staff at her side. She reached out and took Jacquin's hand, the touch surprisingly firm and realistic. She cocked her head to the side, her eyes beseeching.

A flash of images spun through Jacquin's mind, reflected in the changling's eyes. Cold stone floors and towering cave walls veined with lifestone and dotted with holes like a beehive. A fiery, red gem embedded in a long stalactite glowing in the darkness. Rockslides and earthquakes, changlings stumbling and fleeing out of the mountains into the forest. A heavy pain ripped at Jacquin's stomach and head, sickness and death ripping at her skin and muscles, turning her stomach and snapping her bones.

"I don't understand," Jacquin moaned, trying to make sense of the images, the message the changling was trying to place in her mind. She fell to her knees, in too much pain to stand. "Please, I don't understand."

The visions stopped as the changling released Jacquin's hand, her eyes more pained than before. Jacquin could feel her pain, the frustration at their inability to communicate. "I'm so sorry."

The changling stood, shaking her head slowly and walking away, disappearing into a swirl of sand.

Jacquin woke, returning to reality with an icy blast, trembling in the cold. She was half-buried in sand, laying outside the desert walls. She had wandered from her bed in the vision, collapsing in the middle of the desert.

"Jacquin!" Adrian ran for her, her voice ringing in Jacquin's ears, making her smile. She could hear again. Her brief connection with Rox must have given her a small shot of health.

Adrian pulled Jacquin out of the sand, holding her tight in her arms. "Don't make me sleep again," Jacquin gasped, her voice soft, gravely, already fading again.

"Never," Adrian vowed, scooping the fatigued Jacquin in her arms again and carrying her back to Oasis.

Chapter Two

Adrian sat on the floor of the wagon beside Jacquin, her bondmate's hand limp and cool in her grip. She felt her stomach roll with a wave of nausea, her eyelids droop with exhaustion, but she pushed it aside. Jacquin needed her. She wouldn't let Rox affect her. Not with Jacquin near death.

Khalisa crept into the room, a woven bag full of incense and herbs under her arm. "How is she?"

"She's out again," Adrian muttered, rubbing Jacquin's cold hand between her own, trying to warm her. "Even without the tea her visions are taking over."

"Is she still talking?"

Adrian shook her head. "I don't think she can hear me, either."

Khalisa lit a small diffuser full of jasmine oil, the warm, floral scent creeping into the fog of cardamom and neroli that had been lit before. Khalisa fidgeted nervously, her fingers curling around each other in time with her panicked thoughts. "If she's losing her senses, I want to make sure whatever sense she has left is comforting to her. She loves jasmine."

Adrian reached out and touched Khalisa's hand. Jacquin's sister hadn't seemed surprised when Jacquin had returned from the sandstorm with Adrian. In the couple days Adrian and Jacquin had been healthy together, Khalisa had formed a tentative trust for the mage. Adrian's dedication and care during Jacquin's illness had only strengthened their bond. "We'll find a way to help her. I promise."

Khalisa pulled a patchwork quilt from her bag and laid it over her younger sister, tucking the quilt around her like a cocoon. "It was our mother's. Jacquin always liked it."

Adrian and Khalisa knelt together in silence, watching Jacquin's face, hoping she'd open her eyes, take a deep breath, make a sound. Instead she seemed to grow more pale, weaker, more still.

Adrian shook her head, her jaw tight with anger and worry. "That's it. I'm going after Rox."

Khalisa looked up in shock. "You told me she's sick because your bond is breaking. What will happen if you go?"

"She's dying. I have a connection with Rox, I can find her faster than anyone else. If I can bring Rox back, we might be able to save her."

"And if you leave Oasis and she dies?"

Adrian held Jacquin's hand tighter. Her voice was soft, heavy with fear. "If Rox doesn't come back, she'll slowly waste away. You didn't see her in the desert, Khalisa. She's terrified. She's not sleeping peacefully. She's locked in visions, losing her senses along with her mind. I can't watch her like this anymore."

Khalisa fell still, helplessly accepting their only option. Her face fell, her eyes haunted as she tried to find ways to save her sister. Adrian could feel her helplessness and she ached to ease her pain. The sensation surprised Adrian. It was a Blue Sight instinct. Being around Jacquin was pulling her closer to her Blue Sight instincts.

Khalisa brushed hair from her sister's brow, her hands shaking. "What do I tell her when she wakes and you're not here?"

"Tell her I'm coming back with Rox. Tell her we're going to be together. She'll be strong enough to wait."

Khalisa nodded slowly and stood. "I'll have your horse prepared for your journey."

Adrian shook her head. "Dread won't recognize you. She won't trust you unless I'm there."

"I'm good with horses," Khalisa assured her.

Adrian cracked a sad smile, "Dread is a stubborn beast."

Khalisa drew a tense breath. "Then I'll find you supplies. The markets in Oasis aren't selling. Most of their stocks were damaged or used after the raid and during the storm. But I have a few contacts that might be able to help you. I'll have the supplies delivered to the stables."

Adrian nodded appreciatively and Khalisa left, leaving Adrian and Jacquin alone once again. Adrian ran her hand over Jacquin's brow, her heart racing at the thought of separating from her. Try as she might to ignore it, she knew she was chasing after Rox for herself as much as Jacquin. She wouldn't worry Khalisa with the thought that her own health was failing – that Khalisa would likely have two bodies to deal with before the monarc's's end – but it rarely left her thoughts.

Adrian lay beside Jacquin, wrapping her arms around her lover's waist, her head resting on Jacquin's shoulder in a silent plea for her to wake. Jacquin's breath began to deepen, become more steady, but she didn't open her eyes. Still, Adrian knew her presence was a comfort to Jacquin as she wandered the dark realms of vision.

Adrian swore softly under her breath, fighting the urge to

scream, to fight, to cry. She couldn't understand how Rox could stand being away from her bondmates. How she could abandon them for the Circle. Rox had a strong will and wasn't imbued with a particularly strong sense of empathy. She didn't carry the lifestones, only the mark of one. She wouldn't fall ill quickly, if at all, but she would always feel a sense of loss. An emptiness that she'd never be able to ignore. She had to know what she was doing to her bondmates.

After a few hours she heard Khalisa returning and she untangled herself from Jacquin. It was time. She leaned over Jacquin, laying a gentle kiss on her soft lips, closing her eyes and breathing her scent through her nose and over her tongue once more.

"I'll find her, Jacquin. I'll bring her back for both of us." She stood and turned away, allowing her anger to flash in her eyes for the first time as she left the cabin to meet Khalisa. "Then I'll kill her myself."

Adrian ran her hands over Dread's powerful shoulders, admiring the care the groomer had taken with her mare after the sandstorm. Dread butted her human with her nose, the strength of her weight against Adrian's shoulder familiar and comforting.

She'd already prepared Dread for their journey, packing her saddlebags with her weaponry, water skins and the supplies Khalisa had been able to gather for her. She only had enough food for three days. She knew if she didn't return in that time, it wasn't likely Jacquin would survive and Adrian wouldn't survive Jacquin's death and Rox's departure.

Adrian nuzzled Dread's neck. "Ready to ride fast?" Adrian whispered. Dread huffed, stomping her foot once as if to argue that she never did anything else.

Dread could sense the difference in her rider, the oncoming weakness and, even more profound, the stronger bond between them, strengthened by Adrian's stronger Blue Sight abilities. Adrian was softer, lighter. Dread shuffled anxiously, unsure of what to do with the new version of her rider.

"Don't get any ideas, I haven't changed that much," Adrian assured the mare, grabbing her reins and leading her out into the city with as much strength and authority as before.

The sun was beginning to set, the sunlight shifting from a vibrant blue to a paler white. Adrian would make better time riding in the cool night than under the blazing sun. The nightly tribal fire was being lit as Adrian returned to the caravan, leading Dread to Jacquin's wagon.

Khalisa raced toward her as soon as she was in sight of the wagon. Adrian's stomach flipped with hope that Jacquin had awakened and terror that she had taken a turn for the worst. The panic in Khalisa's eyes disintegrated the hope.

"She's gone again. I don't know what happened." Khalisa wept as she reached Adrian, her hands curled over her mouth in terror, her mind racing and chaotic with exhaustion and fear. "I fell asleep beside her and when I woke she was missing. What if she's in the desert again?"

Adrian handed Dread's reigns to Khalisa, a quick look to her horse daring the mare to object. "Watch Dread. I'll find her."

Khalisa took the reigns, the leather straps providing something physical for her to focus on as she trembled. Adrian raced toward Jacquin's wagon, quickly searching the interior and beneath the structure before racing out toward the town gate.

Adrian felt a burning pull on her wrist and she followed the sensation back toward the main town of Oasis. She spotted Jacquin in the distance, stumbling and crawling through the expanse of sand between the town and the caravan. She ran faster, quickly overtaking the sick woman, and pulled her into her arms.

"Jacquin! Jacquin, stop, you're having a vision!"

Adrian gasped as Jacquin looked directly at her, her eyes clear. She grabbed onto Adrian's shirt and cloak, her fingers like claws, desperate and clinging. She was truly awake. "Don't leave me." Her voice was barely audible, broken and distorted, but understandable as she desperately formed each word.

"I have to find Rox. You're going to die if she doesn't return."

Jacquin wept, holding Adrian tighter, burying her face in Adrian's chest, the weakness and grief in her bondmate moving Adrian to tears, her heart a deep ache in her chest. Her strength to leave Jacquin was wavering, nearly gone.

"Take me with you." Adrian shook her head, the idea ridiculous. Jacquin could barely sit up on her own, let alone ride a horse. Even sharing a saddle with Adrian would be dangerous and could possibly make her worse. "My wagon..."

Jacquin's words faded but Adrian paused. Of course.

She scooped Jacquin into her arms and ran her back to the caravan. Khalisa let out an audible gasp, her shoulders sinking as Adrian and Jacquin came into view. Adrian raced to her. "Jacquin's wagon, is it still mobile?"

"Yes, but–" understanding dawned in Khalisa's eyes and she nodded. "I'll help you hitch her. Can your horse pull a cart with another?"

"She'll do what's needed."

Khalisa's face split in the first genuine smile Adrian had seen in days. "I'll find you two cart horses. Your beast can ride untethered."

Adrian sent her a grateful glance as she returned Jacquin to her bed. "I'm bringing you with me. We'll find Rox together."

Jacquin forced a shallow smile, reaching up for Adrian's cheek, running her fingers over Adrian's cheekbone in a gentle, silent request. Adrian bent low and kissed her, her gratitude at having a way to keep her beloved near overwhelming her.

"I love you, Jacquin."

Jacquin couldn't respond, but the smile in her eyes was answer enough.

Khalisa returned with two sturdy, ebony mares. She tethered them to the front of the cart with ease. She peeked in through the door into the wagon's interior, her smile beaming as she noticed her sister, still awake. "You're lucky Jacquin never moved the wagon from the outer circle. I'll take you outside the town gates, then you'll be free to move as you will. Lock the doors and windows. It'll be bumpy."

Adrian jumped to her feet to do as she was told. "Thank you."

The wagon started to pull away from the caravan, creaking and trembling from years of remaining still, but by the time Khalisa had guided the wagon to the town gates, the wheels were turning smoothly once more, remembering how to travel.

Khalisa paused as they exited Oasis and climbed into the wagon. "The desert is treacherous. Don't approach any sinkholes or divots. Sandworms nest underground and can attack your wagon from below. If you see an oncoming storm, stop where you are and take shelter in the wagon until it passes. Don't try to travel through it. More than anything, don't approach other travelers. Bandits stalk the main trade routes between here and the Great Market and they're more vicious than any wild animal."

Adrian kissed Jacquin's hand and stood to meet Khalisa. "The Circle isn't used to the desert, either. Even with Rox to lead them they'll stick close to well-worn paths."

"Do you know where they're going?"

"Rox grew up along the southern coast. The Twins hired her as a guide for a reason. I can only assume they intended her to lead the Circle south. We'll head that way by way of the Great Market."

Khalisa nodded slowly, her mind spinning. "A party that large will be hard to hide. I asked around town. They told the merchants they're mercenaries traveling for a job."

"You're lucky they didn't attack."

"They probably realized we had nothing worth taking after the changlings and the storm."

"More likely they're planning on stopping here on the way north again. If they come back again, that's when you have to worry about them attacking."

Khalisa crossed her arms over her chest. "I'll warn the Council. They're taking me more seriously after the raid."

Adrian's eyes narrowed in mild annoyance. "You should run the Council, Khalisa. You have good instincts."

Khalisa glanced at Jacquin and sucked lightly at her teeth. "Perhaps." Khalisa walked to her sister and kissed her forehead. "Come back alive."

Jacquin wrapped her arms loosely around Khalisa's shoulders, closing her eyes as she drew comfort from the embrace. Khalisa stood and walked with Adrian out of the wagon. "Take care of her."

Adrian pulled her sword from Dread's saddle bags and belted the sheath around her waist. "Always."

Khalisa sized Adrian up once more, her face still, her eyes sharp. It was a face she only showed Adrian when Jacquin wasn't looking, the face of a sister unsure of her sister's new lover.

Adrian stepped closer to her, keeping her voice low to ensure Jacquin wouldn't overhear. "You've kept Jacquin safe her entire life and now you're trusting me with her after only knowing me for a few days. I don't take that charge lightly."

Khalisa took a deep breath and wiped a tear from her eye. "Bring her home safely."

Adrian clasped hands with Khalisa. "I swear on my life."

Khalisa's grip was strong as she nodded. "That's all I can ask. Now go before Jacquin gets any worse."

Adrian nodded and climbed to the wagon seat, grabbing the reigns of the cart horses. She signaled to Dread to follow them and rode out into the desert, Khalisa standing behind, watching them until the cart disappeared into the sunset.

Adrian glanced over her shoulder as the sun started to peak above the horizon. Jacquin was resting again. Adrian wondered what she was dreaming, but she refused to be distracted. The faster she got to Rox, the sooner Jacquin could wake.

She pulled the thick wool blanket tighter around her shoulders, warding off the last of the night's chill. In the distance she could hear wild sandwolves howling, but they were far enough away not to be a threat. Adrian silently said a prayer of thanks to the Mother for their safe passage. If their pace held, they'd reach the Great Market by morning.

Jacquin shifted in her sleep and Adrian glanced back at her again. Even in just the light of the full moon Adrian could see the pained expression on Jacquin's face. Something was unsettling her. Something different than her sickness.

"Jacquin?"

Jacquin let out a soft whimper in her sleep and Dread sputtered in warning. Adrian's head whipped around, searching for the source of both alarms. In the distance she saw a plume of smoke rising into the sky, the charred outlines of a small oasis casting dark shadows across the sand. Adrian led the wagon toward the smoke.

Adrian pulled the wagon to a stop on the outskirts of the charred oasis and leapt down into the sand. She patted Dread's neck. "Watch the cart."

Adrian crept forward, her hand balled into a fist, the energy of her destruction magic making the skin of her palm buzz. The longer she was near Jacquin the harder it was becoming to call on her learned magic. Still, it was easy enough to conjure a fireball in case of attack.

The oasis was barely ten paces across, a tiny watering hold surrounded with a half dozen palm trees. She ran her hands over a blackened tree, the ashy residue clinging to her palms. There were sharp gouges in the trunks, the lines too thin and precise to be animal-made.

The watering hole had been drained, a deep trench in its place. Adrian had never seen a sandworm, but she doubted it burrowed in a square grid. The scent of burnt bark still lingered in the air. The wet sand from the pool's residue held the hole's shape, not yet reclaimed by the billowing sands of the surrounding desert. It hadn't been drained long ago. Days at most. Someone had been looking for something. By all appearances, they'd found it.

Dread whinnied, the high-pitched sound piercing the stillness of the night, and Adrian immediately ran back to the cabin. Jacquin was rustling, bent in on herself as if about to retch, but instead of holding her stomach she held her head.

Adrian bounded into the wagon and held her, hoping the motion would pull her out of her dreams, but as Jacquin turned to her Adrian saw slim trails of blood dripping out of the corner of her eyes and from her nose. Adrian gasped, suddenly unable to breathe, her heart pounding a rapid rhythm against her ribs.

"Jacquin? Jacquin, wake up!" Jacquin's arms flew, catching

Adrian in the side of the face, the strength of the blow shocking her. "Jacquin! Please."

Jacquin's eyes eased open, her irises clouded, another swell of blood rolling down her cheeks. "North. She's going north."

Adrian was struck with a cold understanding. There was only one reason the Circle would turn around so quickly. They had found what they were looking for. They were returning to the Core.

Adrian held Jacquin tightly as she began to weep silently, still trapped in her visions. No wonder she was getting worse; Rox was traveling in the opposite direction and the Circle would be traveling fast if they were bent on home. There was very little chance Adrian would be able to catch them on the way with a sick partner in her wagon. If she was going to confront Rox, it would be in the Core.

Adrian closed her eyes, memories of her first home, her family, flitting through her thoughts, rising from the back of her mind like a gust of icy wind. She had left the barren tundras of the Core behind long ago, both physically when she'd fled for her life and mentally when she turned her back on the way she was raised. Years with the Grey Exiles, those lucky enough to escape the Core with their lives, had made going back a near-impossibility. Now she was traveling back not to kill the Twins, but for a woman.

"I've grown weak," she grunted.

Jacquin clung to her, trembling in her arms and Adrian kissed the top of her head. She might be weak, but her resolve was as strong as ever. And she was going to reunite her bondmates, Twins or no.

She kissed Jacquin again and slowly disentangled herself from the sick woman. "Don't worry, my Love. We're getting closer."

Chapter Three

Rox sat up slowly, wiping her mouth with the edge of her sleeve. The stone floor of her room in the Core was ice cold beneath her hands and legs as she knelt over the small pail. She'd been getting sick multiple times a day for the last three days and her body was starting to feel the effects. She'd lost weight, her muscles tired and heavy. She didn't know where she'd gotten sick, none of the Circle had shown the same symptoms.

"Like morning sickness all over again," she muttered.

Still, it didn't matter. The Circle had found what they were looking for buried in the middle of the desert. Rox had seen the artifact as Calder exhumed it, but she couldn't tell what it was. It had appeared to be a twisted chunk of metal, obviously a fragment of a greater whole. It had taken less than an hour after reporting the discovery of the artifact for the call to return to the Core had been sent to Calder. There had been no raids on the way back, the party barely stopping to sleep. The mission was over and they'd been called home.

Rox stood on shaky legs, steeling herself for her meeting with the Twins. The artifact, even her sickness didn't matter. She had completed her mission. The Twins would pay her, release Serena, and everything would be over. Rox would take her daughter and they'd travel as far from the Core as possible.

Rox closed her eyes and could feel warm sun on her face, the sand beneath her feet, the warmth of Jacquin and Adrian pressed tight against her. Serena could benefit from Adrian's strength and Jacquin's joy. They would both need to heal from their time with the Core. Perhaps they'd return to Oasis. Perhaps Adrian and Jacquin would forgive her for leaving once they knew the truth.

Rox paced the small, windowless barrack. She was still nauseous but she was too anxious to rest. The Twins wouldn't make her a priority – it could be days before they spoke with her – but they could call at any moment.

Rox nibbled at her thumbnail, a nervous twitch she hadn't caught herself doing since childhood. Serena had to be nearby. The Twins didn't leave loose ends. They would want to make good on their contract as soon as possible. If she could find out where Serena was being held... She shook her head. She was too close to do anything that might put her contract with the Twins in jeopardy.

Rox lay on her narrow cot and stared at the ceiling, her face a firm, still mask. She let out a soft breath and her mind instantly drifted back to the desert. She could see Jacquin dancing around a towering bonfire, Adrian sitting in the sand, polishing her sword. She heard Serena's laugh as she bounded through the sand, Fisk peeking out of her pocket. The sun was low in the sky, the night warm and calm, the scents of fire and spice so different than the ice and steel of the Core.

Rox's stomach began to calm as drifted deeper into the paradise in her mind. For a moment everything went still. The heavy darkness of the Core slipped away for a future of safety and love. Serena would love the desert. No one would ever harm her again with Adrian and Jacquin helping Rox watch over her. Rox pushed aside the fact that she had abandoned her lovers, that they might not take her back. For a moment, she let herself hope. She let herself believe that things could get better after being a guardian for the Twins.

A sharp rap on the door pulled her out of her daydream and a young messenger boy stepped into her room. "The masters have called a meeting with all Circle members."

"I'm not a member of the Circle," Rox rebutted.

"They asked that you be there."

Rox drew a deep breath and followed the boy out the door to throne room. She felt a deep stillness as she stepped into the room, the ceilings towering high above her head. She hadn't been intimidated by the grandeur of the room the first time she'd been led there, bound and covered in Core blood, and she wasn't impressed now. Still, it didn't escape her that she'd only walked the throne room floor twice – once in chains, this time as a guest.

She took her seat along the wall, waiting for the Twins to arrive. She didn't understand why she had been invited; she'd never been trusted with the true intent of the mission and her interest in the Twins' plans only extended to her daughter's well-being. She didn't want to be part of their inner circle. The less she knew, the more insignificant she'd be to the masters of the Core. If Rox had her way, her contract and her daughter's life would be nothing more than loose paperwork. If she was important, her potential to damage the Core would be too great for them to let her go freely.

The Twins entered without fanfare, their strides perfectly in sync. They gave off a casual air, always dressing in light armor, refusing crowns or any mark of their birthright beyond their cloaks, but Rox could see through the charade. Their hall was too grand, their act of complete unison too rehearsed. They had carefully crafted their image to enthrall the people of the Core, to maintain their mystery. Behind their calm facades were ruthless eyes. They'd been playing at politics and war for too long to be so still.

Laik, the elder of the two, turned to the Circle. "Foxsen and I would like to commend you all on your successful mission. The set of relics you reclaimed are indeed genuine and complete. The whispers across Aggar are that you were merely a band of marauders. You have done a commendable job. And as a reward, we want you all to be present for the fruits of your labors."

Foxsen clapped and the doors to the throne room opened again. A mage entered, a silver tray in his hands decorated with small, curling and jagged pieces of metal. Rox realized, seeing all the artifacts together, that they were pieces of a puzzle. Her stomach turned, another wave of nausea washing over her. She didn't want to see this. She didn't want to know.

Foxsen took the tray from the mage and placed the pieces on a small table before the Twins' thrones as Laik continued to speak. "Since the dawn of time there has been one great threat on Aggar, one source of power that has constantly led to corruption and foreign invasion: Blue Sights. Blue Sights threaten our entire way of life. Their connection to the *amarin* of every living thing on Aggar has made them some of the greatest manipulators in history. Without Blue Sights, there would have been no Terran invasion, no Amazon inundation. Every nation that has risen on this land has been brought down due in part to a Blue Sight. If we are to grow stronger, to expand our empire, we must see this threat removed."

Rox clenched her jaw, a frozen fear racing beneath her skin. No wonder Adrian was fighting back against the Twins. She must have known their plans. The plans Rox had helped bring to fruition.

Laik continued as Foxsen focused on assembling the artifacts, piecing them back together into an orb-shaped puzzle box. "Their numbers were severely cut down during the Purge but they still exist. Adaptation and evolution has allowed many of them to hide in plain sight, but there is a way to bring them out into the open. A way to end the Blue Sight menace once and for all."

Foxsen finished the orb and held it before his brother. For the first time, the younger twin acknowledged the Circle. "The ancients once used these orbs to call on the mages of Aggar, to gather the powerful to one location in times of great need. They were once used by rebels to massacre a clan of seers, and the elders of magic had them destroyed, the pieces scattered. But we've found one. Assembled it. We can use its magic to call all Blue Sights to the same place and destroy them. We will wipe the species from the face of the planet and, when we take power, we will cull every newborn Blue Sight and the carriers of the Blue Sight gene until it's eradicated forever."

The cold spread to every part of Rox until she was too numb to feel anything anymore. Adrian. She had to warn Adrian.

Foxsen turned to his brother, the orb resting in his hands. Laik placed his hands on top of the orb, both twins instantly surrounded by a bright, crimson red light. The orb, however, remained unchanged. Rox held her breath. Perhaps the orb was too old to be revived or it hadn't been assembled properly.

The Twins looked at each other, their faces slowly sinking into expressions of wild rage, their magic burning brighter until they appeared cloaked in flame. A blast of heat beat against her skin, like standing too close to a kiln, but the orb still remained dead.

The Twins' calm disappeared with their magical flames. Barely-contained rage and frustration etched into their features as they returned the orb to the tray. "Get out," Laik ordered.

The Circle instantly stood, moving toward the doors. Rox followed, trying to escape the Twins unnoticed, her mind spinning trying to find a way to send word to Adrian about the orb.

"Not you, Rox." Rox paused, suddenly paralyzed. The last thing she needed was the Twins calling her name when obviously enraged. A handful of Circle members hesitated, curious about what was going to happen.

She slowly turned. "Sir?"

Foxsen beckoned her closer. "We have your contract to discuss."

Rox approached the dais, her heart a chaos of emotion and warning. "I can take my daughter and go. No homestead. Nothing. I can disappear," Rox assured them.

"Your daughter is being prepped for sale. You didn't hold to your end of the contract."

Rox stopped breathing, her heart falling silent in her chest. "I did everything you told me to do."

"Gryert was killed."

"While on a solo mission!" Rox felt her cheeks color with desperation and fury. "I was with the main party!"

Laik crossed his arms over his chest. A slight smirk tugged at his lips. "He was your charge."

"That's not fair, the contract explicitly states I am not in charge of protection when we are at rest stops."

"Gryert was on a mission, therefore he was not resting. You are free. Your help with the Circle was invaluable. But your daughter is ours."

All logical thought fled Rox's mind, filled instead with rage and grief. She screamed, leaping for the Twins, but a wave of Foxsen's hand instantly made her body too heavy to move. She fell to the ground hard, her head cracking against the floor.

She fought against the spell, trying to get to the Twins, screaming and gnashing her teeth at them like a rabid beast.

Laik shouted. "Guards! Take her to the dungeon."

Circle members instantly surrounded her, grabbing for her. She fought them away, pushing past the boundaries of the spell until she could use her arms again. She swiped and bit at their legs, fighting to get up when she fell back to the floor, a sharp, cracking snap echoing through the room. Rox grunted as another sharp pain spread through her ribs and stomach. She looked up. Calder.

Calder's eyes were bright with maniacal glee, the woman he'd dreamt of killing now unprotected. He kicked her a dozen times, his booted foot finding her ribs and stomach over and over until she retched. He bent and grabbed her face, genuinely smiling for the first time since Rox had met him.

"Not too hard, Calder. Don't damage her. She'll go on the block with her daughter."

Rox fought again, this time in an attempt to flee. She broke through of the magic, lashing out with a new intensity. She was wild. Berserk. She had to get away. Small sprays of blood speckled the Twins' floor.

Three Circle members surrounded her, grabbing her and pinning her to the ground. Calder grabbed her face, pulling her up to meet her eyes. Rox fought him, shaking her head and trying to angle out of his grasp but he fought her, wrapping his arms around her head as if to break her neck.

"Do you feel that, Rox? That weight. That helplessness? You're no longer contracted. Just a slave. I have a new bag of gold and all the time in the world."

"Enough, Calder," Laik called. "We'll let the stocks decide."

Calder released her as the rest of her captors bound her and lifted her off the ground, keeping her tightly contained as they dragged her out of the throne room toward the dungeons. She continued to fight, nearly slipping one of her bonds when Foxsen approached, moving unnaturally fast, his hand reaching out to grab her throat. A flash of burning heat spread up to her face and she instantly fell unconscious.

Rox woke in darkness, a cold breeze flooding across her skin. She recognized the sensation, the smell. She was in the Core prisons again.

She pushed up on her hands and knees, struggling to find her strength. Her body screamed at each movement, a dozen or more bruises sprouting across her body from where the Circle had beaten her. Her skin was already numb with cold. She'd been stripped of everything but her underclothes – her knife, her leathers, all gone.

She heard a sharp chirp and the scurry of tiny feet and she felt a small burst of relief. Fisk had always been smart. He must have hidden as she was taken into the prison.

Rox leaned back against the stone wall of her cell as Fisk squeezed through the bars and raced into her arms. He was warm and soft, something familiar as her world shattered around her. She wondered where Serena was, if she was still safe, if she knew what had happened. She held Fisk tighter. When would Serena stop hoping for her mother to return?

Rox held Fisk tighter and for the first time since her village had been attacked by the Circle, Rox wept. Fisk chirped and hummed, snuggling close, trying to give his human some comfort, but Rox couldn't feel anything but grief, loss, hopelessness. Every emotion she'd been suppressing seized control of her body and mind, every death she'd facilitated, every questionable moral call, every weakness, every fear. She should have searched for Serena the moment she arrived. She shouldn't have trusted the Twins to honor their contract.

Rox curled in on herself, her sobs hard, body-wracking bursts that shot from her lungs and stung her mouth. She felt another swell of nausea and she succumbed to whatever sickness raged in her body. It didn't matter anymore. She'd failed.

"Not so strong without the Twins to protect you, are you?" The voice invaded Rox's privacy, instantly pulling her emotions deeper inside, quieting her sobs. She nudged Fisk away, her pet silently taking her direction and running to hide in the furthest corner of the cell. "Oh please. Don't stop on my account."

Rox stood slowly, grief turned to a deadly, quiet rage. Calder chuckled low and dark as he leaned forward against the bars of Rox's cell. He was nothing more than a shadow, Rox would never have been able to make out his features if it wasn't for her night vision.

Rox walked toward him, slow and predatory, stopping just out of arm's reach. "Are you happy, Calder? Is this what you wanted?"

"It's a start."

"I won't cry in front of you again."

"Good. I was afraid losing your contract would break you. I want to be the one to break you."

"If you touch me I'll–"

"What?" Calder pressed tighter against the bars, "You have nothing. No one to protect you. A few gold coins and you're mine. You think anyone else will bid on you? A wild, damaged, willful mother past her prime? You will be mine. You have nothing."

"You're making a very dangerous assumption, Calder. You think having nothing makes me weak but it's the opposite. I have nothing else to lose. And I warn you – I'm at my most deadly when I'm desperate and you know it. It's why you don't have the courage to face me without metal bars between us."

"Then perhaps I'll have to use the rest of my coin on your daughter."

Rox's hand shot out on instinct, grabbing Calder by the throat and slamming his head into the bars between them. He fell back a step and grabbed his head, laughing hard and loud. Rox sucked in a deep breath at the insanity of the sound. "I'm so glad this turn of events hasn't broken you. It's a pleasure I wanted for myself."

"Touch my daughter and I'll kill you."

"I would very much like to see you try."

Rox charged forward, reaching out to grab him. She slammed her fists against the bars, snarling and throwing her weight into her reach as if she could move the wall with nothing but the strength of her will. Without hesitation, Calder retaliated, drawing a knife and stabbing it through Rox's hand.

Rox screamed as the blade split through her skin, the blade hitting the bars so hard sparks flew. Calder removed the blade and Rox crashed backward, scrambling away from the wall. She trembled with pain and shock as she examined the hole in her hand, blood sliding down her arm and pooling at her feet. She could taste bile in the back of her throat.

Rox voice was shaken and soft. "The Twins said…"

Calder rose, still holding his knife, wet with Rox's blood. "The Twins have given me permission to defend myself. I can't kill you. I can't damage you in any way that appears voluntary. But I can strike back when you attack."

Rox's hand began to shake, her muscles rebelling against her injury, her body too weak from stress and illness to process the wound properly. "I could get an infection," Rox grunted. "What then?"

"Then I'll happily pay for you post-mortem. You're nothing but a small payout to the Twins now. Killing you in self defense will earn me a small slap on the wrist."

Fisk crept forward, crouched low, worried about his human and angry at Calder. Rox raised one hand, her face defiant. She wouldn't let Calder realize she wasn't alone. She couldn't lose her beloved pet as well as her daughter.

"Then it's just the two of us."

"It always has been, Rox."

"Then come in here. I'm wounded. Sick. Unarmed. You might stand a chance."

Calder chuckled again, wiping his blade on his shirt. "There's no rush. We'll meet again without bars, without rules or regulations. Then this will end."

Rox held her hand close to her chest, the wound burning, her head starting to spin from the pain. "I'll kill you."

"The desperate words of a wounded animal. Growl and snarl all you like. Before the year's out you'll be groveling at my feet."

Rox curled her knees to the chest, sitting as far from Calder as possible, clenching her jaw to remain silent. A deep loneliness settled over her like fog, paralyzing her.

"No one can save you, Rox. Not even yourself. Give up now."

Chapter Four

Jacquin leaned back against Adrian's shoulder as she sipped at a bowl of warm broth, her hands finally steady enough to hold the bowl on her own.

Adrian smiled and kissed her cheek. "You're healthier every day."

Jacquin took another long sip of the broth and smiled gently. She would never tire of hearing Adrian's voice. "We're getting closer to Rox."

The door to the wagon stood open, the cool dawn air drifting into the main cabin. The horses whinnied softly as they grazed, tethered to nearby trees.

"This pocket of woods is a brilliant hiding place. How did you know it was here?"

Jacquin set the broth aside and turned, wrapping her arms around Adrian's waist and resting her head on her chest. She was slowly regaining her senses, but her strength still hadn't returned. Just sitting up, even with Adrian for support, was exhausting.

Jacquin stared out the door at the twisting, ancient silverpines. She'd never seen a forest before, only imagined what they were like when she read old stories from the north. The stories didn't do them justice. She'd never seen anything more alive. "The Purge wasn't the first time the Amazons were hunted. Back when the Amazons were still a presence on Aggar, they established Shea holes. Hidden camps tucked away across the planet where hunted Amazons could hide for a time. The stocks are dust now, but anyone who has studied the old records knows what to look for. There are a number pocketing the Great Forest."

Adrian ran her fingers through Jacquin's hair. "We have to leave the wagon here. The paths are becoming too steep, too treacherous."

Jacquin could tell Adrian wasn't being completely honest. There were major merchant routes that would take them safely through the forest to the Core. Adrian tensed beneath her as she sensed Jacquin's thoughts and Jacquin laughed, tipping her head up to kiss Adrian's neck. "Your Blue Sight abilities grow stronger the closer we get to Rox, too."

Adrian blushed lightly. "It's a strange sensation."

"It's who you are."

Adrian looked up at the ceiling and sighed softly. "I'm not trying to hide from you, Jacquin. I'm trying to protect you."

"I think we're beyond that."

Jacquin held her tighter. "We're not. I have a lot of enemies. Powerful people who could do a lot worse than a band of raiders."

Jacquin pushed away from Adrian just enough to draw her attention. "If they really want to hurt you, everyone you care about is a target, no matter what they know. And I fear it's rather obvious that you care about me."

Adrian chuckled and kissed her, the embrace tender and gentle, her lips soft against Jacquin's mouth. "I'm still worried about you."

"Then tell me what you can. Tell me what may affect our journey."

"I am... known in the Core. My illusion spells won't always work and if I'm recognized, I'll be killed on sight. We have to enter stealthily. The merchant routes are watched. We have to cut through the forest by horse, cross the river Ma'naur and work our way into the Core on our own."

Jacquin chewed her lower lip, deep in thought. "Will we need a guide?"

Adrian shifted uncomfortably and Jacquin could tell the question had angled too close to Adrian's truth for comfort. "No. We won't need a guide. I know the way."

Jacquin took her hand. "I promise not to ask any questions."

Adrian kissed her forehead in thanks. "The real question is if you're strong enough to travel. You'll grow stronger the closer we get to the Core, but that won't mean anything if you fall ill from riding outside."

"Can I ride with you?"

"Yes."

"Then I'll be sure I'm strong enough."

Adrian nodded slowly. She knew they had no choice. Jacquin wouldn't continue getting better unless they were traveling closer to Rox. "Alright. We can leave the wagon here. It'll be safe. We can return for it later. We'll take the horses, one for each of us."

Jacquin nodded and fought to come to a kneeling position. Her stomach turned once and her head spun, but she held herself upright. "Let's go."

Adrian tethered the Oasis cart horses to a nearby tree. "We aren't far from the Ma'naur. About an hour on horseback. I know a ferryman who can take us to the Core discreetly, but then we have to be more careful." Adrian ran back to join Jacquin on Dread. She leapt up onto the saddle wrapping an arm around Jacquin's waist and grabbing Dread's reigns with the other. "You stayed up on your own."

Jacquin smiled and leaned back against her lover. "I almost feel like myself again. The color has returned to your cheeks, too Adrian."

"Rox is very near. We just have to find her." Adrian clicked her heels and Dread rode forward. "The Circle stays in the military barracks in the main castle, but if Rox is seen as independent she may be staying in town."

Jacquin shifted, her body aching from riding for so long. "How will we find her?"

Adrian sucked in an uncomfortable breath. "I have... allies in the city. Allies who can give us information and hide us for a time. Still, we'll have a day, possibly two, to find her and convince her to leave with us. Anyone harboring us for long is putting themselves at risk. The Twins have eyes everywhere and a violent sense of revenge."

Jacquin tensed, remembering the way the Twins had treated Rox in her visions. She hadn't told Adrian what she knew of Rox's involvement in the Circle. She never revealed the information she learned in her visions without permission. "What if they target Rox?"

Adrian's grip around her waist tightened. "Do you have any reason to believe they would?"

"No."

An awkward silence fell between them, each realizing the other held secrets they didn't want to share. Finally, Adrian spoke. "If they turn on her, she'd be in the prisons or the slave yards."

Jacquin shuddered. "Perhaps we should travel faster."

Jacquin and Adrian stood along the banks of the Ma'naur, more than a league up river from the main ferry crossing. The banks were crusted with ice, only the rapidly flowing water kept the river from freezing over as well. Jacquin trembled, hugging close the fur cloak Adrian had purchased for her in a small town at the base of the mountains. She shifted uncomfortably, her legs aching from finally being able to stand on her own, her body nearly numb from the frigid cold.

She missed the desert. The clouds hung low and heavy, closing in on Jacquin like the lid of a box. She missed the sun, the heat, the sand of her home. Only Adrian's presence kept her from being completely miserable.

Adrian knelt along the bank, her fingers in the water, small streams of pale blue light spreading from her hands out into the river like tiny snakes. Adrian sighed and stood, wrapping an arm around Jacquin's shoulders. "Gavin will see my call soon. We have to give him some time."

Jacquin shivered again, her jaw tight and aching. "I never knew I could be so cold. Not even winter nights in Oasis are like this."

Adrian chuckled and kissed her cheek. "That's how I felt my first few nights in the desert. I never knew I could be that warm. I admit I prefer the cold."

Jacquin smiled mischievously. "We must be highly incompatible."

Adrian turned her, pulling her close, pressing tight against her until Jacquin could feel every line of her body even through her fur cloak. "Yes. Totally incompatible." She kissed Jacquin gently, warming Jacquin from the inside out. "I'm so happy you're walking again. That you came back to me."

"Thank you for saving me. I couldn't find my way on my own."

"I think that makes us a bit more compatible than our taste in weather."

They kissed again, Adrian guiding Jacquin back against a black pine, her mouth finding its way down Jacquin's throat and chest. Jacquin arched her head to the side, making the lines of her body easier for Adrian to reach, when she spotted a forest green light float back on the water, riding the waves like a trail of slime in a swamp.

Jacquin grabbed Adrian's shoulder, nudging her away. "Adrian! Look!"

Adrian turned and smiled as she ran back to the shore and touched the trail of light. It instantly disappeared beneath her hand. "It's Gavin. He's on his way."

Adrian raced away from the shore into the forest to check Dread, whom she'd tethered to a tree.

"Are we taking him with us?" Jacquin inquired as Adrian returned.

Adrian shook her head. "Not now that you can walk on your own. The main town of the Core is a maze of waterways. Dread would never be able to get around unseen. When we get Rox, we'll have Gavin take us back here and we'll take Dread back to the cart horses."

The boat slid against the bank, the ferryman using his pole to drag the boat closer, his thick biceps taut beneath his heavy wool shirt. Gavin leapt to shore, his tall leather boots crunching against the rocks, his dark cloak billowing with the motion. He brushed a lock of ebony hair from his eyes as it fell out of the tie at the nape of his neck.

Gavin pulled Adrian into a tight hug, nearly lifting her off her feet in his burly embrace. "It's so good to see you again, Adrian."

Adrian hugged her friend tight, slapping his back as she pulled away. "I'm glad you're still willing to ferry rogues and scoundrels into the Core."

Gavin brushed her compliment aside. "I'm not brave enough to join the Exiles, but I'll help their cause as long as I can."

Adrian turned to Jacquin. "This is my friend, Jacquin."

Gavin shared a knowing look with Adrian and scooped Jacquin into his arms, squeezing her hard, his beard brushing against her neck. "It's good to meet you, Jacquin!"

Adrian ran to her friend and touched his arm. "Gavin! Please. She's been sick."

Jacquin laughed. "It's alright. I feel fine."

Gavin released her gently, his eyes apologetic. "Forgive me, it's just been years since Adrian traveled with anyone, let alone a beautiful woman."

Adrian blushed lightly. "Gavin, a friend of ours is in the Core. We need to get her out."

"Do you need me to deliver a message?"

Adrian hesitated. "I think we're going to need to see her in person. Negotiating might prove difficult."

"Where is she?"

"She works with the Circle."

Gavin's eyebrows rose in shock. "You want to infiltrate the Circle? You?"

"I know it sounds insane."

"It sounds like suicide."

Jacquin raised a brow at Adrian and Adrian pulled Gavin aside, stepping far enough away that Jacquin could barely hear her. "I'll be fine. I need to get in and out, that's all. She may not even be in the Circle's barracks."

"Then you need to get to the inner-city Exiles."

"Yes. Ariana will know who I'm looking for."

Gavin shifted uncomfortably and glanced back at Jacquin. "How much does she know?"

"Not much, and I want to keep it that way."

"You want to bring her into the world of the Grey Exiles without knowing where she is?"

"She's from the desert, Gavin. She barely knows about the Twins. The less involved she stays, the safer she'll be."

"Then why is she here?"

Adrian's eyes narrowed into a fierce glare. "Just get me to Ariana."

Gavin grunted disapprovingly, but he nodded. He turned back to Jacquin and waved her forward. "Come on. I have a stack of empty crates you can hide in."

Adrian and Jacquin loaded their supplies into an empty crate and climbed into crates of their own. Jacquin held her legs close to her chest, resting her head against the wooden wall. The distinct smell of fish and tar was nearly overwhelming. Gavin dragged an oiled skin over the crates, hiding Jacquin and Adrian from view before pushing off back into the river.

The ferry swayed back and forth as they moved through the river. The motion made Jacquin's stomach turn. She'd never been on a boat before, and she quickly decided she didn't like it. She'd thought the desert was unstable, but she'd take sudden sandstorms over ice and the rolling rivers any day.

After nearly an hour of traveling, the boat began to slow, sliding over stone as well as water at they entered the waterways of the Core. The boat slid to a stop and the sound of boots on wood echoed through the crate wall.

Jacquin tensed, but when the guard spoke he sounded more bored than threatening. "Hunting again, Gavin?"

"Yeah, just getting a bit of rabbit for the missus. Her cravings have become chaos with this child."

"Third child now, yeah?"

Gavin's voice was calm and familiar, without a hint of nervousness. Jacquin wondered how long Gavin had been smuggling people into the Core to remain so calm with the guards. "Yeah. Midwife says it's another boy."

"You must be proud! Three boys in a row."

"Tell you the truth, after the chaos of the first two we were hoping for a girl."

"Well, maybe the midwife got it wrong."

Gavin laughed. "We can only hope. See you and the wife for dinner next week?"

"Sounds good. Have a good day, Gavin."

The boat pushed off again and moved slowly through town

before pulling to a stop again. Gavin pulled back the tarp and beckoned Jacquin and Adrian out of the crates, a finger to his lips. They had pulled to a stop beneath a tall porch built like a dock over the waterway. A trapdoor was open above them, a rope ladder hanging down.

Adrian pointed Jacquin toward the trap door and Jacquin scaled the ladder, Adrian close behind. They climbed into a small, dark pantry. Adrian pulled the ladder up and closed the door behind them, walked to the door and knocked four times. The door opened and a willowy, elderly woman with long silver hair guided them into her home.

"Adrian!" the woman exclaimed, pulling Adrian into a tight hug. "I never thought I'd see you again."

Adrian pulled away with a smile. "Aw, you know I always intended to come back."

"Yes, but I'm an old woman."

"You'll outlive us all."

Jacquin looked around Ariana's home in awe. The plank wooden walls were lined with charms and spells, scrawled on paper, the walls, embedded in talismans and spell bags. The only furniture in the room was a cot, a small fireplace, a stove and a massive table covered with notes, messages, a large map and series of scrying crystals.

Jacquin wandered the room, examining every spell. She could feel the lives of dozens of people in the notes on the table, stories and information scrawled in a series of different handwritings. Jacquin glanced back at Ariana and knew in an instant she was a master informant, a hub for a series of spies and rebels. She could see it reflected in every spell, in her crystals, in the letters. Her life was open to Jacquin in a way she'd never experienced before and Jacquin found herself suddenly hesitant to delve into her world anymore.

Jacquin found a relic from the Great Market, made of sandstone and glass. She ran her fingers over it and for a moment she thought she could feel the heat of the desert sun, smell warm sand, from the talisman and she smiled.

"It's a protection spell. It keeps the Twins from seeing what goes on in my home."

Jacquin turned as Ariana stepped behind her, her brown eyes warm and haunted all at once. "I can tell."

"You're from the desert, yes?"

Jacquin nodded. "From Oasis. Near the Great Market."

"I've never been that far south myself, but I've seen it in my mirrors. It looks warm."

Jacquin smiled softly. "Much warmer than here."

Adrian stood over Ariana's map, spinning one of her scrying crystals but the gem never stopped over a particular spot. Adrian grunted in frustration. Ariana walked to the table. "Stop grunting, Adrian. Use your words. What are you looking for?"

"Jacquin and I are seeking a friend. Rox. She works with the Circle."

Ariana's face fell and the warmth in the room vanished. Jacquin's stomach clenched in fear and she moved to stand beside Adrian, sifting through a tall stack of paper until she reached the information she wanted. Ariana's voice was low and tight. "Everyone in the palace knows Rox. The Twins refused to honor her contract. She attacked them and they had her imprisoned in the old Seer's Tombs. That's why your scrying won't find her. She's to be sold in the slave markets tomorrow."

Jacquin gasped, her face twisting both with worry for Rox and sorrow for Rox's daughter. Adrian's hands balled into fists, her eyes reflecting rage. "We have to get her out. You have to have men in the guard towers."

"Adrian, you know as well as I do that the Twins' prisons are heavily guarded. It's nearly impossible to break someone out."

"Nearly, but not entirely. Rox is crucial to the rebellion."

Ariana's lips turned down at the corner. She didn't believe Adrian. "Breaking out a woman who has been personally marked for slavery by the Twins' themselves carries enormous risk."

"Then get Jacquin and me into the prisons. We'll break Rox out. You'll only need your contacts to create a diversion, give us some time to work."

Ariana paced, her chin in one hand. I could buy you minutes at most."

Adrian shook her head. "That's all we need if we can have a straight shot. I know the castle like the lines of my palm. I can make it happen."

"I'll not take responsibility for you if you're caught. You're a grown woman now, not a foolish Blue Sight child stumbling into bigotry and harassment. I can't protect you." Adrian looked Ariana in the eye, the woman flinching slightly at the strength of Adrian's Blue Sight, even when masked with illusion. Ariana gasped and reached out, touching Adrian's cheek like a mother might a returning child. "You've changed."

Adrian rolled back her sleeve, revealing Rox's lifestone. "I'm bonded. And my bondmate is buried in a prison cell beneath the Twins' feet. I have to get her out."

Ariana's eyes fell, solemn and thoughtful. She tapped her fingers against her lips and finally nodded. "I know how to make this happen. You'll have a half hour at half past midnight. No more. You'll enter and leave through the servants' quarters in the west wing. You won't encounter any guards, but you'll have to leave the Core. The Twins will be searching the moment they realize Rox is missing."

Adrian smiled wide and pulled Ariana into a tight hug. "That's more than I could have asked for."

Ariana held Adrian tighter and kissed her cheek. "You'll drive me to madness, my child."

"You were mad when I met you."

Ariana chuckled softly. "Too true."

Jacquin crept forward, following Adrian through the stone hallways of the main palace of the Core. She held her arms close to her chest, a heavy, overpowering sense of wrongness flooding every stone. With each step she could sense the past, different buildings, different people, but always the same result. Pain. Fear. Death. Regimes had risen and fallen on this land, entire tribes massacred, people enslaved and oppressed since the first people of Aggar started to build on the ice. She could almost smell the blood in the air, the sweat and tears of uncountable victims.

"This land is cursed," she muttered under her breath.

Adrian turned, looking at her nervously. "What?"

Jacquin shook her head. "Nothing."

Adrian led her down silent hallways to the main doors of the prison, massive metal structures that didn't even allow air to slip around their sturdy frame. There was immediately a blast of smell, mold and human musk, rancid and sour.

Adrian curled her nose. "They fell into disrepair long ago. Only the bars remain strong."

They crossed the threshold and Jacquin nodded. "These caves are far older than the Core."

Adrian nodded. "The castle was intentionally built over them."

A squeak and scuffle caught Jacquin's attention and she laughed aloud as Fisk raced toward her, trilling with glee and climbing up her dress to her shoulder.

Adrian and Jacquin descended down stone steps into the prisons, Adrian calling a ball of flame into her palm for light. They instantly spotted her, lying still in one of the closest cells to the front door.

The women ran forward to their bondmate, Adrian shredding

the lock to Rox's cell with a magical twist of her hand. Jacquin raced to Rox's side, pulling off her cloak and draping it over Rox's ice-cold body.

Rox turned, her eyes clouded, her body bruised. She reached up for Jacquin as if in shock, her hand running across Jacquin's cheek. "Jacquin?"

"I'm here, Rox. Adrian, too."

"You came for me?"

Jacquin took her hand and kissed her palm. "Always. We're here to save you."

Adrian strode toward them from the door and glared at the sick Rox. Rox's face twisted with grief and sorrow. "Adrian, I'm sorry."

Adrian shook her head. "We can discuss your abandonment later. We need to get you out now."

Jacquin tried to help Rox stand but the woman was weak on her feet. Jacquin gasped as she noticed a festering stab wound through Rox's other hand. "Adrian! She's hurt!"

The anger in Adrian's face dissipated as she took Rox's hand, holding it out to the light. "Someone stabbed you?"

Rox trembled and shook her head. "It's not important. You have to help me find my daughter."

Adrian flinched in shock, glancing at Jacquin to see if she was just as surprised. "Daughter?"

"The Twins have her. They're going to sell her if they haven't already. We have to find her."

Adrian shook her head. "We have to get out. The path is only clear for a few more minutes, then the Twins will begin their search. We need to be across the river by nightfall."

"I won't leave without Serena," Rox growled.

"Stay and you'll die. We all will. Leave and we may be able to formulate a proper plan," Adrian rebutted. "We don't have time to argue."

Jacquin assessed Rox's injures. "Adrian, she can barely stand, let alone run with us. We have to carry her."

"Or heal me." Rox sat up, grabbing the front of Adrian's shirt. "You're a Blue Sight and a natural healer. I felt it when we locked eyes. Heal me."

Adrian took a step back in shock. "I don't heal. I'm a destroyer."

"You can heal and you know it. Use your Blue Sight as a channel. Heal me."

Adrian's eyes softened in grief and pain. "I want to, Rox, I do, but..."

"Just look me in the eyes and do it."

Adrian move uncomfortably, looking to Jacquin for support before finally looking into Rox's eyes.

Adrian began to glow blue like hot flame, her magic rising around her, flooding through her into Rox. Jacquin gasped as Rox's injuries began to fade and disappear. The infection in her hand melted from her like water and the skin knitted back together. Just as Adrian was starting to get winded, her breath coming in rapid shots, Rox broke their connection, both women gasping as their bond was severed.

Adrian fell to her knees, her muscles jumping beneath her skin. Rox smiled and grabbed her, kissing her hard and deep. "I knew you could do it."

Adrian and Rox helped each other to their feet. Rox tied Jacquin's cloak around herself. Jacquin took Rox's hand. "We'll find Serena. I promise. But for now we have to get you to safety."

Rox's face fell. "I won't leave the Core."

"You have to," Adrian retorted sharply. "The Twins' first course of action will be to try to track you. If you're in the Core, they'll know. Then we'll all be back here. You have to get to the forest at least."

Rox huffed and growled in frustration, her eyes moving back and forth as she thought through her options. Tears fell from her eyes as she realized Adrian and Jacquin were right. "Fine. But I'm coming back for her with or without you."

Adrian glanced out the cell door, nervous about time. "Fair enough. But let's go. We have a ferryman and horses waiting for us."

Rox kissed Adrian, then Jacquin and nodded. "I trust you both. Let's go."

Chapter Five

Rox sat beside the fire, holding her arms close to her chest as she trembled. Even beneath a blanket of furs and wrapped in Adrian's cloak she couldn't stop shaking.

The forest towered high above, blocking out much of the night sky, the trail of smoke from the fire barely making it past the woven canopy of black and silver pines. They had made it across the river, back to Adrian's horse and through the forest to the cart horses where they'd set up camp and Adrian had drawn a protection circle to block the Twins' scrying efforts.

The scent of the rabbits Adrian had trapped roasting over the fire wove through camp, making Rox's stomach twist. She was starving; she'd barely eaten in days, but somehow the scent of food made her feel sick. Rox twisted her hands together, her nails digging into her skin. She felt her daughter everywhere, could smell her in the forest, see her dancing wild in the flames, feel her soft curls in the silken furs around her shoulders. What was happening to her? Was she still in holding or with an owner? Would she still be in the Core when they had a viable plan to go after her?

She thought of the psychological and sometimes physical torment Calder had subjected her to over the last few days. She couldn't imagine her daughter in the same situation. Serena had always been an emotionally sensitive child despite her wild nature and she'd never been hurt by another human before coming to the Core. She wouldn't know what to do as a slave, especially in the hands of Calder.

Rox trembled and swallowed hard. Calder. What would he do once he discovered Rox had disappeared? Would he go after Serena?

"Can I sit with you?" Jacquin stepped silently beside Rox, her eyes heavy with worry. "I'm cold."

Rox could see through the lie, but she didn't care. "Yes, please."

She opened her blankets and Jacquin slid behind her, cocooning them both in the cloaks and blankets. Rox leaned back against the taller woman, encircled by Jacquin's arms, her scent sweet and spiced against the earthy scent of the forest. For a moment

Rox felt sheltered, safe in the harbor of blankets and Jacquin, protected from the Twins and the Core in ways not even Adrian's spell could match.

Rox turned and buried her face against Jacquin's chest, huddled beneath the furs, hidden from the rest of the world, and once again she wept. She held Jacquin tight and the woman responded, holding her close, running her hands through Rox's hair, kissing her head and brow.

"We've got you. You're safe. We love you." Jacquin's voice echoed like whispers from the Mother, attempting to soothe Rox's fears, but it wasn't herself Rox was worried about. Her traumas, her heartache, could wait. Every moment they delayed was a new trauma for Serena.

Rox felt Adrian's strong hand on her shoulder through the blanket, her touch cautious and concerned. "Rox?"

Rox shifted, opening her blanket again and Adrian curled around her from behind, wrapping Rox completely between her lovers. Adrian laid a soft kiss on the back of her neck. "I'm sorry, Rox. I didn't understand. I should have guessed after you released the Circle's slaves. I should have known you had a reason for being with them."

Rox reached back with one arm and wrapped it reassuringly around Adrian. It didn't matter anymore. Their feuds, their frustrations meant nothing faced with the new reality of the Twins and Serena's enslavement. She didn't owe the Core anything else. She was free, yet she had never felt so defeated.

Adrian and Jacquin held her until her weeping subsided. Rox furiously wiped at her eyes and her nose, embarrassed at the display of emotion, her blotched face and red eyes. Adrian shook her head, sensing Rox's emotions. "Don't be embarrassed. Not with us."

Rox held her face in her hands, still leaning on Jacquin's shoulder. "I'm sorry. I didn't mean to fall apart."

Jacquin kissed the top of her head. "If you can't fall apart in our arms, where can you? We love you."

A new wave of shame washed over Rox. She should trust them. They were her bondmates. Still, she couldn't help but feel weak, especially with Adrian. They shared a warrior's bond. They both knew what it meant to be hard, untouchable. She didn't want Adrian to see her so defeated.

Adrian tensed as she felt Rox's emotions and understood her fears. "I understand you, Rox. Feel whatever you feel. Just know we will never look down on you for being vulnerable. It's not a weakness." The rabbits spat and sputtered on the fire and Adrian kissed her again. "You need to eat something."

Rox shook her head. "I already feel sick."

"You were just healed. Your body needs help recovering. I'll make you tea. I think I saw some wild mint deeper in the woods. It'll be good for both of your stomachs."

Adrian detangled herself from their pile, grabbed her sword and a knife, and traveled into the woods.

Jacquin chuckled lightly. "Being useful is the only way she knows to show her love."

Rox looked up at Jacquin in concern. "Both our stomachs? Have you been sick?"

Jacquin kissed her cheek. "It's fine. I'm better now."

"You came after me when you were sick? You should have stayed behind."

Jacquin shifted uncomfortably. "Rox, were you sick at all while you were in the Core?"

Rox leaned back in thought. In the pain and grief about her daughter and Calder's attack she'd forgotten about her flu. "A flu. Nothing more."

Jacquin brushed a long curl from Rox's eyes and Rox spotted the lifestone mark on her wrist. Adrian's words about the bonding returned and Rox paled. "It was me, wasn't it? I left and you the lifebond made you sick."

Jacquin kissed her, long and slow, cradling her head with a gentle grip. "It doesn't matter. Truly. You went after your daughter. I would have hated it if you abandoned her for me, even if I died."

Rox pulled her into a hug. "Serena would have loved you."

Jacquin leaned forward, her lips close enough to brush the lines of Rox's ear. "We'll save her and bring her to the desert. I'll teach her to dance under the moonlight with her family and tell her stories of how brave and selfless her mother is. We'll be a family. Safe. Free."

Rox's heart pounded in her chest, aching for such a future. She brushed tears from her eyes. "I dreamed that every night in prison. How did you know?"

"Because I saw it every night I was sick."

Adrian returned with a handful of mint leaves and set about preparing tea. Rox pulled away from Jacquin and walked to her, pulling her into a tight hug. "I'm sorry. I know you aren't expecting a warrior out of me."

Adrian relaxed in her arms and smiled. "The lifebond and the combination of my Blue Sight and Jacquin's seer abilities makes us feel like we already know each other. But you and I don't. You might be surprised what I think of you and how I judge people, Rox."

"I'd like to get to know you better, Adrian."

Adrian chuckled and threw a handful of mint in the boiling water. "Well, if the rocks in my wrist mean anything, we have a lifetime to make that happen. Now rest. We need you and Jacquin strong if we're going to break into the Core."

Rox tossed in her sleep, the tangle of furs and her bondmates' bodies suddenly tight and oppressive, drawing her out of her dreams. She sat up, damp with sweat despite the cold. Her legs ached, cramped from being too still. She wanted to run, wander, leap.

In the distance she could hear a warm hum, cresting like the gentle lapping of the sea on the shore. She could almost hear her name entwined in the sound, like the whispers of a lover, beckoning her deeper into the woods. The sounds pulled at her on a primal level, making her eyes sharp and her mind clear. It was the same sensations she had when she was in a rage, but her body was calm.

She crawled out of the pile of furs and canvas that served as her bed, careful not to disrupt her lovers or Fisk, and jogged into the forest. She moved aimlessly, searching for the source of the sound, the ground soft and giving slightly beneath her feet as she ran across pine needles and soil. She moved swiftly, dodging and weaving around the trees as if she were made for it, her natural instincts whispering where to go, how to move.

Rox reveled in the feeling of a clear mind, her thoughts full of nothing but the song of the forest, the call in her heart and the feeling of movement. No more prison walls. No more fear. She felt powerful. Brave. Settled. There was nothing that could keep Serena from her now; not Calder, not even the Twins. This was her land. Her home.

Rox blinked, the absurdity of her thought slowing her run. The north had never been her home. She was from the coast, a fisherman's daughter and a desert scout. The ice plains of the Core had always been foreign to her. Still, she was somehow able to navigate the forest with little effort, her body naturally knowing what to do and where to go, like memories from another life, imprints in her DNA.

She came to a small clearing, the moonlight streaming through the hole in the trees, bathing a gathering of changlings in pale blue light. Rox froze, her breath quick with fear as a dozen changlings, sitting in a close circle, turned to her as one. Their soft feline fur swayed gently in the light breeze that slipped through the open canopy, their eyes glowing like amber and emeralds in the moonlight.

Rox reached for her knife, but it wasn't there. All her weaponry was still back in the Core. She stumbled back, her fear overriding the primal instincts that had given her such joy running through the forest.

The changlings didn't move or stand, just continued to stare at her. Their faces were still, their arms loose at their sides. They didn't seem surprised or threatened by Rox's appearance. Their weapons sat untouched in a pile at the center of the circle, more like a stack of crystals than glass weaponry.

Rox slowly began to calm and took a step forward into the clearing. She waited for one of them to react, to lunge, to hiss, but the only sound she heard was the gentle, rumbling hum that had awakened her. It took her a moment to realize the sound was being emitted by the band of changlings.

The primal sensations from before began to reclaim her mind, lulling her into a heady calm. A ginger-striped changling woman holding a wooden staff stood slowly, reaching out to Rox. Rox could read her expression, an invitation to join the circle.

Rox sat between a human-like changling man with thick, soft grey hair over his taut muscles and an ebony female that reminded Rox of the changling she had battled in Oasis. The standing changling let out a rumbling sound that could only be described as a purr as she sat back in the circle, looking up through the clearing in the trees at the moon.

The music swelled and Rox closed her eyes, her mind drifting out of her body, floating through the wilds of the north and the caverns of the nearby mountains. She felt rough stone and bark beneath her hands, a twisting tension of muscles smaller and tighter than her own beneath her skin. She stretched long before a fire and mined lifestones in the roots of the mountains. She could smell sulfur and lava, pine and fresh soil. For a moment she was flying, her wings unfurled behind her back, Aggar drifting away from her far below her paws.

She touched hundreds, thousands of lives, swimming through a sea of emotion and sensation buried deep in her blood. She knew in an instant she was wading through the lives of her ancestors and kin, all of changling history open to her and, deep in the beginnings of time, the imprints of the eitteh that started her line. She had never felt so connected to Aggar or to herself. In a moment, her heart seemed to shift, to fall into place.

"Rox?"

"What are you doing?"

Adrian and Jacquins' voices broke through her wandering

mind and she opened her eyes. Adrian stepped forward, her sword held high. The ebony changling beside her hissed in warning, the entire circle growing agitated, their hands angling for their weapons. The music had stopped.

Rox leapt to her feet, her hands outstretched to her lover. "No! Stop! They're safe!"

Adrian hesitated, her sword wavering. "They're changlings."

"So am I." Rox's words hung heavy in the clearing, a palpable silence that caught everyone's attention. "At least partially. It's in my blood." Jacquin smiled, wide and dazzling. Rox glanced at her sideways, a mischievous smile turning up the corner of her mouth. "You knew."

"Only after you left. I saw your ancestor. She wasn't visited by a ghost. She had a changling lover and birthed his child."

Adrian slowly sheathed her sword and the changlings began to calm. Adrian was still tense, obviously unsure. Rox wondered how many of Adrian's childhood nightmares had featured changlings. It seemed every human in the north had been raised to fear them.

Finally, Adrian forced a laugh. "It explains your temper, Rox." She looked Rox over, her eyes teasing. "And your height."

Rox shot her a playful glare. The ginger female stood again and took a step toward them. Rox felt the gravity of her presence and her playfulness dissipated.

Jacquin's face grew serious and she shared a look with the changeling. "I thought you were a spirit. A guide."

The changling shook her head and reached out a hand to Jacquin. Jacquin hesitated. "I can't understand your messages. They're overwhelming."

The changling looked to Rox, then to Adrian. Rox could hear the whispers of the changling's intent in the corner of her mind, distorted and broken like a message read in the rain. "She wants me to interpret for her, but I'm not changling enough to receive her message clearly. But you can, Jacquin. You're a seer."

Jacquin shook her head. "I can't interpret. It's just a barrage of images and emotions. I don't understand."

The changling glanced up into Adrian's eyes, her gaze instantly flicking away like a hand pulling back from a hot stove. Adrian clenched her jaw. "I see."

Rox took Adrian's hand. "What is it?"

"Jacquin can receive her message. You can interpret it. And I can act as a link between you. Jacquin can reach into my mind without meeting my eyes, and you, Rox, can withstand my full gaze. We're the perfect conduit."

The three women exchanged looks, the changlings waiting patiently beside them. Rox could feel their anxiety. They had been waiting for these three women for a long time.

"I want to help them," Rox admitted. "I don't think they have anyone else."

Jacquin took Adrian's hand and nodded. "They need our help."

Adrian shifted uncomfortably, but Rox angled herself to meet her eyes, her *amarin* pleading. "They're my family, Adrian."

Adrian tightened her grip on Jacquin's hand and nodded. "For you, Rox."

Jacquin took the changling's hand and Rox's mind was instantly flooded with images and messages, the wave of information sorting and organizing with the species' memory she'd awakened sitting in the circle, filtering through generations of changling language, customs and symbols. As if sharing a single voice, Rox began to speak the changling's words.

"We have been searching for you for generations. The Divine Triad. Our only link to the human world. We have laid waste to dozens of human settlements that stood in our way. There was once a time when we communicated with your kind. The speech was halting, simple, manipulative, but we could still speak. Millennia hiding beneath the mountains in the presence of the lifestones, beaten and broken by the humans nearly to extinction, has changed that. We are now bonded. Silent. We need you as our mouthpiece."

"I don't understand," Adrian grunted, trying to translate and filter the rush of images and emotions from Jacquin and the translation from Rox.

The changling – a shaman – didn't understand Adrian's question. "We are bonded. One," Rox repeated.

"The beginnings of a hive mind," Jacquin gasped through the pressure of her visions. "They're telepathic as a species. Linked across the planet."

"Yes. One." Rox felt a swell of pleasure from the shaman at communicating with the women. "We need your help."

Adrian grit her teeth. "What do you need?"

"The core is in the mountains."

Adrian shook her head. "The Core is nearly a day's ride north."

Rox shook her head, trying to understand. "The mages' core is in the mountains. It's poisoning our home."

Adrian's brow furrowed in confusion. "Jacquin?"

Jacquin moaned, losing the strength to continue their

connection. "I don't know."

Rox felt the shaman's desperation rise. She could see a glowing red orb embedded in a stalactite, emitting sickness and death, the bodies of thousands of changlings at its base.

"I'm sorry!" Jacquin wept and released the changling's hand, falling to the ground. The connection between the four women instantly disintegrated, leaving Rox dizzy and ill, her mind exploding with the presence of the shaman, fighting with her own thoughts for control of her mind.

Adrian helped Jacquin sit, holding her as she recovered from her contact with such a foreign mind. As Rox's own thoughts and memories returned she realized the truth about what the changling had meant. "I know what the core is."

All eyes turned to Rox and she shook her head to clear it. "The Twins have a device. They've culled together the pieces from all over Aggar, it's what the Circle was looking for. It's supposed to call together all Blue Sights. They intend to eradicate them."

Jacquin grabbed Adrian's waist in a vice-like, possessive grip and Adrian's face twisted with rage and grief. "They what?"

Rox looked at her apologetically. "I'm sorry. I forgot during my imprisonment. But the device doesn't work. They couldn't activate it." Rox looked up at the shaman, her face hopeful, urgent. "It's missing a piece. Its core. Buried in the changling's mountains." The shaman bowed, tears in her eyes. Her message was delivered. "The device is leaking without its shell, poisoning the changlings' home. It's what finally drove them back out of the mountains, what's been making them crazy. The poison has affected their entire telepathic network, poisoning even those changlings that have escaped. We need to remove it and store it in its proper casing. We need the Twins' device."

Adrian snorted, the sound violent and full of unspoken emotion. "Good luck. The Twins are vicious. Cruel. They won't give us anything by choice and they're too clever for us to take their prize by stealth."

Adrian's voice broke with unshed tears and Jacquin placed a hand on her shoulder, her brow furrowed with worry. Rox tried to meet Adrian's gaze, to give her strength and read the source of her sudden emotions, but Adrian pointedly refused to catch her eyes, covering her eyes with her hands, the motion infused with decades of shame.

Rox felt her lips curl as a violent sense of protectiveness flooded her. "Then we take it by force." She turned to the shaman. "Changling warriors are some of the swiftest, most cunning and vicious in Aggar. You have a force large enough to help us storm the Core?"

The shaman nodded, her people ready for battle for generations.

Rox looked back at Adrian and nodded with sudden decision. The Twins would no longer threaten her partner, her daughter, the world. "Then we invade the Core. We finally dethrone those tyrant Twins and we save our world and the changlings. Their reign is over."

Chapter Six

Adrian crouched low in a the large cedar tree, a simple illusion camouflaging her in the evergreen's branches. A small group of travelers from the Core climbed off the ferry barge, leading three horses and a merchant's cart onto the main path through the mountains. Rox spied a maroon cloak, the traveler's hood pulled high over his head. All of Ariana's messengers wore red.

The messenger walked deeper into the forest, glancing up through the low-hanging branches. He lowered his hood and Adrian felt a sharp pain her chest as she noticed how young he was, barely adolescent. It was a smart move. The Twins would be less likely to track him. But he was too young to be caught up in a revolution.

The messenger hissed into trees, flashing a small, silver leaf medallion in his palm. "Adrian?"

Adrian dropped to the ground and released her illusion spell. Ariana's messenger jumped in surprise and turned around, holding out the medallion for her to see. "Who sent you?" Adrian questioned, already knowing the answer.

"Ariana of the Grey Exiles."

"Were you followed?"

The boy shook his head. "Ariana sent merchants with me. I helped unload the horses. No one will think twice about my being here."

Adrian walked toward him, one hand on her sword, the other touching his shoulder, a blue light shining beneath her palm, temporarily running beneath the messenger's skin, making him glow with Adrian's magic.

The messenger tensed, frozen with fear, but the magic reached his feet and seeped back into the earth, never changing color or brightness. He wasn't sent by the Twins. Adrian nodded. "What's her message?"

"She says the Exiles are awaiting your command."

Adrian nodded. "Good. Tell her to watch the river."

The man nodded. "Consider it done." He pulled a package from the pack on his back and handed it to her. "She also wanted you to have this."

Adrian slowly took the heavy, paper-wrapped package and unwrapped it to reveal a thick, silver-grey wool cloak identical to the one she'd lost in the raid on Oasis. Adrian ran her fingers over the fabric, the color and weave bringing back hundreds of memories. The cloaks were banned in the Core, a symbol of the Grey Exiles.

"You shouldn't have brought this. If you'd been caught with it–"

The boy raised his hand. "She told me you should wear it when you return. You are an exile, Adrian. You should wear your colors proudly."

Adrian unfurled the cloak and tied it around her throat, the weight familiar and comforting. "Thank you."

She pulled a gold coin from her pouch and offered it to him. He put up his hand and shook his head. "I volunteered for this mission. I wanted to thank you for taking a stand. This revolution wouldn't exist without you. You were so brave, leaving the Core like you did. You're an inspiration to us all."

Adrian stiffened with his praise, instantly transported back to the snowy tundra, watching a mob leave the Core, bent on killing her. She hadn't left voluntarily. She'd lived for years, emotionally and physically abused for her Sight, never taking a stand. She wasn't brave. She wouldn't have gone if it weren't for the backlash against her Blue Sight. She'd left the Core to save her own skin, not to make a statement. It hadn't been until Ariana had found her a home among the other exiles, until she'd lived among the truly brave, those who had left the Core by choice, that she'd become a revolutionary.

Adrian had become a symbol not because she was a real inspiration, but because her name was recognizable. None of the Core's nobility had publicly abandoned the city until Adrian. She was an easy message to spread, a symbol to hold up, but it was a lie.

Adrian swallowed hard. "Thank you. But you're the brave ones."

The man bobbed his head with a smile. "It will all be over soon."

Adrian nodded tensely. "Yes. Now get back to Ariana. The longer you're out here the more suspicious you look."

The boy nodded again and raced back out of the trees for the ferry dock.

Adrian watched him go, a tension forming in her chest that spread to her stomach. She had never wanted to be an inspiration for revolution. She wondered what the young messenger would think if he knew she still wasn't sure she wanted to invade even as plans were quickly falling into place; that part of her heart, her allegiance, her home was still behind Core palace walls, her shame and guilt irrevocably bound to the opinions of the vicious nobles who had raised her. She wondered what the Grey Exiles would think if they knew the deepest roots of her grudge against the Twins were not in their atrocities, but in the way they had broken her heart as a child.

Adrian sucked in a deep breath and rolled her shoulders, trying to relieve a tension that wasn't in her muscles. She tried to cast another illusion and the words burned her tongue, the symbols hazy in her mind as her magic clashed again with her Blue Sight. She closed her eyes with a grunt. For a time her magic had been at peace, but not anymore, her abilities mimicking her heart.

She grabbed her sword at her hip and trudged deeper into the forest, making her way to where she had tethered Dread. It would be a long ride back to camp.

Adrian strode into the changling camp, the cold nipping at her nose, carrying with it the scent of damp fur and earth. The changlings had been pouring in for days, traveling in packs from the mountains and further south. They swarmed like bees, filling the forest, sharpening swords and knives, fletching arrows and preparing meals without speaking a word.

Jacquin stepped up behind her, running her fingers over Adrian's new cloak. She was being fitted for light armor. It was the first time Adrian had seen her in pants. "This looks familiar." Adrian didn't know how to respond. After a moment of silence, Jacquin glanced out at the camp. "It's unsettling isn't it? The silence?"

Adrian glanced at her. "You can't understand them?"

Jacquin chuckled. "Ever since we reunited with Rox my mind is at peace. The visions don't come nearly as frequently. It's everything I always wanted, but it's much quieter than I'm used to. To me they're completely silent. Only Rox has been able to communicate with them. Our magics combined seems to have awoken a dormant part of her species memory."

Adrian leaned back against a nearby tree. "I can tell what they're feeling, their intentions, but not words or thoughts."

"That's your Blue Sight, my love."

Adrian folded her arms over her chest and glanced down at her feet. "It's getting fainter."

Jacquin turned to her, her slender brows knit with concern, her lips pursed. "What do you mean?"

Adrian sucked a deep breath past her teeth and sighed. "Ever since our first meeting with the changlings my magic has been chaos again."

Jacquin hesitated, choosing her words carefully. "Your Blue Sight connects you with the world. Are you trying to separate yourself?" Adrian's skin turned cold, her muscles tensing. She popped her jaw. Jacquin nodded. "I see. Adrian, I promised not to push for information about your connection to the Core and I won't. But know I'm here if you want to talk, so is Rox. Perhaps sharing some of your concerns will help you find some peace."

Adrian wanted to talk, wanted Jacquin and Rox to ease her fears, but she could feel her truths sinking deeper into her heart, guarded and hidden from the women she loved. They knew so little about her. She couldn't risk their opinion of her changing if they knew her truth.

Adrian held her arms tighter against her chest. "Ariana is ready. Her soldiers will be ready to open the gates for us when the time comes and sneak us into the palace while the changlings fight."

Jacquin sighed softly at Adrian's retreat. "They're taking a great risk."

"They're willing to die for us to succeed."

"They trust you," Jacquin attempted to assure her, but the words only made Adrian more unsure. Memories of her adolescence in grey tarp-tents, traveling as a refugee through the Ramains. She saw the first people who had raised her with love, patiently erasing her ignorance, her prejudices and easing crippling insecurities with their love and steadfast refusal to give up hope. People with debilitating illness, missing limbs and traumatic emotional scars. Escaped slaves, activists and jaded soldiers with their families, bound together in their rejection of the Core.

Adrian didn't want to involve them in a war. She'd done terrible things, sacrificed her entire life, to ensure they wouldn't enter the fight. "Either way, it will all be over soon. Either we defeat the Twins and retrieve the artifact or we fail and every rebel will be hunted down and executed. Not even the exile camps further south will be safe. The Twins will kill them all."

Jacquin squeezed Adrian's shoulder. "We'll succeed. Every sacrifice will be for the greater good."

Adrian pushed off from the tree. "They're still dying, Jacquin. Pray to the Mother the battle is quick. The Goddess knows she won't hear my pleas."

The boat cut through the waters of the Ma'naur, slicing through the waves like a knife, chasing the long line of magical light Adrian had cast into the river as a sign to Ariana to secure the gates. Jacquin and Rox stood on either side of her, her cloak billowing back behind her shoulders. She took a deep breath as the Core loomed closer, clenching the hilt of her sword. The day of the revolution had finally come.

The changlings stood behind her, their energy frantic and tense, ready for battle. Their glass weapons, many dotted with lifestones, glowed in the moonlight. Adrian spotted hand-made bombs in many of their belts. The changling shaman stood near Jacquin, her fur seeming to buzz with magic. She was ready to lead her people. She had been for a long time.

Adrian squinted, trying to see the waterway gates to the city through the pre-dawn haze. Had Ariana been successful? Had the resistance already been massacred? She knew Ariana would begin with a quiet takeover. She'd place her sympathizers in the guard on duty at the right time, use her spies to quietly assassinate any of the Twins' loyalists who'd get in the way. She wouldn't want anyone to be aware of the attack until the changlings poured into the city, targeting defensive strongholds, opening gates and waterways for the rest of the waiting army and drawing as many soldiers from the palace as possible. Still, if they had been discovered early, if someone had sounded the alarm, they could be sailing into a trap.

Adrian took Jacquin's and Rox's hands. "Once we enter the city we'll meet up with Ariana's men. I'll know how to recognize them. They'll lead us secretly through the back alleys of the Core so we can hopefully infiltrate the palace undetected. We will undoubtedly have to fight in the palace. The Twins will be on high alert. No one will be able to enter unnoticed, not even with Ariana's charms."

Jacquin glanced around Adrian. "Do you know where they're keeping the device, Rox?"

Rox shook her head. "They took me away before I could see anything."

Adrian clenched her jaw. "They'll be keeping it in their tower. I know how to get there, but it will be dangerous. You shouldn't follow me." Rox and Jacquin instantly started to argue, their voices a blend of shock and refusal. "I'm not trying to be proud, but the tower is warded on the best of days. Neither of you is a trained mage. Neither of you knows them as well as I do. You wouldn't survive. I want you to find Serena. Jacquin, you can try to have a vision, read the minds of the guards, and Rox, you defend her. You know the slave yards. You're the best team for the job."

"I don't want to separate the triad," Jacquin announced, using the word Rox had reported the changlings had taken to calling them.

Adrian shook her head. "We don't have any choice. I promise, if we could stay together I would, but it's too dangerous."

Jacquin balled her fists at her sides, trying to think of a better argument, but Rox clasped Adrian's shoulder firmly, her eyes sad and vicious all at once. "Make them pay for what they did to my daughter?"

Adrian clasped her shoulder as well, the two women finally sisters-in-arms as well as lovers. "I swear it. Find Serena."

Rox snarled, the expression pure changling. "If I have to rip apart every slaver with my bare hands."

They closed in on the Core and to Adrian's relief the gates opened, red cloaks rippling in the early-morning air. Ariana had been successful. The boat slid into place and the changlings immediately disembarked, following their shaman into the shadows of the city. Two red-cloaked guards, their silver leaf pins glowing at their throats in the torchlight of the city gates, beckoned Adrian forward.

Adrian, Rox and Jacquin approached them, Adrian scanning each with her magic to guarantee they held no magical trace to the Twins, and then followed them away from the changlings.

The revolutionaries led the three women down a winding path around the Core, keeping them to the shadows and far from main roads as they eased up to the palace. Halfway through the city a sentry post along the city wall exploded.

The city erupted in chaos. More explosions went off, waking every resident and calling streams of guards out of the towers and from the palace as the changlings began their invasion. Screams and the striking of steel on glass filled the air, rising to a deafening pitch as the western gate blew open, letting in another contingent of changling soldiers. The city quickly smelled of nothing but ash and blood.

"They've secured the western gate but are having trouble with the east," Rox reported, interpreting the network-mind of her people, their thoughts and messages filtering through the pieces of her brain open to their communication. "More guards are backtracking to the palace. They realize it's an invasion, not an isolated attack."

"Then we have to go faster," one of the exile scouts prompted as they ran for the palace.

The palace grounds were as chaotic as the city. A pack of changlings had beaten them to the main gates and the grounds were already smeared with blood, the bodies of guards and changlings alike littering the path.

"This way," one of the exiles beckoned, leading the women away from the main gates toward a vine-covered hole in the wall, leading toward the kitchens. "Enter through there. We have people among the servants. They'll get you into the palace proper unseen.

From there it's up to you."

Adrian clasped their hands in a tight grip. "Thank you."

The exile on her right nodded sharply. "End this madness, Adrian."

Adrian steeled herself, her adrenaline already pumping, her focus sharp for battle. "I promise."

The men took off back toward the city and Adrian led her bondmates through the hold in the wall and into the kitchens. Servants in red cloaks ushered them instantly through narrow, dark servants' walkways, the maze-like hallways built to allow the servants to move without disturbing nobility. They exited near the throne room.

Adrian nodded to Rox, who took Jacquin's hand and led her toward the slave cellars. Jacquin hesitated, looking back at Adrian, her eyes sad and pleading. Adrian met her gaze briefly, trying to send her as much love and assurance as possible, before drawing her sword taking off in the opposite direction. To her relief, Jacquin didn't try to follow her.

Adrian was instantly met by palace guards, their weapons at the ready. Adrian didn't hesitate. Her sword flew, stabbing one guard in the throat instantly and blocking the blow of another. The two remaining guards froze in shock, their eyes wide in recognition. "Adrian?!"

The hesitation was long enough for Adrian to behead them both, her bespelled blade slicing through muscle and bone like butter.

She fought her way through the castle, viciously, silently attacking every threat, silencing most before they could call for help. She didn't dare try to disguise herself with magic. The Twins would be drawn to a casting mage like moths to a flame. She didn't want to face them until her hands were already on the artifact.

The Twins' tower, where they practiced their magic and stored their spells, stood at the most northeastern corner of the castle, the enchantments protecting it so thoroughly it was often invisible to anyone who had never visited it. Adrian, however, was intimately aware not only of its spells, but the path to reach it.

The guards became fewer the deeper she got into the castle, their focus on securing the doors and palace grounds. The hallway leading to the tower door was completely empty. Adrian called out a word of power, drawing a rune in the air with her finger as she ran at a seemingly empty wall and the door to the tower appeared, already unlocked. The door handle was warm in her hand, almost inviting. It recognized her. The newer spells wouldn't be as inviting.

The stairway to the Twins' magical study was long and winding, curling tight as a spring along the walls of the narrow spire. Adrian pushed every shred of her Blue Sight aside, pushing away even thoughts of her bondmates and the Grey Exiles in her deadly focus, calling on her most powerful protection spells. She glowed blue and gold as the Twins' spells attacked her shields, burning and firing at her, attempting to push her off the stairwell and crush her against the wall. Adrian countered every spell she recognized, but most were new, crafted from the minds of the maniacal Twins in the years Adrian had been away.

The stairs leading to the tower door crumbled beneath her feet and she leapt, grasping desperately for the hearth, pulling herself back to her feet. Sweat poured down her skin, her breathing coming in sharp gasps as her shields sapped her energy. Soon they would begin drawing on her life force to remain intact. All her illusions disappeared, including the one over her eyes. If she was to have any hope at winning a battle with the Twins, she would need to find a way to conserve energy.

She pushed open the main door and stumbled into the Twins' study. The large, circular room was filled with tables stacked with notebooks, ancient tomes, runes and talismans. Racks holding ingredients for potions cast a chaotic, foul scent into the air. Out of the corners of her eyes Adrian could see magical contamination everywhere, built up from constant exposure to the Twins' powers and experiments.

She spotted the artifact Rox had described, the puzzle box sitting on a tall stone dais near the center of the room. She could sense the magical wards around it, the Twins not even trusting the wards around their tower to protect it. Adrian stood before it, studying the spells, her magic carefully picking at the threads of the spells, trying to unbind them without alerting the Twins. As she worked, her mind roamed back to what Rox had said about its purpose.

She muttered angrily under her breath, "You want to kill the Blue Sights? That's your grand plan? That's what's more important than conquest?"

Adrian scowled as she caught sight of the far wall. Runes as tall as she was were etched into it. She recognized the design, structured long ago. It was the root of the Twins' illusion that made them appear identical.

A burst of primal rage broke in her stomach, her emotional barriers so carefully constructed to contain a lifetime of shame and anger demolished in a flood of rebellion and she threw a powerful, shining blue fireball at the symbols. It exploded against the Twins' protection spell, burning in a wall of flame as the magic battled but the strength of Adrian's emotions won through, her spell cracking the bricks beneath the symbols, erasing sections as the top layer of stone turned to dust, destroying the spell.

In an instant the Twins appeared, burning with rage as their illusion melted. Foxsen's eyes moved closer together as he grew taller, Laik's nose became more hooked and his shoulders more broad. Their cloaks fell back revealing silver hair like starlight.

"Adrian!" Laik shrieked, his voice deeper, yet his tone unchanged since he used to scream her name with rage as a child. She could see every accusation in his eyes, every burning hatred he'd stoked over the years. Adrian was the reason they were fraternal, the reason they weren't perfect like every midwife and prophet had predicted of the princes of the Core, the future rulers of the Core's empire.

Adrian was tainted. The woman. The Blue Sight. The third sibling who never should have been. The missing Triplet.

Adrian grabbed the artifact, the magic in her hands hot and searing like acid ripping mercilessly through the Twins' protection spells, leaving stripes of burns across her palms. She held the artifact before her brothers, her hands shaking. "Is this for me? You couldn't kill me naturally without losing some of your own skills, so you formed armies and delayed the plans of conquest laid out before we were born to find a way to get rid of me?! I was already banished!"

Laik growled, always ready to fight. "You're a disgrace. A blight. You had to be removed."

Adrian turned to Foxsen, her tall, slender, magically brilliant brother who had been so much gentler than Laik, sometimes even a friend. "You went along with this?"

Foxsen's voice was less sure but just as firm. "You weren't supposed to exist in the first place, Adrian."

Adrian's face twisted and crumpled, his words bringing out a hurt she had buried long ago. She had expected conquest. She'd expected slavery and pain. She expected banishment and cruelty. Somehow, however, she had never expected her brothers to so vehemently want her dead.

Adrian set the box aside and drew her sword with a snarl. "Then kill me yourselves. Don't delegate my murder to a magic box."

Laik didn't have to be invited twice. He lunged, drawing his sword but leading with his fist, the blow catching her in the face. The feeling was familiar, bringing back dozens of memories of taking beatings from her brother as a child. Instead of staying down, she lashed out, battling with swords, fists and magic, nearly a perfect match for Laik.

Foxsen stood to the side, a tome of spells clenched in his hands as he formed runes in the air, creating his own spells with the pieces of ancient text. Adrian spun away from Laik and threw a fireball, aiming not for Foxsen, but his book. The spell rebounded off the book and Adrian dodged as it zipped past her hip and exploded into the shelf of potions, the glass bottles shattering, herbs and spices going up in smoke creating a thick, sour haze in the room.

"Look me in the eye when you try to kill me, Foxsen!" Adrian screamed.

Foxen shouted a magical word, clearing the smoke from the room just as Laik struck, a bolt of crimson lightning shooting from his hands. Adrian raised her sword to defend herself, the spell protecting the blade turning red hot and deflecting the spell, sending the bolt flying across the room into Foxsen.

Foxsen screamed, the sound gurgling in his throat as he fell to the ground, a black, scorched hole through his book and chest.

"Foxsen!" Adrian and Laik both screamed, rushing to their brother on instinct, but Foxsen was already dead, his face frozen in a look of shock, the smell of scorched flesh assaulting Adrian's nostrils.

Adrian felt her heart sink, the only member of her family she'd hoped would grow to love her lying dead on the floor. Laik, however, was nearly doubled over, both at the loss of his brother and the sudden loss of magic the two had shared.

Adrian watched him in shock. Foxsen was her brother, too. Their magic was permanently entwined. She should have felt a loss of power as well, but she felt as strong as ever. She glanced down at her wrists and spotted her lifestones. She grinned. She was no longer woven with her brothers. She was part of a new triad now and their power, combined with her Blue Sight, would keep her strong even after her brothers were gone.

Laik turned to her, enraged beyond reason, his eyes glowing red. He charged, his sword raised, but Adrian was ready for him. With her heart a chaos of anger, defiance and pain she struck, her sword cutting through his magical wards and spearing him through the heart. He grasped at her sword for a brief moment in shocked surprise, his eyes finding his sister as he fell, dying draped over Foxsen's burned corpse.

Adrian let out a broken cry as she felt her last brother die, the feeling like a piece of her heart was falling from her chest. She dropped to her knees and leaned over them, weeping into the bodies for a long moment, allowing herself to mourn for her family, for what could have been if they hadn't been raised in prophecy and war. For her brothers who shared her birth.

"I'm sorry," she gasped. "I'm sorry it had to be this way."

Outside the palace shook as another bomb went off closer to the palace. The motion brought reality into the front of her mind and she slowly stood. There would be time to grieve properly later. For now, she had to return to her bondmates.

With their spells shattered with their deaths, Adrian had no trouble grabbing the artifact and racing down the stairs back into the palace. Her Blue Sight felt like a throbbing hum, a buzz spreading beneath her skin. Her magic was slowly changing, the toxic effects of her brothers' powers draining away. She didn't dare try to throw a fireball or bolt of lightning. Her destructive powers were leaving, a part of her dead along with her family, boosting her natural abilities to heal and sense.

She could feel Rox and Jacquin near. Her heart pounded at the knowledge that they were still alive. She raced for the courtyard near the slave yards, finding her lovers near the palace gardens.

Jacquin limped, her sword and covered in other people's blood. Rox was a beast, her sword missing, her skin and clothes stained with carnage, but her eyes weren't wild, her body still. A young girl of no more than five tenmoons with long, blond curls huddled beside her, a sword in her hands, her eyes more steady and brave than any child her age should possess. Adrian knew instantly she was Serena.

"You found her!" Adrian called, rushing to support Jacquin. "Let me help you."

She led Jacquin against a garden shrub. Jacquin clung to Adrian's shoulders. "Rox massacred them, Adrian. Every slave trader in the square. Most with her bare hands."

Adrian wasn't surprised. "She's a changling."

"Her daughter fought with us."

Adrian glanced back at Serena, wrapped tightly in her mother's arms, both women a mess of blood and grime. Somehow, despite the carnage, Adrian had never felt safer.

Adrian sank to her knees and held Jacquin's ankle, a flood of healing magic easing into her wounds. Jacquin let out a sharp cry of relief as her injuries disappeared. She looked down at Adrian in awe. "You've changed."

"The Twins are dead," Adrian confirmed, holding out the artifact. Jacquin pulled her into a tight embrace and kissed her, her love a flood of relief after the deaths of Adrian's brothers.

Rox tipped her head to the side, listening for the changlings' reports. "Something's changed. The changlings are taking the Core. Soldiers are beginning to surrender."

Adrian nodded, a burst of relief in her chest. "Their obedience spells have fallen. A handful of their higher officials will be waking up."

"We need to get out of here. The battle will be ours, but we have to get this artifact out before someone else rises to claim it," Jacquin declared.

"I'm getting Serena out of here," Rox agreed.

Adrian nodded sharply. The battle was done. The Core had fallen. "To the river."

Adrian descended down the narrow stone walkways slowly, her eyes just barely adjusted to the darkness of the path. Jacquin moved ahead of her with more grace, Rox behind her, her night-eyes reflecting the light of the only torch far ahead. Behind Rox, clenching her mother's hand, was Serena. The girl had refused to be left behind and Rox had been unwilling to part with her.

Adrian looked on the child with pride. Serena had proven to be strong and brave in the days since the overthrow of the Core. Her mother's instruction to be a brave girl, a warrior girl, had sunk home, her willfulness keeping her alive. Her captor, a man named Calder, had been stabbed to death before Rox had even arrived.

The towering caves of the changlings loomed like the gaping jaws of the mountains themselves over the small band of travelers. The changling shaman led them deep into the lifestone mines after the bleeding core that would complete the Laik and Foxsen's artifact.

Adrian looked at each cave in awe. Tiny homes pocketed the walls like a stone beehive, a complex city dug into the lifestone caves themselves. At one time there must have been thousands of changlings living here, and Rox had hinted that there were other communities spread throughout the mountain range as well.

The lifestones in her wrists buzzed lightly, recognizing the deep veins of more lifestone threaded through the caverns. Her senses were heightened, her Blue Sight reading memory and emotion embedded in every stone. It was no wonder the changlings had evolved so quickly here. It would be impossible to live here for long without being somehow changed.

The shaman turned and beckoned to the Triad. "We're almost there," Rox translated. They reached the end of the walkway and the shaman paused, handing her torch to Rox. "She says she can't take us any further. The core has poisoned her too much already. If she goes any further while it's still active, she'll die."

Jacquin clasped the changling's hands. "Thank you. We'll take care of it from here."

The changling bowed low, her eyes never leaving Adrian, Rox, and Jacquin. Rox blushed slightly. "She called us her saviors."

Jacquin smiled gently and Adrian recognized the stillness in her, the peace in her eyes. She'd had a vision, probably about this journey. "We're all doing our part to make a better world."

They left the shaman behind and journeyed deeper into the caves. Jacquin stepped with surety and Adrian took her hand. "You've walked these steps before?"

Jacquin nodded gently, her eyes soft. "I know this place, yes. I know what we have to do."

It didn't take long to reach the core. Adrian immediately recognized it from her visions from the shaman. It pulsed red like a beacon through the middle of the massive stalactite, the air around it warm and heavy. The puzzle box in Adrian's hand tugged gently, like attracting magnets calling to each other. Adrian coughed hard, the toxic taste of the core coating her mouth.

Jacquin reached back and took Adrian's sword from her belt. In three swift chops the magical blade severed the core from the stone and the core leapt into the open box in Adrian's hands. Adrian instantly closed it, the lines of the box sealing and the artifact glowing a pale, white light. The air in the room instantly changed, not yet humming like the rest of the caves, but the fallout of the core dissipating.

"What do we do with it now?" Serena questioned, her young voice asking what everyone was wondering.

Jacquin took the box and smiled. "We call the Blue Sights."

Adrian did a double take in shock, her heart speeding in her chest. "What?"

Jacquin laughed. "Adrian, think about it. The Blue Sights are spread across Aggar, most hiding their gifts or tormented into suppressing it. People don't understand the power of the Sight. The Blue Sights don't even understand what they can do. They deserve to be safe and, more than anything, they deserve to be taught about bonding, about their abilities."

"How would we do that?" Rox questioned.

"Long ago there was a place to train seers and Blue Sights alike, to keep magical peace in Aggar. These caves are a veritable wellspring of energy for the mages of Aggar." Jacquin looked at Adrian and grinned wider. "I think it's time we re-establish the Council's Keep."

Epilogue

Jacquin walked slowly through the hall of seers, her pupils sitting behind her on silken pillows, the incense and deep thrum of harps lulling them deeper into their visions. Jacquin leaned forward on the railing of her balcony and looked out over the new Council's Keep, the stony honeycomb once so barren and unwelcoming now a bustling city thriving in the roots of the northern mountains.

Below her changlings and humans mingled, trading and studying. The changlings had proven to be masterful teachers for many of the seers and Blue Sights who were particularly drawn to their telepathic form of communication and connection with the earth. Already Jacquin could see the first changes among the students, the melding of human and changling in the psychic bonds of the lifestone caves. She didn't doubt the merge would one day create something new and wonderful. The magical children of Aggar.

Since the rise of the Triad, the icy north of Aggar had settled into a rare time of peace. Blue Sights and seers had flooded the new town, enough to allow Jacquin, Adrian and Rox to open a school and sanctuary that eventually attracted mages of every field. With Rox to oversee changling and human relations and Adrian to protect and train the Blue Sights, the mages of Aggar had never been better prepared to establish an era of peace.

Jacquin smiled lightly, rubbing her swollen belly absent-mindedly. The child would be her third; her Amazon genetics growing children out of the power of her bond with both Rox and Adrian, the children truly born of all three women and loved by their mothers and older sister, Serena, herself a mighty warrior for the Keep. She'd discovered the power in the changlings' archives, the records full of their dealings with the Amazons of Dey Sorormin.

Four tenmoons ago, Jacquin had finally made contact with the home planet of the Amazons. The sisters had been rejoiced to hear that the ancestors of their lost kin had survived. The first ships started appearing a tenmoon later.

The clash of swords and swell of music in the lower stories of the Keep echoed the presence of the first Amazon colony on Aggar in a millennia. The pound of dancing feet keeping rhythm to the music was a soothing bit of home, Khalisa's classes in full swing as her sister, the representative from Oasis, visited.

Jacquin turned to look on her pupils and let out a contented sigh. She had never imagined a peace so profound, had never hoped she would be part of making such a change to the world. Even far from her beloved desert, nestled in the snowy tundras she swore she could never love, she had found home.

"Continue to breathe. Find your guides. You don't have to rush. You don't have to see anything. Just be." Jacquin directed her pupils, her voice soft, growing deeper with age.

She could feel it in the heartbeats of her students, the song of the Keep, the smell of lifestones and incense and the taste of hope and magic in the air. The effects of the new Keep would expand and multiply, changing the landscape of Aggar forever. For a time, if even a short time, there would be true peace in Aggar.

Jacquin felt the child in her womb toss and kick beneath her arm and she laughed aloud at the sensation. Even a temporary peace was worth fighting for. Every change was new life and she couldn't wait to see what the future would hold.

The End of Book 3

DICTIONARY OF AGGAR TERMS

amarin: The amarin is the essence of life, the empathic imprint of animate existence which results in a cumulative pattern of feelings, thoughts and reflexes. It is one's aura.

basker jackal: a sleek, scavenger canine, native to the Ramains' plains and renowned for its blood lust; semi-domesticated by militia for chase and guard chores

black glass: a ceramic-glass compound of especially durable strength that hones to a sharp edge; commonly used in making knife blades

blackpine: A valuable hardwood conifer with a black, barkless trunk and green-black needles which is common to Maltar's lands.

Blue Sight: The Sight or Blue Gift is a sixth sense genetically linked to blue eyes; an awareness of and ability to manipulate life auras and amarin. The terms also refers to a person possessing the Blue Sight.

bondmate: any eitteh, human, or sandwolf who has been empathically bonded into a sandwolf's familial unit (see pack bond; sandwolf)

boko: A food native to the Ramains, boko is a vegetable-meat paste wrapped in boiled leaves.

braygoat: a short-horned goat native to Ramians' southern districts

brushberry: an evergreen bush with a sweet-tart berry; a Ramains wine

bunt: A tall, stemmed grain which yields red-brown seedlings and whose husks are often used for animal fodder. The term also applies to the grayish flour produced from the seedlings.

buntsow: a carnivorous, hooved mammal; a scavenger native to the northern forests; a non-venomous cousin of schefea

"By the Mother's Hand": (idiom) "Done with the Goddess' blessings."

Changlings: Sentient half-human, half-feline beasts native to the Northern Continent, Changlings are a race of people known for their amoral selling and reselling of information. They are also miners of lifestones.

Circle, The: The elite soldiers of the Core, bands of bandits and warriors who do the Twins' bidding

Clan, the: people of the Clan's Plateau; descendents of off-worlders who were stranded on Aggar at the fall of the Galactic Terran Empire; renowned for their weapons technology and raiding activities

Clan Lead: legislative representatives chosen by and from among the Clan folk; (plural) a governing assembly; civil servant

Clantown: the governing settlement and militia corp of the Clan's Plateau; a village in the ancient Terran Quadrant, located at the edge of the eastern plateau adjacent to the Ramains' Great Forests

commons: A Ramains' term for a tavern housed by an inn.

Core, The: The nation risen from the ruins of the Clan's settlement, once the Maltar's realm.

Council of Ten: A collection of ten Masters and Mistresses educated in the history and humanity of Aggar who are guardians of the planet's integrity.

Crowned Rule: the designated heir of the Ramains' Royal Family; usually chosen for skills of statescraft rather than warfare

cucarae: A small, extremely poisonous scavenger, this crustacean is found in the wastelands of both the Northern and Southern Continents.

cucarii: A group or nest of cucarae.

Desert Peoples: Also known as The Southerners, the Desert Peoples are loosely organized nomadic tribes native to the Southern Continent and renown for their distilled liquors and merchant ventures.

Diblum: a small Ramains' village southeast of Khirla

dracoon: A governing marshal appointed by the Ramains' King.

early moon: The first of the twin moons to rise on any given evening.

eitteh: A sentient feline native to the Northern Continent. The term eitteh usually refers to the winged females of the species as males are never seen. See also winged-cats and men-cats.

Eldest Prepared: These individuals are the best of the Shadow trainees at the Council's Keep and are the preferred choice for assignments and lifebonding. They also instruct the younger recruits.

Fates, the: The male deities of evil mischief, the Fates are mystical rulers of the dark underworld. Their primary figures include Malice and Ambition while their secondary figures include War, Ire, Greed and others.

Fates' Cellar: The legendary home of the Fates, Fates' Cellar is the mythical place where evil souls go after death to suffer in a punishing afterlife. Also known as hell.

Fates' Jest: (idiom) A malicious turn of events attributed to the Fates.

Firecaps: These intersecting, volcanic mountain ranges comprise the northeastern third of the Northern Continent. They are uninhabited and controlled by Seers in order to stabilize continental land masses.

grubber: A generic term for ground rodents in the Northern Continent. Grubber generally refers to smallish, nasty-tempered mammals.

harmon: a soul-spirit; self-image projected by a Blue Sight to another

honeywood: a deciduous hardwood with rough, red bark; yields a golden grain of decorative value; common to the southern Ramains

Jezebet: Usually given to a woman, this title is bestowed upon someone who is a resident of the Council's Keep and is trained in the arts of lifebonding Shadowmates.

jumier: a fowl native to the Ramains' northern districts

Khirla: Dracoon's capital in the Ramains' southeasterly district Khirlan

lexion: A domesticated fowl common to farms of the Northern Continent which is raised for its meat.

lifestone: An opal-like energy stone often found in limestone deposits in the Northern Continent and used by the Council in the practice of lifebonding Shadowmates.

mala': A female slave or bond-servant of the Ramains whose duties are restricted to the household and the bedroom.

Maltar: The ruling family of the northern half of the Northern Continent.   The term may refer either to the ruling family member or the country itself.

men-cats: The male of the eitteh species, these cat-like savages inhabit the mountain ranges on the Northern Continent.

mesta: A thick-skinned, amber fruit with a tart, meaty pulp in the seed pods that is cultivated by farmers in the Northern Continent.

midnight moon: The second of the twin moons to rise on any given night.

Min: A generic title given to free-born women in the Ramains. It is comparable to the Terran term ma'am.

milkdeer: middle-sized, long necked mammal native to the Ramains; frequently domesticated for its milk

monarc: A standard calendar division, roughly equivalent to a Terran month, which is comprised of four, ten-day periods.

Mother, the: A nurturing female deity who is seen as the birthmother of the universe.   Aggar's twin moons are associated with her watchful light.

mumut: a spice leaf grown chiefly in the lower districts of the Ramains

pack bond: empathic understanding of personal commitments; empathic bond of sandwolves used to define familial units (see sandwolf)

pripper: A small, tree-dwelling mammal known for its comical antics and bushy coat.

Purge, The: The last attack on Aggar by Terran forces that culminated in the use of biochemical warfare that massacred nearly every Blue Sight. The battle also destroyed the Council's Keep and Valley Bay, scattered the seers and Amazons.

Ramains: The southwestern third of the Northern Continent which is united beneath a liberal monarchy and shares a border with the Council's lands.

Royal Marshall: special emissaries of the Ramains' Royal Family; originally banded to protect travelers; duties expanded to provide districts with legal and military resolutions, to supply the Royal Court with information from outlying districts

sandwolf: sentient canine, originally native to the Southern Continent, which instinctively imprints at birth to one or more sentient others to provide an emotional, empathic bond in developing protective behaviors and communication skills (see pack bond)

schaefea: A hoofed scavenger of middle size native to the northern mountains. The schaefea has protruding tusks and venomous saliva glands.

Seers: Those individuals gifted with the Blue Sight who are bound to Aggar's lifecycles and no longer capable of individual thoughts or actions. They are directed by the Council of Ten and are the crafters of Aggar's landscapes. Sometimes referred to as mystics.

silverwood: A hardwood conifer with a smooth, silver-green bark and gray-green needles which is common to the Ramains foothills and mountain regions. Also called silverpine.

single moon: The night at the end of each monarc in which only one of the twin moons is visible. Term is synonymous with monarc.

Tad: Generic title given to free-born men in the Ramains which is similar to the Terran term sir.

tinker-trade: a traveling merchant member of the Traders' Guild

ten-day: A division of days within a monarc, roughly equivalent to a Terran week.

tenmoon season: A period of time roughly the same as two Terran years. The name comes from the fact that ten single moon nights will occur during the time it takes for Aggar to complete one orbit around its sun.

torin: An edible, broad-leafed fern commonly found in the wooded rangers of the Northern Continent.

Traders' Guild, the: a merchant union supported by membership dues that promotes the fair exchange of market goods; endorsed by the Desert Peoples, Ramains, Council and Valley Bay the union may provide arbitrators, bonded transport agents, and travel lodging to supplement regional resources

twin moons: Two planetoids orbiting around Aggar's globe. The term is also associated with the Mother's watchful care.

Twins: The tyrannical, magical rulers of the Core

Unseen Wall: An unidentified energy field which was ordered by the Council of Ten and is controlled by the Seers; the Unseen Wall comprises the border around the Terran Base Quadrant.

Valley Bay: the settlement of the Sisterhood; located near the White Isles, isolated from the Northern Continent by the Firecaps; governed by the Ring of Valley Bay and bound to the home world through the Blue Sighted gifts of the Ring's Binder.

waterferret: amphibious ferret with both scales and fur; often used to aide fisherman and common along coastal towns; very intelligent, but often sneaky and prone to theft.

White Isles of Fire, the: The group of volcanic islands off the eastern Firecaps of the Northern Continent. Sometimes called the Archipelago, it is the native homeland of the Council and the Seers.

Wine of Decisions: A spiced wine containing a natural drug which prompts the visions of the Blue Sight.

winged-cats: Generally used as another term for female eitteh.

DICTIONARY OF SORORIAN TERMS

Amazon: a Sister choosing to work/settle outside of the Sisterhood's jurisdiction

ann: (idiom) A word used to emphasize thoughts or ideas and function as a verbal exclamation point. Ann might also be translated as "Take note!" Other meanings include to be far away or distant.

be: far, distant

beasties: Large, hoofed mammals, these horned animals have copper-colored, wooly coats and are descended from the Highland Cattle of old Terra.

bin: A preposition meaning between. Sometimes means to or from.

Cee: A word that refers to the customs or ways of any given people.

cheroan: to make safe, to protect

Coramee: daughter

corean: A verb meaning to find precious, to treasure.

crone: a wise elder among healers n'Shea

dey: This word can be used as either an article as in "the" or a pronoun as in "we" or "our" and is meant to connote respect.

duen: to do kindly; to act with concern

Dumauz: (plural: —en) a kind-hearted individual; a concerned friend

Feast of Helen: This anniversary celebration of unity and independence marks the birth of the Sisterhood's firstborn child.

felan: A verb form meaning using, doing or creating.

Founding, the: the original planetary colonization of dey Sorormin under the Galactic Terran Empire; settlement of the home world

Helen: This name refers to the Red star of dey Sorormin's solar system, the firstborn of dey Sorormin's original settlement and the leader of n'Sappho during early negotiations to retain Sorormin independence. The word means "light."

Houses of dey Sorormin: surnames of Sisters, designating family and/or skills; six of Seven Houses recall ancient goddesses of Terran lore (n'Athena: guardians (Greek), n'Awehai: crafters (Iroquois), n'Hina: agricultural providers (Polynesian), n'Huitaca: artists (Chibcha), n'Minona: historians/teachers (Dahomey), n'Shea: healers (Irish); First House of dey Sorormin (n'Sappho: legislative leaders) recalls a Terran stateswoman of Greece

Kahmee: little daughter; a very young girl

kahn: A noun meaning sunrise or dawn.

kamak: A verb which indicates something is brought to completion or finished. It may also be used in place of is made.

kau: A pronoun referring to the second person singular (you).

ki: A word indicating possession (yours).

kumin: A verb meaning to join together.

m': A preposition denoting as or of (from).

m'Sormee: birth mother; (literally) from the woman's life

mae: A word indicating that something is dear or precious.

"Mae n'Pour": (idiom) An expression which means "Give me strength." This term is often used as a curse to express frustration or anger but can also be used as a genuine prayer to the Goddess.

mau: A noun meaning heart.

mauen: The plural form of mau (hearts).

mee: A noun which denotes life.

minmee: A word meaning birth, minmee also carries the connotation of the sacred connection of life-giving or creating.

n': This expression denotes possession. It is usually used to indicate an individual's House.

n'Athena: One of the Seven Houses of dey Sorormin, members of this house are traditionally the guardians of the Sisterhood. The term also recalls a Terran goddess from ancient Greek lore.

n'Awehai: One of the Seven Houses of dey Sorormin, members of this house are traditionally the builders and craftswomen of the Sisterhood. The term also recalls a Terran goddess of Iroquois (Native Northern American) lore.

n'Hina: One of the Seven Houses of dey Sorormin, members of this house are traditionally the agricultural providers of the Sisterhood. The term also recalls a Terran goddess of Polynesian lore.

n'Huitaca: One of the Seven Houses of dey Sorormin, members of this house are traditionally the treasurers of music and arts of the Sisterhood. The term also recalls a Terran goddess of Colombian Chibcha (Native Southern American) lore.

n'Minona: One of the Seven Houses of dey Sorormin, members of this house are traditionally the historians and teachers of the Sisterhood. The term also recalls a Terran goddess of African Dahomey lore.

n'Sappho: First House of the Seven Houses of dey Sorormin, members of this house traditionally make up the legislature and leadership of the Sisterhood. The term also recalls a Terran stateswoman of ancient Greek citizenship.

n'Shea: One of the Seven Houses of dey Sorormin, members of this house are traditionally the healers and earthwitches of the Sisterhood. The term also recalls a Terran woman-deity and/ or the white witches of ancient Irish lore.

n'Sormee: parenting mother or guardian; (literally) of the woman's life nehna: (idiom) A prompt for more information meaning and then, then it happened that or so then.

Niachero: Daughter of the Stars; descriptive of Sisters who genetically resemble those n'Athena who negotiated the settlement of Valley Bay; Amazons who led the space protectors to save Aggar during the fall of the Galactic Terran Empire

nor: An word that indicates an event happened in the past.

puor: An word meaning strength, stability or virtuousness.

quinn: A word denoting peace, tranquility or the absence of violence.

quitan: to nurture; to tend with compassion

ret: A word meaning cruelty or harm.

sae: Another term for please, this word denotes a request.

sak: This word means intelligence or cleverness.

shea: This noun refers to a healing witch from the House of n'Shea. A member of this house will frequently be one who is closely bound to nature. She may also be a mistress of love potions and possess the evil eye. See the term n'Shea.

sheaz: A noun meaning the earth or world, this term may also refer to the components of a nurturing Earthmother Creator.

Shekhina: The moon of Helen's second planet. This moon is home to Helen's high-tech base where diplomatic contacts between the dey Sorormin and the Galactic Terran Empire occur. It is also the home of the Immigration offices and the orientation/screening facilities for new Sisters. Historically, the term refers to an ancient Terran goddess of Judaic lore and sometimes connotes the divine image of a woman.

sor: The noun meaning woman.

soroe: The noun denoting friend or dear companion.

Soroi: loved one; lover; beloved

Sororian: The woman-made language of the Sisterhood. The term
     derives its root meaning from the ancient Terran word which
     refers to sisters.

Sorormin: A noun that is synonymous with the word Sisterhood.

Sorormin, dey: The word which represents the proper name of The
     Sisterhood. The term also refers generally to the culture of
     women who settled on Helen's second planet. dey Sorormin
     are recognized members of the Senate in the Third Galactic
     Terran Empire.

sueht: A past tense form of the verb to lose or to misplace.

tau: A pronoun denoting me.

ti: A word that indicates possession (my).

tizmar: A verb which means to remain, to settle or to unite and/or
     join together.

vu: A term meaning very little, a small amount.

z': A term indicating for or with.

"Z'ki Sak, Diana": (idiom) An expression of regret or disbelief which
     translates as "By your wits, Goddess."

www.ingramcontent.com/pod-product-compliance
Lightning Source LLC
Chambersburg PA
CBHW070538100726
47907CB00004B/1165